Six Guns South

Fawcett Gold Medal Books
by Robert MacLeod:

THE APPALOOSA   13971-9 $1.25
THE MULESKINNER   14054-7 $1.50
SIX GUNS SOUTH   14235-3 $1.50

Six Guns South

by

Robert MacLeod

FAWCETT GOLD MEDAL • NEW YORK

To DAVE REES, gifted historian of Arizona and old western railroads, journalist, photographer, moviemaker, and good companion, whose outstanding collection of reference data and photographs is no greater than his generosity.

SIX GUNS SOUTH

Published by Fawcett Gold Medal Books, a unit of CBS Publications, the Consumer Publishing Division of CBS Inc.

All of the people and places in this tale are fictitious, except a few cities and towns, and a few historical personages who are merely incidental to the story.

ISBN: 0-449-14235-3

Printed in the United States of America

12   11   10   9   8   7   6   5   4   3

CHAPTER 1

I got up just after daylight, and Uncle Frank already had a fire going and was taking a bath in the wash boiler. For all he was going on sixty, and kind of stringy and knobby, he was tough as leather. The two bullet scars on his ribs were red and knotted.

I looked out to see what kind of a day it was going to be. The twins were already mounted up and riding out. They looked over at me and one of them said something and they both laughed, to let me know it was something about me. I'd had the feeling before, in the last year or two, but now I got it real strong—I'll have it out with those two one of these days.

Still naked as a jaybird, Uncle Frank was standing in front of the mirror shaving, stopping every half minute to strop the old straight-edge, and whistling to himself like this was the finest day that ever was. It was a nice morning—May seventh, 1912, and the State of Arizona only two months and three weeks old—but it didn't seem so nice to me, because for the first time in my whole twenty-two years, he'd forgot my birthday.

That was a damn fool stunt, whistling while he shaved, because, with his mouth all puckered up, of course he cut his lower lip. He began to swear, because he was getting ready to drive Letty to Douglas in the surrey, and a razor nick like that just never stops bleeding, even if you stick a piece of newspaper on it, like he did.

But he got dressed and put on his boiled shirt and a paper collar and a ready-tied bow tie on an elastic band, and when Letty hollered from her and the twins' veranda across the yard, "Frank Kelly! What in the world is holding you up

5

now?" he yelled back, "Just a minute!", and then said to me, "Kel, hook up the team, will you?"

My first name is Kelly. My mother hung it on me, after her family, and I'd a lot rather been named Jack Adams, or Frank Adams, instead of Kelly Adams.

I hitched the team to the surrey and brought it around to the cabin and put a jug of water in it. Letty was stamping up and down on her veranda and getting madder, and Uncle Frank came out with his bow tie crooked and that piece of newspaper stuck to his lip. He said, "Boy, I gotta run! You know her! And Kel, just once, don't get in any tangle with the twins while me and Letty are gone, will you?"

He climbed on and shook up the team, and turned so sharp the front wheel scraped the box. I watched him jump down and help her up, with that big hat of hers with the cherries on it flopping on top of her piled-up hair, and her trying not to let him get a look at her ankles when she climbed over the wheel. They went rattling off down the lane.

I rolled a smoke, and sat awhile, feeling all alone and left out. Then I did up the breakfast dishes and made up the bunks. I hung on the gun Uncle Frank gave me on my twenty-first birthday a year ago, when he said I had sense enough, now, to carry a good gun and know when not to use it. I remember I was all choked up, because it was his favorite gun, not the nickel-plated Smith and Wesson he packed around the ranch. I already knew everything about that gun —"Colt's New Military & Frontier Revolver, Weight 2 lb. 8 oz., Length of barrel $7\frac{1}{2}$", takes the .450 and .455 Regulation Service Cartridges. This same revolver without the movable bar sight is called the Bisley Model 1894." There was a lot more, all printed on the cardboard box the gun came in. That Bisley had a trigger pull smooth as silk.

I went to the corral and saddled my little gelding. I'd seen the twins ride off toward the tank, for sure not heading out to do any work that day, with Uncle Frank gone to Douglas. And I thought, if everyone else can just go play, why I can at least take my birthday off.

The last few months, I'd been getting sicker and sicker of the sight of those twins—well, really, ever since I first saw them eight years ago, when Uncle Frank and old Charlie Hunt and Tex Warner and the other ranch foremen and owners up here in the Pedregosa Mountains decided all us kids were running too wild. They brought in the widow, Leti-

tia Greenfield, from Missouri or some place, to set up a
school. The widow was real good-looking, big and yellow-
haired and green-eyed, and Uncle Frank just let go all holds
the first time he saw her, like she was the last woman there
was ever going to be on earth. He wanted to marry her, even
with those twin brats of hers, a couple of years younger than
me.

Uncle Frank persuaded Old Man Murchison he ought to
give her the house me and Uncle Frank lived in. The Turkey
Track was a real cow outfit then, and Uncle Frank was foreman. So we moved into the cabin. Then when Murchison let
all the hands go and sold off the stock, and finally the ranch
to Horace Goldsby in New Jersey, Uncle Frank talked
Goldsby into letting the widow stay on here. Goldsby didn't
care. He had all the money in the world, and he let the leased
pasture land go, but he kept the whole ten patented sections
just for a place for him and his friends to hunt and fish in.
And he kept Uncle Frank on as a sort of caretaker-foreman,
and Uncle Frank got him to hire me and the twins when we
got big enough, just to take care of about fifty head of real
fine Herefords and twenty or so real good horses—and
maybe twice a year we had to pack Goldsby and three or
four of his dude friends into the Chiricahuas for a hunting or
fishing trip.

It'll show how hard Uncle Frank got hit by the widow—
why, he sent Guadalupe packing after he got a look at Letitia
Greenfield.

Guadalupe—Lupe, we always called her—was cooking for
old man Murchison and Uncle Frank, when my father and
mother got killed in the train wreck, on their way to El Paso
where we lived then. We were staying on the ranch with
Uncle Frank for the summer, and they were going home for
a week to take care of some business. I was three years old,
and they left me with Lupe so they'd have a few days' vaca-
tion from me, too, I guess.

And of course, Uncle Frank just took me in like I was his
own kid. Then the easiest thing all around was for Lupe, who
had to take care of me, to move into Uncle Frank's house.

Well, she was really the only mother I ever had, you might
say, and I wouldn't talk to Uncle Frank for a month after
he ran her off when the widow came. That was when I was
fourteen and the twins were twelve.

I guess Lupe really wasn't very good-looking. Her face was

pockmarked and she was a little bit bowlegged, but we loved each other, and to me she was beautiful. She kept us a clean house and fed us good, and you couldn't have found a better woman, for all she was ignorant and prayed four or five times a day to a little plaster Virgin Mary. And she loved Uncle Frank.

She mended my clothes, and taught me to keep clean, and hugged me when I was bad and Uncle Frank took the razor strop to me, and she physicked me when I got bound up from green apples, and tonicked me in the spring, and treated me for everything I caught, from the chicken pox to wasp stings, and all out of the one bottle, some kind of medicine called *Virilidad* that Uncle Frank used to buy for her in Agua Prieta, in Mexico, right across the fence from Douglas. I learned Spanish from her as good as English. All the kids talked Spanish some, living so close to Mexico like we did, but none of them as good as me.

It took me a long time to get over it when Uncle Frank sent her away, and that was part of the reason, I guess, why I never got along with the widow Greenfield. But not all of it, not by a long shot! Not with those twins of hers around, and the way she favored them and thought the sun rose and set in them.

So that morning, after her and Uncle Frank left, and feeling low like I was, I thought I'd just take me a ride somewhere. And I got on Brownie and pointed him off toward Ruyker Canyon, with Dodson Peak on our left, and Chiricahua Peak sticking up ten thousand feet into the sky, north of us.

There was a million quail in the brush and scattering out in the oak and piñon, and up higher, in the Ponderosa pines. We scared up some turkeys, which was an excuse for Brownie to do some pitching. We'd been through that before, and when he found out he wasn't going to dump me, he settled down. We went over and had a look at the spring in the draw, and there were big, fresh lion tracks. I thought, well, I better have a look at those calves up in the big pasture, but first we'll go back and get the .30–.30, and just then I heard Polly and Cassie laughing, over the hill in the next draw.

I knew they'd be all eager if there was any chance to kill something, and the three of us would have a better chance for the lion than me alone, so I rode over the hill.

And I forgot about the lion.

They dressed alike, and both of them wore their damn yellow hair down to their shoulders so they'd look like Wild Bill Hickok, and I couldn't tell them apart even yet, except Polly wore his two guns reversed with the butts sticking out in front for a cross-draw, the way Bill Hickok used to do, and Cassie had a scar at the corner of his mouth that I put there three years before.

They were always fooling around with traps, and wolf poison, and now they had a bitch coyote caught by the hind leg in a number 2 trap.

The chain was staked down, and Cassie had roped the coyote around the neck and stretched her out. She was kicking and her tongue was stuck out, and he eased up so he wouldn't choke her to death. The two of them were talking and laughing and didn't see me till I was almost up to them.

Polly was saying, "You hang onto her, and I'll go back and get it."

They both stopped still, and Cassie grinned at me and said, "You're just in time for the fun."

I said, "What fun?" and Polly turned his horse and banged the spurs in hard, and the horse wrung its tail and went into a gallop.

"What's he goin' after?" I said. I knew it would be something mean and dirty. They were great ones for practical jokes, and somebody always got hurt or shamed. Only if someone pulled one on them, then it was something to fight about.

Cassie said, "You'll see," and we sat there on our horses, him keeping his rope just tight enough so as not to kill the coyote, and me just looking at him.

They weighed about a hundred and fifty and stood maybe five foot eight, and they were wiry and strong. I was a good five feet eleven, and weighed about one eighty, and I could always whip either of them because I was bigger, and just as tough. And where they were kind of pale faced and light blue eyed, with pursey little mouths, I was black haired and dark eyed, and burnt good and dark. And I couldn't stomach the way they'd sometimes go around holding hands or with their arms around one another. They were really just one person in two bodies.

They'd lived on the Turkey Track eight years, and had been to their mother's school with the rest of us kids, up to about tenth grade, I guess. And they went to the barn dances and rodeos and sometimes down to Douglas on the border, and they'd got to be top ropers and riders because Uncle Frank took time to work with them, like with me—but the truth was, they didn't have a friend in the world, only their mother, and they couldn't care less.

And like I said, I could lick either one of them, whenever I had to, but never both of them together. Nobody around could do that, because they never paid any mind to fighting fair, or saw anything wrong with two against one. And it was rocks and kicks, even teeth. It really seemed like they tried to kill anybody in a fight. They'd only been on the ranch a couple of days when I found that out. I was joshing Cassie about that girl name of his, and he came at me so mad he was squalling, and calling me names I never heard any kid use, and clawing and kicking. I hit him some good ones, but he wouldn't quit. And then Polly came out of no place, as wild as Cassie—and they gave me a beating, because I wouldn't quit either, not if they killed me. And when Uncle Frank broke it up, he gave me a hiding, too. And the widow, she hugged her little darlings and said I was a vicious little beast. Uncle Frank made me say I was sorry and sent me to bed without any supper. I caught Polly alone a couple of days later, and I let him have it good. And of course, that got me another hiding from Uncle Frank, the worst he ever gave me.

That wasn't the last fight with the twins, either. Half a dozen times over the years we had it out again. The two of them would tease me into a fight and lick me good. I was too stupid stubborn not to go for them even when I knew what they were doing. But afterward, every time, I caught one of them alone, and I bloodied their nose, and gave Cassie a swelled ear one time, and knocked two teeth out of Polly, and just three years ago I smashed Cassie's mouth for him and gave him that scar. So the last couple of years we'd left each other pretty much alone.

And of course Letitia—Uncle Frank wanted me to call her Aunt Letty, but I never would—of course, she had no use for me at all. Only lately, like with the twins, I managed to get along with her, and there was a lot of visiting back and forth, us going over to eat dinner with them, and Uncle Frank cooking up Dutch oven dinners for picnics and things like that. She was kind of sickly-sweet-nice to him sometimes, and other times wouldn't give him the time of day. But he never quit hoping. I guess he proposed to her about once a month. I guess, too, while she never said yes, she never turned him down flat, either.

I used to wonder if things would have been different if she'd named them Joe and Elmer or something instead of Castor and Pollux. She was a great one for astrology and reading horoscopes. She believed all that! I really don't know if I do or not. I used to think it was a lot of foolishness, but some funny things have happened, some mighty queer things after her horoscopes.

In school she taught us kids multiplication tables and spelling and arithmetic and geography, but she spent a lot of time talking about the ancient Greeks and the Hindoos and Egyptians and their old myths, and about black magic and spells. And I got so I half believed it all. And she named the twins Castor and Pollux, because they were born in June under the Zodiac sign of Gemini. And of course everybody called them Cassie and Polly, and it started fight after fight, and I always thought it helped make them the mean, vicious, nasty little sons of bitches they were.

And me, born on May seventh, I'm a Taurus, a Bull. She always said I'm a *black* Taurus, with my black hair and dark complexion and eyes, and that I have a black soul. That's because she knew I never liked her worth a damn, and I never let her precious little bastards run over me.

So after while, Polly came back. He had the turpentine bottle out of their medicine chest. He got down off his horse and him and Cassie got to giggling, and he walked over to the bitch coyote that was just lying there, now, about worn out fighting the trap on its leg and Cassie's rope on its neck.

I got kind of sick inside, because I knew what they were going to do. I said, "For Godsakes, why don't you just shoot her?"

Polly said, "Man, she'll go off like a rocket when I pour this on her ass! Hold her steady, Cass! Hey, how we gonna get your rope off when I turn her leg loose?"

"Leave it on," Cassie said. "She'll go round me like a big old Fourth of July pinwheel, about four feet off the ground. *Whooee! Pour on the coal, Polly!*"

I pulled my Bisley and shot her through the head. I had to miss Polly's head about two inches to do it, but I did it. The coyote didn't even kick.

All three horses jumped, and Cassie near went off. I hauled Brownie up short. Polly dropped the turpentine bottle and grabbed his reins, then stared around at me with his mouth open. Cassie got his horse stopped and swung around to face me, and his hand was on his right-hand gun. I backed Brownie, to keep both of them in front of me. Polly was so mad he was slobbering, and Cassie was calling me the dirtiest names I ever heard.

Polly began to ease his right hand across his belly to his left-hand gun, and I turned the Bisley square on him and cocked it. He let his hand drop, and quit cussing me, then I stared into Cassie's eyes for what seemed like five minutes before he took his hand off his gun.

I think when they got that mad they were actually a little crazy. I think they'd have really shot me, before they cooled down. The trouble was, they knew me. They knew what a stubborn damn fool I am even when I'm scared. And I had my gun in my hand, and they didn't.

Polly walked over and took Cassie's loop off the dead coyote. Then they rode off for home. I watched them go around the shoulder of the hill, and they turned in the saddle and looked back at me just before they rode out of sight.

I went slack like some kind of knot had come loose, and the sweat broke out on the back of my neck. I knew this wasn't the end of it. This wasn't just getting back at them for one of their real funny jokes, like handing you a branding iron with the handle heated up. No, I'd shamed them good, this time. They'd got to believing they were pretty fast with a gun, and here I'd faced the two of them down with my gun in my hand, which was even worse than spoiling their fun with the coyote. They'd get even for this one! And whatever it was, it would be bad. And when they pulled it on me, I knew I wouldn't just take it. I was scared now, because I figured this time somebody'd likely to get hurt, really hurt.

CHAPTER 2

I built a smoke, and let it burn down to my lips, watching the empty place where they disappeared, and letting myself calm down.

Well, I couldn't just sit there, so I headed for home. First, I was going to ride wide around their house so as not to run into them. Then I thought, Kel, you better not start that! So I rode right past their open door, and I was ready. Their horses were tied to the veranda railing, but I didn't see the twins. I stripped Brownie in the corral, and walked back to the cabin.

I didn't take my gun off when I built up the fire and put the coffee on to boil. I looked out the front window a couple of times, but nothing was stirring over at the Greenfield house, so I made a bacon sandwich and poured a cup of coffee and sat down at the table. When I reached for the sugar bowl, that's where Uncle Frank had left the note.

KEL,

Aunt Letty says all the right stars have finely got themself in the right position, for the first time in 8 years, I take it. Like when its your break playing pool and the 15 ball drops in the side pocket and the other 14 are all laid out nice so you can run the table. Only happens once in a life time, maybe, I mean the stars in one of her horoscopes. Anyway she finely said she would marry me and that is where we went, down to Douglas to get married. Now boy I know sometimes you don't get along so good with her but you are app to be kind of hard on people being so young like you are. So for your Uncle Frank's sake and all the good years we ben together I want you to get along with

13

her. She likes you almost like her own kids and said if you will just straighten up and be friends with Cassie and Polly why she will be a mother to you too. We can all be one happy family.

UNCLE FRANK

Then way down in the corner in small writing he put "Anyway I hope so. I sure hope so."

The first thing I thought was, I'll get out right now. And if I have to walk around on tiptoe being nice to that old biddy and a brother to them two slimy rats, I'll end up fighting with Uncle Frank, too. Then I thought, hell, that would be like running away from trouble. I'll stay around and see if it will work out somehow. Only right now I got Cassie and Polly on my mind. And just then I heard them coming across the yard.

I was of a mind to get the Winchester and talk to them through the crack of the door, but then I couldn't do that, either, and I loosened the Bisley in the holster and stepped into the open doorway bold as brass and cold as ice inside.

But they were peaceful. Cassie had a note in his hand, and they looked so upset, I guess our feud had actually slipped their mind for now.

Polly said, "My God, Kel, you won't believe . . ." and I said, "I got one, too, from Uncle Frank. So what's the trouble?"

"Why, hell," Cassie said, "we can't let them get married! I mean, my God, all of us livin' in the same house like a tribe of Yaquis. That damn uncle of yours, he don't like me and Polly worth a damn. We sure don't want our mother married to nobody! An' we sure ain't gonna live in the same house with you!"

"Well, that's one thing we agree on," I told him. "Nobody could pay me to live with you two! But, hell, you're lucky, getting Uncle Frank! Look what I'm getting!"

Well, that boiled them up again. Cassie said, "Now you listen here! Don't let's hear no talk from you about our Ma!"

And Polly put in, "We don't like the way you talk to her, and if you don't cut it out . . ."

"Aw, shut up!" I told him. "I never said nothing bad about Letty. It's just I can't stand her. But you're off on the wrong track. I don't like it any better than you, but it's their business, and if you don't like it, why just get the hell off the ranch. If you go making trouble for Uncle Frank, you got me to answer to."

"We already got you to answer to for this morning," one of them said. "We're not forgettin' that! Only right now, we're all three in the same trouble, and we better play along together."

Well, we jawed about it most of the afternoon and got nowhere, but at least the trouble between us was set aside for later. Finally Polly said, "She left supper in the fireless cooker for the three of us. Come on over."

So we went and had the roast and beans and cornbread Letty fixed. After supper, Cassie said, "Well, I guess we can't do nothing till they get back, anyway. We'll let it ride a while —but I s'pose it means you and him will be moving in here with us, so you damn well better mind your p's and q's."

"You wouldn't have any place at all if it hadn't been Uncle Frank put in for you eight years ago with old man Murchison, and later with Goldsby, and if he takes a notion, he'll just run the two of you the hell off the ranch."

"Take more'n that old fart to run us off," Polly said. "He ain't our uncle, nor he ain't running our affairs."

Well, there was no use stirring up more trouble, so I got up and went back to the cabin. I lit the lamp and stripped down to my underwear, and cleaned my teeth and blew the lamp out and climbed into bed. And right away I felt something squirming around between my feet. I went straight up, and landed on the floor, all tangled up in the quilt. When I got the lamp lit, I almost hollered. They had tied a centipede to the foot of my bed with a piece of string. Those things give me the chills worse than any snake! This one was about seven inches long, sort of copper-colored, with a fake head on its rear end just like the real one, pinchers and all, and you can't tell which way they're heading—and all those pale, horrible legs squirming around. It was all I could do to make myself get my gloves on and pick it up by the string and smash it with a length of stove wood. Some folks say they're not poison, but somebody else can prove that out!

They had done it, of course, before they went home and found the note. And here I'd actually been feeling a little friendly to them, because I knew their mother marrying Frank had really hit them hard, like she was a traitor to them. It would never enter their head that they were grown up men and ought to be leaving home and go on their own.

They had a lot worse shock than me, because they couldn't imagine she would really up and do it after all those years she had turned Uncle Frank down. But me, I'd been scared all that time that it would happen.

But one thing, I wasn't going to leave now, like I felt I wanted to, till I got even for that centipede. Those critters actually make me sick at my stomach. And they knew it, and I couldn't let it pass, whatever happened when Uncle Frank and Letty came home.

I guess almost being sick to my stomach reminded me, and gave me the big idea. I went to the medicine chest and there it was, where Lupe had left it eight years ago—that Mexican Virilidad tonic, that dynamite she used to dose me with for everything from measles to a kick from a horse, and for diarrhea and constipation, both.

I hardly had to read the label, I'd read it off for Lupe so many times, whenever I'd squawk about having to take it, and she had to prove to me it was the perfect cure for whatever ailed me at the moment—*"para condiciones debiles, para mejorar la capacidad fisicomental y enfermos de agotamiento general,"* and a lot more. Then it ended up *"También efectivo como purgativo blando."* Which meant something like this—For conditions of weakness, for improving physicomental capacity, and infirmities of general exhaustion. Also effective as a mild laxative.

Mild laxative! That stuff was about as mild as sixty percent dynamite! It didn't taste bad, sickly sweet and loaded with alcohol, but after a couple of spoonfuls of Virilidad, a body better not get farther than jumping distance from the privy!

I looked across the yard, and they still had a lamp lit. They were so lazy they'd eat breakfast with the devil if he'd cook it and they didn't have to. I hollered, "Come on over for breakfast! I'll make pancakes!"

I pried the lid off the can of corn syrup and stirred in a cupful of Virilidad and tasted it, and I thought it would pass. It sort of sharpened up the flavor of the corn syrup. I put the syrup on the table and the Virilidad bottle back in the medicine chest, and went back to bed.

I slept fine and got up early and stirred up a pitcherful of pancake batter and put the coffee pot on the range and sliced bacon. I was just going to yell for the twins when I heard them coming.

I said, "Now, pancakes are no good if they cool down, so I'll keep 'em coming till you holler. I'll fix mine after."

The soapstone griddle was hot and I poured the batter, four good dollops, out of the pitcher, and when the little bubbles showed on the cakes, I flipped them over, and cooked them thin and brown the way they liked them. And those two innocent bastards slopped on the butter and poured on the Virilidad syrup and made hogs of themselves till they had to take off their gun belts and let their pants belts out a couple of notches. And they never noticed anything funny about the syrup.

So when they took toothpicks and went out and sat on the porch, I had me a good breakfast of coffee and bacon and toasted leftover biscuits.

Cassie belched, and hollered in through the door, "Kel, boy, how you sleep last night?" and I could hear Polly snort, real tickled.

I said, "I gotta admit that was a good one. You boys know nothing gives me the shakes like one of them thousand-legged sons of bitches. I near went through the roof. If I'd've got bit, believe me, you'd be sorry. But I guess we're all square for the coyote now, huh?"

They quit laughing, then, and Cassie said, "Not by a damn sight we ain't! That's one you're gonna be sorry for! That's the first coyote we trapped in two years, an' you knew it."

So here we went again. And I was sick of trying to keep the peace for Uncle Frank's sake, and sick of the two of them and their stinking practical jokes and their never learning they'd always get it back, whatever they pulled on me. And I thought, Kel, you better get the hell off this ranch before something bad happens.

Then Cassie said, "I'm feeling too low to do any work. Can't get up no ambition. C'mon, Polly, let's go round by the hayshed and practice some." And he stood up and patted his belly and buckled on his two guns, and said to me, "Well, one thing you're good for, you can cook pancakes. What you say we marry him, Polly?" And he cackled, and Polly strapped on his guns butt foremost in that stupid show-off way, and said, "He's too Goddamn ugly."

I didn't give a damn, and I sure wasn't going to miss being there when that Virilidad went to work, so I said, "I'll be right with you," and went in and hung my gun on, too.

The hayshed was a high roof held up by long poles, with the hay stacked under with plenty of air circulation. It was boarded up around the bottom like slats, about fence-high to keep the stock out. About forty feet away was the privy, a two-holer. I never could see why they build them with two holes, because I sure don't want anybody in there holding *my* hand. Maybe it's for real emergencies.

There was a garbage pit full of bottles and tin cans back there, and we set some up, and they practiced quick draws. They were pretty good for a couple of twenty-year-old kids, faster than me, and good shots to boot. But I was better at aimed shooting because I took my time, the way Uncle Frank taught me.

He used to teach them, too, until I told him something they bragged to me about, then he gave us all a real stiff talking-to and wouldn't teach us any more. And one other thing he did—he strapped on his gun and took a silver dollar in his right hand and held it out straight in front of him. And when he dropped it, he pulled the gun and got a shot off before the dollar hit the ground.

Then he unbuckled the gun belt and laid it down, and pulled his shirt off and his underwear down to his hips, and there were those two knotted-up scars on his right side.

He said, "Listen, you knotheads! I was about your age, and faster than you are or ever will be. And I thought, people will sure look up to Frank Kelly when he's a famous gunslinger. And I went looking for trouble, to build me a rep. And I prodded a real one into a shoot-out, and he did this to me before I cleared leather. He could just as easy killed me. And ever since, all I pack a gun for is snakes or some cow on the prod, and to defend myself if I ever need to. And *that* I can do, in case you get to wondering some time."

Then Polly said, "What the hell's the lecture for?"

"Kel told me," Uncle Frank said. "I should've knowed, with the lack of brains you two got. You think you're going down to Douglas and prod old Long Tom Mundt into a shoot-out, so right away you'll be famous. He's old and way over the hill, but I ain't at all sure you could do it, even whipsawing him two to one—You ain't no more bullet proof than any other fool I ever seen."

Then they called me a snitch and said they'd get even for

me telling Uncle Frank. And I said they didn't have the guts to try it one at a time, and Uncle Frank shut us up.

But it was true. That was what they planned—to gun down Marshal Long Tom Mundt in a shoot-out, or some other law man, or some famous gunfighter if they could find one. But believe me, those scars on Uncle Frank made me think, even if it didn't change their minds at all.

Well, anyway, so there we were, the three of us packing guns and shooting at cans and bottles and me waiting for the Virilidad fireworks to start, and all of a sudden Cassie's face twisted up and he made a run for the privy, trying to unbuckle his gun belt and his hip-britches belt all at the same time. He slammed himself inside, and Polly said, "What the hell got into him?"

I grinned at him and said, "You'd be surprised!"

He said, "That Goddamn syrup!" And he shoved his guns into the holsters and started to walk to the privy, fumbling at his buckles, and then he broke into a run, too, and crashed into the privy door where it had swung shut like it always did, and jerked it open and fell inside.

I leaned against the hay shed, hugging myself and almost choked to death laughing. I think that old Virilidad had got even stronger, laying around for eight years!

I was wiping my eyes with my bandanna, and one of them took a shot at me. It knocked splinters off the plank right beside my head, and I dropped face down. And I wasn't laughing any more.

One of them stuck his hand out the door with a gun in it, and I shot three times through the door just above where I figure his head was. Then it was quiet for half a minute, and I backed around the corner of the hayshed.

And Polly came out with his pants down around his ankles, his trapdoor underwear seat flapping open, and both guns in his hands, looking back and forth. And just when he spotted me looking around the corner of the shed, he gasped like someone had stabbed him in the guts, and whirled around and made a dive back into the privy, dropping his guns. In a couple of minutes, his hands came out and grabbed the guns, and right away, he kicked the door open and took two shots at me. They missed by a mile.

I didn't want to shoot anybody, not them or anybody else. But I was full up to *here* with trying to hold back around

them, and dodge brawls—but they never held back. And lately, Uncle Frank had got to halfway taking their side. It was
that miserable woman, of course, that Goddamn witch with
her horoscopes and crazy, half-sick love for those two sons
of bitches of hers. I was sick of always being on my guard
and never having a nice, friendly time with anybody—and
sick of the ranch, too, and even Uncle Frank with all his wise
advice, and never do this and don't say that or it'll hurt her
feelings, and don't make them mad, Kel, because you know
how she takes it out on me.

I decided I'd go, right then. Maybe out to California or up
to Utah. Because if the shoe had been on the other foot, and
they had pulled a real bad one on me, I'd never left till I was
even. But it wasn't me sitting in that privy with my guts tied
in knots. I was way ahead of the game.

I heard Cassie say, "Get ready! We'll bust out when I say.
You all loaded? Can you make it yet?"

They were going to come out shooting and kill me if they
could.

I figured where their heads must be. If they were standing
up, I guessed they'd get hit—but right then I didn't give a
damn. I reloaded, and let go all six through the boards, high
up on the privy. And while I reloaded fast I yelled at them,
"I'm gonna lay out here till you throw your guns out. You
ain't fooling any more, I know that. Well, I ain't either! If
you don't believe it, come out shooting! I'll cut you down!"

I tiptoed away, and got Brownie and saddled him. At the
cabin I got my coat and hat and fifty-six dollars I had in a
cigar box. I refilled my shell belt, and looked out toward the
hayshed, but nobody was in sight. I packed some clean underwear and a couple of shirts and and a razor and tooth-
brush in a satchel, and tied it behind the cantle. I wrapped
some biscuits in a bandanna and put them in my saddlebag.

When I rode down the lane, they were still in the privy, I
think, and I guess they took me serious. I never will know
what I would have done if they'd've come out after I warned
them.

I turned Brownie onto the road for Douglas, thirty miles
south and nearly a mile lower down. And up here in the
pines and piñon and oak and grass valleys with the springs
and streams and the quail and turkeys and foxes and deer, it
was like heaven. And I had the feeling maybe I'd never see it,
or Uncle Frank, again.

Down on the desert floor, it was beautiful, too. The mesquite was loaded with fuzzy little yellow cattails, the long spikes of the *ocotillo* had a blossom like a red fire on each tip, and the palo verde were just clouds of yellow flowers. The dark green creosote were spattered with yellow flowers, too, and all the cactus showing those big, beautiful flowers that you can hardly believe belong to them, even the big stumpy *saguaros* with wreaths of waxy flowers on the very tops, crooked like they'd been hung on by a drunk. And quail calling and thrashers chasing each other and cactus wrens running around like today was the last day to find a little soft grass to make their four or five nests, and cottontails thick as fleas.

And up ahead was Douglas, in that tremendous wide flat, under a blanket of thick, strangling, yellow, poisonous smelter smoke, stinking up the whole world.

I felt real funny. On the one hand, I was real low and sad inside, leaving the Turkey Track and the Pedregosas and Uncle Frank and everything I'd known all my life. And on the other hand, I was glad the break had finally come. I didn't have any idea what I was going to do—I supposed I'd hang around Douglas a few days, and go across the line into Agua Prieta for some of that good Mexican cerveza, then go looking for a job on some ranch or maybe just set out traveling.

CHAPTER 3

It wasn't more than ten-thirty when I left. Brownie went into his jog trot that covers the most ground and gives you the worst pounding. I wouldn't get to Douglas till maybe seven in the evening, and I just settled down to take it. About two o'clock, where Blue Creek crossed the road, I got off and slipped the bridle and let Brownie chew some grass, and I ate my biscuits and rolled a smoke and rested my behind.

When we were about ready to start, I saw the surrey coming, way down the road. I thought, well, that's about the shortest honeymoon on record, and when Uncle Frank pulled up and stopped, I could tell by the set of Letty's jaw that they'd been arguing. She wasn't saying a word, now, though, and I grinned and said, "Well, you sure gave us a surprise. Congratulations, Mrs. Kelly!"

She snorted and looked away in the distance. Uncle Frank just said, "Well, looks like you're traveling. Anything wrong back home?"

"Everything was quiet when I left," I said. "I just figured I oughta go find a job somewhere else, Uncle Frank. I've never been anywhere except Bisbee and Tombstone and once to Tucson and a few times to El Paso. There really ain't enough to do on the Turkey Track. Cassie and Polly can handle it, easy."

He looked at me a long time and didn't say anything.

Then, not looking at me or him either, she said "Frank!" and he sighed and said, "Well, you come back whenever you're a mind to, Kel. There's always a place for you."

He shook up the team, then hauled them up again and turned around to me and said, "The Gadsden's a good place to stay till you make up your mind where you're goin'. Tell you what, you stay there till I bring you your back pay. You got four months coming, ain't you?"

It was five months, and I was about to say why didn't he write me a check right then, but he stared at me real hard, and I figured he wanted a chance to talk to me without her around, so I said, "Sure. I'm in no hurry," and he turned around and flapped the reins and they started off. She moved as far over from him as she could get on the seat.

The closer we got to Douglas, the more the sulphur smoke from the smelter got in my throat. Before we rode into town, I took my gun off and put it in the saddlebag, because Douglas had a town law that you couldn't wear a gun.

We rode down to the Gadsden Hotel and I went in and signed up for a room on the third floor. The lobby was real fancy—great big marble columns stretching up two stories, and a double stairway opposite the desk, up to a balcony. The furniture looked expensive. There were doors from the lobby into the dining room and the bar, and there were a lot of people, mostly men.

A bell boy grabbed my saddlebags and satchel and we went up in the elevator, and he opened the window and hung my coat up for me and gave me the key. I gave him a dime, and put my gear in the closet.

Then I went down and rode Brownie over to Andy Henning's Livery Barn to arrange for his keep.

In the hotel bar I had a drink of rye, and then a steak in the dining room, and afterward I bought the El Paso *Herald-Post* at the desk, and a sack of Bull Durham, and sat in the lobby. The paper said that one of Madero's generals, Victoriano Huerta, had defeated General Pascual Orozco in a twelve-hour battle and killed six hundred rebels and the rest ran away.

Like everyone else, I knew there had been a revolution a couple of years ago, and Francisco Madero had run that bloody old dictator, Porfirio Díaz, out of Mexico, and then had been elected president himself. But then some of Madero's own rebel generals revolted against him—General Zapata down in the south and General Pascual Orozco in Chihuahua, and others, and they were fighting again, all over Mexico. Nobody could keep it straight—that is, no American —who was fighting who, and nobody was much interested, anyway. Uncle Frank and other people said we ought to take over Mexico and run it right—and that was about all it meant to any of us *norteamericanos*. And they used to laugh because there were so many generals, and say that no Mexican knew how to fight, anyhow, except maybe Pancho Villa.

But I was too tired to read, and when I was getting up to go up to bed, the marshal, Long Tom Mundt, came in with a long skinny deputy, and went through the lobby, looking around and saying howdy to people. He sure looked me over when I crossed to the elevator, and I guess he kind of checked on everyone he didn't know personally.

I had me a hot tub bath, and it sure was wonderful after that copper wash-boiler me and Uncle Frank used on the Turkey Track. The sheets smelled fresh, and were smooth against my bare hide, and I thought, I'll sleep till noon!

And then I couldn't get to sleep. I suppose a man would get used to it—but a freight wagon went up the street with the skinner cussing the mules, and I could smell the dust it

kicked up, and an automobile went by with an awful racket.
Then just when I was dozing off, a street car went around the
corner with its wheels screeching on the dry rails, and the
trolley came off the wire and banged around, and the conductor was swearing, trying to get the trolley wheel back on the
wire. After that, some drunks started arguing just below my
window, and swore at me when I stuck my head out and told
them to shut up. So I filled the water pitcher and dumped it
onto them, and one of them fumbled under his coat and
pulled out a short gun and went to cursing and trying to figure out which window the water came from. Mundt's skinny
deputy sort of drifted out of the shadow of the hotel and
went up to him.

He said, "Elmer, you know better'n that. Gimme that gun!
You're gonna get ten dollars or ten days."

Elmer was of a mind to get tough with him, but the deputy
had a sawed-off double shotgun hung from his shoulder on a
string, under his coat. When he swung it up level, you can
believe there wasn't any more argument. Elmer's two friends
disappeared, and the deputy shoved him around the corner.

So then, of course I couldn't get to sleep at all. A church
bell across in Agua Prieta went "Bonk, bonk" like any Mexican church bell that never seems to ring, but just makes a
dull clank. It was hot, and I laid on top of the sheets, sweating, and got to thinking about the Turkey Track Ranch and
Uncle Frank and the Greenfields, and how sour it all went
right from the start, when those two vicious little monsters
came to live there. And Letty, and how she hated me from
the first time she ever cast my horoscope chart and told our
fortunes, me and the twins, with the Tarot cards.

She said she had cast the twins' horoscope charts right
after they were born, and that the first chart would cover
their first twenty years, maybe, kind of like the maps sailors
have to sail from here to there. And after that, you kept up
to date with what she called "progressed" charts. Oh, I
learned a lot about astrology because she was forever chart-
ing horoscopes and explaining what they meant. It was sure
confusing—like "the eighth house is the natural house of the
sign Scorpio," and it's supposed to be the house of Death,
and Gemini people under *that* sign—well it isn't the best
thing in the world for them! It's supposed to show sort of
sneakiness and harping on death and sex, and maybe revenge, and never forgiving an insult. I used to try to under-

stand her explanations, and I'd sneak her astrology books and star charts and try to make head or tail out of them, and I got so I knew a lot of jumbled-up things and, like I said, I don't know, yet, if I believe it or not. And what I've been saying, that's all about the twins, because they were Geminis, in the sign of Scorpio. And Letty said the planets Mars and Uranus were "posited" in the twins' signs of Gemini, and if there happened to be an eclipse of the sun any time around their twentieth birthday, it meant something pretty awful was going to happen—but not necessarily to them. She used to figure out from their charts all the good things about them, how they'd be strong and fearless and tough, and be able to stand a lot of punishment.

Only I read her books, like I said, and the reason they were supposed to have those good sides to them was that they were born only two days out of Taurus and into Gemini. And Taurus, that's me! Born May seventh about six A.M., that's what Uncle Frank told Letty when she asked—in the rising sign of the first house. And that meant I would most likely be "physically strong, magnetic, self-centered, practical, sometimes stolid, capable of great patience," according to her books.

Well, Letty sure didn't brag up those things about me! But she did say my birth sign was intercepted by Aries, which put fifty degrees influence in Taurus, instead of the usual thirty degrees. And I looked that up, too, and it seemed to mean I would be lonely and disappointed. And that I wouldn't ever forget a wrong, and could be patient a long time before I blew up, but that once my temper let go, it would be pretty bad. My earth sign could be real bad if I ever got in any tangle with a Gemini. And she said that the Saturn in my Taurus was in bad conflict with the Uranus in the twins' Gemini. And whatever anyone thinks about this astrology stuff, it sure seemed to be true when it came to me and the twins. I'm sure that's why she hated me, because of what she read in our horoscope charts, as much as the fights and trouble we had. And two things had happened that scared the hell out of her and the twins, too, and turned the three of them even more against me.

About a week before their nineteenth birthday, in April, 1911, we had an eclipse of the sun, and it was scary. The birds quit singing and there wasn't a breath of breeze, and everything had a kind of coppery color in the gloom. Letty tried to say something, and couldn't, and pulled the twins against her and hugged them. Her chin was quivering and she began to cry. And she'd look at me and bite her lip and look away. The twins were scared, too, I could tell, remembering what she'd said about if there was to be an eclipse.

And that night she cast new horoscopes for both of them, but it didn't make her feel any better. She cast mine again, too. She said she'd try me again and see if the *malefic* influence had left. That's the word she used, and I had to look it up in the dictionary, and it means evil, causing disasters. But when she had the chart done, she tore it up and said I never should have been born.

But since then, until yesterday, everything went along pretty smooth.

Well, I laid there remembering all the trouble, for eight solid years, and I was glad I was finally out of it. I didn't like to think I ran away from trouble. That bothered me. But I thought, well, I had the last laugh on those two bastards, and it was all finished.

So I finally got to sleep.

CHAPTER 4

I didn't get up till ten, and I had another bath and a good breakfast. I would have to wait around till Uncle Frank came to bring me my pay, but I wasn't in any hurry. It was only a mile or so to Agua Prieta, so I walked over. The border guards didn't pay me any attention—Mexicans and Americans were crossing back and forth all the time, and they hardly ever stopped anybody.

It's funny what a difference a few feet of ground made—as

soon as I stepped across into Mexico, everything felt different. The houses were built along the narrow streets like a solid wall with doors and windows in it, and you could hardly tell the homes where people lived from the bars and restaurants that were swarming with flies. Pack burros were going by loaded with firewood, and there was a creaking water cart, just a big barrel on wobbly wheels, pulled by a burro. Everything was dusty and looked run down, with plaster falling off the adobe walls, and people walking in the middle of the streets. And sometimes a door in the wall would be open, and you'd get a look into a patio, with flowers growing everywhere, in kerosene cans and tomato cans, and wash hung on lines and kids and skinny dogs and goats all over the place.

I sat in the little plaza a while, where there were concrete sidewalks between the grass and the flower beds, and benches, and a bandstand with the paint peeling, and old men sitting smoking or playing dominoes. There were a lot of Federal soldiers in town, and I saw a few *Rurales* in their big, felt sombreros and short, round-cornered jackets, and the big spurs dragging when they walked—except nearly all of them were horseback. And good horses. Really fine horses. They all had that Mexican insignia on a badge, an eagle sitting on a prickly pear chewing on a snake. And one thing about them, they were tough boys. Not that they were swaggering around showing off—but sometimes you meet a man, and there's a feeling, a kind of invisible little cloud around him that tells you, don't start anything! Well, those Rurales had that feeling around them, every one of them.

I found a cantina, dark and cool, inside three-foot adobe walls, and had a bottle of fine, dark Mexican beer. And that's where I found Concha. Or rather, she hitched onto me like a cholla stub that hooks onto you and you can't shake it off or kick it off—only I didn't try to fight her off.

She didn't come up to my shoulder. And she was pretty and round and brown and black-eyed, and her teeth were white. What I liked about her, she was clean, and her hair was shiny, and black as ink. And a purple *rebozo* wound around her head and shoulders. Her blouse didn't have any sleeves, and it didn't cover much of her chest, either. Her red skirt barely covered her knees, and even her feet were clean, in her sandals.

Puta is even a dirtier word than whore in English. I don't know why. Of course, that's what she was, a pretty little seventeen-year-old puta. But she didn't give me any sad story about how she had to go on the streets because her father got killed in the war and there were eight little orphan brothers and sisters that had to be fed, but in spite of everything, she was still a virgin in her heart. Nothing like that. She just said if I would buy her a drink I could sleep with her for two pesos, and if I wanted to stay all night with her it would be five. Silver pesos, she said, not paper money. And all the time, she was hanging onto my arm and pushing her round little belly against me and grinning up into my face and flapping those black eyelashes that must have been an inch long.

I had another beer and bought her a tequila, which I knew was tea when the bartender brought her the little glass, but I didn't care. Then we went to her room. I guess you'd call it a crib. It had its own door, onto a patio full of flowers, inside high adobe walls. Three families lived there. There was a burro asleep in a corner and some fighting roosters strutting around and fat little brown kids, boys and girls both, not wearing a stitch.

Her neighbors, nice fat Mexican ladies, said, *"Buenos dias"* to us and went on about their business, slapping tortillas and yelling at the kids. Concha shut the door and barred it. There was one window opening onto the patio, with no glass in it, just some crooked bars of mesquite limbs. There was one chair with a woven rawhide seat, a Saltillo *serape* on the floor, a rickety dresser with a red candle on it burning in a glass under a crucifix hanging on the wall. The bed was a big double one, the kind the Mexicans call a *cama de matri- monio.*

While I was looking for some kind of curtain to pull over the window, Concha got all her clothes off and jumped onto the bed. That blouse and skirt and sandals was all she wore. She didn't pay any attention to me being embarrassed, just sat there sprawled out and grinning, watching me take my clothes off. I guess I blushed the full length of my five feet eleven.

She was a real eager little puta, who enjoyed her work, and she didn't get tired. But I did. Sometime after lunch time, which we forgot all about, I just went flat like a punctured tire, and she snuggled her head against my neck and pushed up against me, shiny and slippery with sweat. She made me happy for the first time in a long time, and I was grateful to her. We slept until dark.

We had supper in the Restaurante Sonorense on a back street somewhere, and I was the only norteamericano there. It was a good place, and I like Mexican food, like it good and hot, with a lot of that hot sauce that will blister the inside of your mouth. It was cheap, too.

After supper we walked to the little plaza, with people we passed saying politely, *"Buenas noches, Señor, Señora."* We sat in the plaza a while, digesting the *chile relleno* and the *frijoles refritos* and the *carne asada,* and then went back to her place.

She was sure set on giving me my money's worth, and I hadn't even paid her yet. And what with dogs barking and burros winding up to bray and one of her neighbors beating his wife and the kids screaming and church bells going "bonk, bonk, bonk" every hour or so, and five hundred roosters crowing before I could even see it getting light, but mostly Concha so dead set on earning her pay, I didn't sleep at all. And I left her asleep and got dressed and put five dollars on the dresser, then went back to that restaurante and had eggs ranchero style, which means hotter than boiling oil. Then I walked back across the line to the Gadsden Hotel.

I went to sleep in the bathtub and only woke up when the water got cold. So I hung the Do Not Disturb sign outside my door and slept till dark. When I got up I had a shave, and after supper, I read in the paper where that General Huerta had attacked the rebels in their trenches at Rellano, six thousand rebels under General Orozco and ten thousand Federals with cannons and machine guns, and there was a big slaughter and the rebels broke and ran away. And down in the south, in Morelos, the rebel Zapata was getting stronger against Madero's army.

But I was still too worn out to finish reading the paper, and I went back to bed. And when I woke up about ten in the morning, there was Uncle Frank asleep in my chair. The hotel people knew him, and let him have a key. He'd rode half the night or more, and he looked old and tired, slumped down in the chair.

I woke him up, and he stretched and yawned and said, "How about lending me your bath tub and razor?" So he had a bath while I got dressed. Then he gave me a check for my back pay. It was supposed to be three hundred and sixty dollars for the last six months. I didn't look at it, just put it in my poke. I knew that wasn't all he rode thirty miles for, but he didn't say anything till we had our breakfast and came back to the room.

We both rolled a smoke, and he said, "I guess you knew when we met you at Blue Creek the honeymoon was over, already."

I just said, "Well, it didn't look like either of you was dying of joy."

"I think she's part witch," he said, "with them horoscopes and all. She must've put the Injun sign on me when she first came. We hadn't hardly said 'I do' when she told me how she was gonna move things around so's I could move in with her and the twins. And I said, 'Oh, no, Letty! I'm movin' in, all right, but they're movin' out! What kind of life you think we'd have with them two under foot night and day?' Then she said she'd never give up her boys, and I got mad and said I'd run 'em the hell off the ranch, if that's what it took. So, anyway, that's the story of my marriage, I guess."

I said, "You mean it's busted up already? She ain't gonna budge?"

"Well," he said, "I won't go into the details, what she said and what I said, but my God, Kel, can you imagine me living in the same house with them two? Anyway, when we got back, they started yelling that she was a traitor to them for marrying me. Then she told me if I wouldn't treat them like my own sons, why she wouldn't even let me in the house. I said, 'Letty, how'd you get the idea this house belongs to you? If it wasn't for me putting in for you when you came here, you wouldn't've had it at all! Now I'll tell you something. *I* run this outfit! Me—Frank Kelly! Cassie and Polly got twenty-four hours to get the hell off the ranch! And lady, if that don't appeal to you, why you get off with 'em!'

"I was standing by the surrey, and you know, I always got the Winchester carbine under the seat. Well, Cassie said, 'You Goddamn old bastard, don't you talk to her like that!' and he had the nerve to lay a hand on one of his guns. I fetched him a clout on the ear that near knocked him down. And while he was staggering back, I picked the Winchester up, and Polly—my God! Thinks he's a gunfighter! He was just standing there with his mouth hung open. I put the muzzle of the Winchester against his wishbone and shoved him against the house and told him to either unbuckle his guns and drop 'em, or pull 'em, whichever he was of a mind to do.

"Well, he was of a mind to drop 'em. Cassie was of a mind to go for his, and I told him, I said, 'Cass, boy, all I gotta do is twitch my finger and blow a hole in Polly's wishbone.'

"Then Letty screeched at him to drop his guns, and he unbuckled his belt and let 'em go. But I still shoved Polly against the wall, and I said, 'Cass, do me a favor. Go in the house and fetch me both your carbines and the shotgun. Now you can take a whack at me out the window. But I got the trigger pulled back on this Winchester, and the only thing holding the hammer from dropping is I got my thumb on it. So if you was to plug me, why my thumb would let go, wouldn't it?'

"Letty squawked, 'I'll get 'em, Frank! I'll get 'em!' and she fetched me those guns.

"I sat on the cabin porch most of the afternoon and thought things over. They didn't come out of the house. And then, yesterday afternoon, I made up my mind, and I hid all their guns. I went over and called Letty out and said, 'I'm going down to Douglas and take Kel his pay. I'll be back day after tomorrow, and if they're still here, I'm gonna kick their ass off the place.'

"She said along with everything else I didn't need to use obscene language.

"I said, 'You be here when I get back or not, just as you like. But them boys better be gone.'"

Uncle Frank stopped talking and looked at me, but I didn't know anything to say. After while, he said, "I expect she'll go with them, Kel. So you come back."

It wasn't easy, but I said, "No, Uncle Frank. I hate leaving you, but it's time for me to get out. If the Turkey Track was still a working cow outfit, maybe—but hell, I don't earn my sixty a month and found."

He didn't argue. He said, "I didn't think you'd come back. And I'm sorry I forgot your birthday, so I put a extra twenty-five dollars on the check. Ain't much of a present, kind of cold-blooded like, but well. . . ."

So I said, "Thanks, Uncle Frank. I know how it was."

"Well," he said, "I'll get going. Now you listen, Kel. I got Cassie and Polly bluffed, and they won't go for me. But I meant it, I won't have them on the place no more, and I don't expect Letty will stay with me. Now, I've gotta give back their guns. Can't keep 'em, it ain't right, and anyway, they'd just get some new ones. Most likely they'll show up here in Douglas, 'cause there's no place else to go till they figure out what to do. So you watch out! They'll have to get even for me runnin' 'em off. They'll take it out on you, if they get a chance, 'cause you're my own flesh and blood."

Then I told him about the coyote bitch and the centipede in my bed and the Virilidad I put in the syrup. He started laughing and said, "I thought they looked a little peaked! And I sure wondered how that privy got shot up. Well, Kel, all the more reason to be on your guard."

He put his arm around my shoulders and gave me a squeeze and said, "You take care, now!" and walked out.

After while I went over to the bank and cashed the check. I bought a money belt and put the bills in it and buckled it around my middle next to my skin, except fifty dollars in gold I put in my poke.

I bought me a whole new outfit, head to toe, all except underwear and my spurs and gun belt. A three-X beaver Stetson, a brown one, and a black silk handkerchief to tie around my neck, a white broadcloth shirt with pleats on the chest, black wool pants, and handmade boots with three inch heels. I got a black coat with kind of long skirts, I guess you call it a frock coat, and I got a barber shave and haircut. I looked like some rich young rancher or a gambler. And I had to show off to somebody, so I went across to Agua Prieta and hunted around the cantinas till I found Concha.

She climbed all over me, squealing and hollering, and I really think she wasn't putting it on. So we went to a store and I told her she could have anything she wanted. So she got a new yellow rebozo and a hand embroidered blouse with flowers on it, and an orange-colored skirt and a pair of red shoes with high heels. She went in the back room and put all the new gear on, and wrapped her old clothes in newspaper.

She said she couldn't thank me right, not there in the store, and we went to her place. She didn't have her new outfit on fifteen minutes when she took it off again. She sure thanked me, all right. Right past dinner time and clear till suppertime. And then she wouldn't let me pay her, not a cent. That's hard to believe, I guess, but it's the truth.

We got dressed and sort of stumbled over to the Restaurante Sonorense, and I had a plate of *enchiladas* with real hot sauce on them, and *sopapillas* light as air, with honey, and of course, refried beans and fried potatoes and a tomato salad. And we both had beer, her one bottle and me three.

Then back at her place, we slept a while, and she felt grateful again. And I never thought I would ever get too much of a woman that way, but I sure did! About one o'clock, I got up and got dressed. She didn't ask me for any money, but I gave her ten dollars.

She said, "You'll be back tomorrow?" and I said, "I don't know if I can stand you being so grateful," and I went out.

I was too tired to walk, so I hired a coach, a rickety old victoria with wobbly wheels and a skin-and-bones horse, and went back to the hotel.

CHAPTER 5

I managed to get undressed and fell into bed, and next thing I knew, a maid was coming in to do up the room, and it was nine o'clock. I chased her out and slept till eleven, and took a bath and shaved, and had my breakfast brought to my room, like I was a rich man.

So it wasn't till maybe half past twelve I got into my new outfit and stepped into the hall. Brownie needed exercising, and I was going to just ride him around. I was heading for the elevator, and a door opened down the hall, and there was Letty Greenfield in a red wrapper and her hair in paper curlers.

I stood still. She hustled down the hall to another door and knocked and said, "It's mama, boys." Then she looked around and saw me.

She gasped like somebody had pinched her on the rump, and shoved the door open and went in. I tiptoed back and put my ear against the door, and I heard her say, "He's right here! He's just down the hall!" And somebody mumbled something, and she said, "Kel!"

One of the twins said, "Hey, that's fine! We'll have us a talk with ol' Kel! He kind of represents ol' Frank, too, wouldn't you say?"

So Polly said, "Get dressed, Cass!"

I went back to my room and started putting stuff in my satchel, but I stopped. But then, because it began to seem to me that whatever I called it, I really ran away from them on my birthday, back on the Turkey Track, and I damn well wasn't ever going to run away from them again!

I left the gear scattered on the bed, and all I took was my big Bisley six-gun, hung in the holster on my right hip. My new frock coat halfway covered it.

I locked the door and walked down the hall past their door, and went down on the elevator and gave the clerk my key. Then I walked across the lobby and out on the sidewalk, on my way to get Brownie, and if they saw me . . . well, so be it.

I waited for a street car and a truck to go by, and stepped into the street to cross over to the livery barn, and somebody yelled from the hotel entrance, "Hey, you!"

I stopped, and it was the marshal, Long Tom Mundt, and he stepped off the curb and came toward me. He was pretty old, with knobby wrists and his chest kind of caved in and a pot belly on him. He was a big, broad, husky man once, you could tell that. And maybe he had lost his speed and his sharp eyesight, but he wasn't missing any guts! He always had sand in his craw, Long Tom Mundt, and he still had it.

He come up to arm's length of me, and said, "How come you're packing that hideout gun?"

I said, "Mr. Mundt, I ain't trying to hide a gun the size of this Bisley. It's just this long coat of mine."

"Well, kid," he said, "you don't pack no iron in my town! So use your left hand and hand it over, and then you come with me."

I backed up a step, and he took a step right with me. I said, "I'm Kelly Adams, and . . ."

"Never heard of you," he said.

He had seen me with Uncle Frank, all right, but I guess he forgot.

I said, "Listen! Those Greenfield twins are in the hotel, and I think they're gunning for me. I ain't gonna be empty-handed!"

"Never heard of them, neither," he said. "Now, gimme that iron!"

I wasn't making any move for my gun, and he shouldn't have, either, because when he pulled his, my old mule-headed stubborn streak came out.

I stepped in quick and grabbed his wrist and shoved his gun hand aside. And he was grunting and swearing and trying to jerk his hand loose, but he wasn't strong enough any more, and I hung on. I said, "You damn old fool! I ain't going to your damn jail and I ain't paying any damn fine, and I ain't giving you nor nobody else my gun! Not now, nor any other time!"

We were glaring at one another, and I couldn't figure how to turn him loose and not get shot, because I couldn't let go of him and grab his gun, and he sure wasn't going to hand it over to me, either! He said, "I ever lock you up? You carryin' a grudge against me?"

People were beginning to stop—a couple of riders and a buggy, and people on the sidewalk, and some came out of the hotel to watch. Me and the marshal, we were at a stand-off, and just then one of the twins hollered from the hotel entrance, "Hey, Kel! Didn't quite make it, did you! We're gonna have a little talk, Kel, boy! About that pancake syrup! An' then your God damn Uncle Frank!"

Me and the marshal both swung around, and when I let go of his wrist, *he* forgot all about me, because here came those two pushing through the crowd and already they were crouched over with their hands just over their guns—those four big guns, Polly's waist-high with the butts sticking out in front, and Cassie's tied down almost to his knees. And behind them, Letty was in the front of the crowd, with a queer kind of smile on her face.

Long Tom Mundt said, "You Goddamn babies, gimme them guns! You know the rules!"

They looked at one another, and Cassie gave a little nod, and Polly began to drift over to one side while Cassie kept coming straight for Marshal Mundt.

They had forgot about me, too, and I got a sick feeling inside, because I remembered their big plan, and I knew what they were going to do.

I guess Mundt didn't want to give them any excuse, because he put his gun back in the holster. If it had been just one of them, like with me, he'd probably have kept it in his hand, but with two of them, and separating the way they were, he must've figured he'd better talk them out of it.

He held his empty hands out to Cassie and said, "Gimme them, youngster!"

Cassie patted his guns and said, "You want 'em, old man, you take 'em!" And Polly was still sliding off to Mundt's right.

How could I stay out of it? I pulled my gun, then, and stepped up beside the marshal, between him and Polly, but I looked at Cassie, and I yelled, "You two hold on, now!"

The marshal took a quick look at me, then back at Cassie, and he was muttering to himself, "Damn me for an old fool, gettin' boxed like this!" He seemed to figure I was in with the twins, some way, on a three-way plan to kill him. He kept looking back and forth over his shoulder, trying to watch the three of us all at the same time.

Well, I stopped Cassie. He straightened up looking at my gun. But Polly, he slid over a little behind me and the marshal, and to our right. I had to swing clear around to face him. And while I was turning, he jerked both guns out.

There was a hell of a blast from the front of the hotel, and Polly dropped onto his face, kicking and wallowing around, screaming like hell. I stood like I was petrified, and Cassie did, too. But not Marshal Mundt—he slugged him over the ear with his gun barrel. Cassie dropped onto his hands and knees, knocked silly but not clear out.

There wasn't one sound in that street. I watched Mundt's skinny deputy step out from the crowd, stuffing a buckshot shell into the right-hand breech of his sawed-off shotgun. And then Letty Greenfield went swooping past him like a big bird, screeching and squalling, and flung herself down beside Polly. She hauled him up to her chest and sat there rocking back and forth hugging him, with the awfullest screams coming out of her wide-open mouth, and tears running down her face.

So while I stood there like a clothes store dummy staring at her, and then at the deputy walking up to her and Polly with the shotgun pointed at them—in case Polly was faking, being dead, I guess—Long Tom Mundt kicked Cassie in the head and knocked him onto his side, and took both of his guns. He tossed them toward the deputy.

Then he sort of strolled up to me like he was gonna make some remark about the weather, and all of a sudden he stuck his gun in my belly and said, "Now, you son of a bitch, gimme that gun!"

It was still in my hand, and he made me wild mad after my siding him, there. And he wasn't fast enough any more, and he came too close to me. I batted his hand aside, and he fired too late. It scorched my coat—and I buffaloed him! I whacked him good, and he dropped onto his face and laid there.

The deputy was picking up Cassie's guns, and he straightened up with a jerk, and looked first at Cassie, who was getting up to his feet, and then at Marshal Mundt lying on his face, and then at me. Then he raised the shotgun and told me to drop my gun. Then Letty slung her big cloth purse at Cassie, and it slid up to his feet, and he began fumbling in it and pulled out a little Colt .38 pistol.

She was screaming, "Kill them, Castor! Kill them!"

The deputy swung around to look at her, and Cassie shot him in the back. The way he fell, I knew he was dead.

Cassie was still half-silly from that knock on the head, and he fell to his knees, and Letty dumped Polly off her lap and scrambled over to Cassie and kneeled down beside him and got one arm around his shoulders. She pointed at me and screeched, "There, Castor! There's Kel!"

He raised the pistol with both hands and took a shot at me, but he was still wobbly and she was pulling at him, and he missed. I was backing away, and I would've killed him, but I was afraid I'd hit her, and I sure would have hit somebody in the crowd. The hotel clerk was in front of the crowd with a shotgun, but I guess he didn't shoot for the same reason, and now some of the others had hand guns.

Letty scrambled on her hands and knees to the dead deputy and picked up his shotgun. She had to jerk and yank to break the string around his shoulder, but she did it, and trotted back to Cassie and helped him stand up, and took the pistol out of his hand. And now nobody was bothering with me, because she gave him the shotgun, and they stood there back to back, him swinging the shotgun back and forth and her waving the hand gun. The people were yelling and cursing, but they quit moving in, and Cassie and his mother began going sideways toward the cross street. The crowd split and made way for them, and that's when I slipped down the opposite street and walked slow and let people go around me that were running toward the hotel.

Nobody noticed me. I got out of town and into the chaparral.

I wondered more how much of a damn fool I'd been not giving up my gun to Long Tom Mundt, and even worse, how hard had I hit the old man? The deputy had killed Polly Greenfield and Cassie had killed the deputy, and most likely the crowd would kill Cassie if they hadn't already. The question that had me really scared was, had I killed Long Tom Mundt?

CHAPTER 6

So I was what they called a fugitive from justice, and it was my own stubbornness that put me where I was. If I'd've just gave my gun up to Mundt and told him about the twins being after me, why it would've been up to him and that deputy with the shotgun. But he didn't have any right to take my one gun, when the twins were gunning for me. I would've done the same as I did, all over again.

I laid out in the chaparral till it was nearly dark, then I walked through the brush to Agua Prieta. It was full dark when I got to where Concha lived. She wasn't there, but one of her neighbor ladies recognized me, and hollered at her husband, and he grumbled and put on his shirt and went out to find Concha.

In about an hour they came back. She was real glad to see me, and I said thanks to the man, and he smiled and said, "For nothing!" Concha and I sat on her bed and she started to take her clothes off, but that wasn't what I was there for, not that time. I asked her if she heard anything about the shooting over in Douglas.

She said, "Oh, yes! Three *contrabandistas* tried to kill Marshal Mundt, and there was a great battle. The deputy killed one of them, and one of them killed the deputy, and the third one killed Marshal Mundt, and their woman was trying to help them get away, because everybody was shooting at them, and imagine! Three of them with only one woman! And the two that weren't killed left her to be captured, to gain time so they could get away."

"Well," I said, "did they both get away?"

"Oh, no," she said. "Justice triumphed as it always does in the end, and they are both caught and they will be hanged tomorrow."

I could see she didn't know as much as I did. I said, "I have to know what happened in Douglas. Will you go and find out if both contrabandistas got away, and if the mother . . . I mean, the woman, if she got put in jail, and most important of all, find out about Marshal Mundt, whether he got killed or not."

I gave her five dollars, and she went out, and I laid on her bed and went to sleep.

When she came back about nine o'clock, she hadn't found out what I really wanted to know. Cassie got away, for sure, but they caught Letty when she tried to get into the funeral parlor to see if they had Polly there. But nobody Concha talked to knew anything about Marshal Mundt, whether he was dead or not. They had taken him to the company hospital, and some said he was dying and some said he had already died.

Concha said that in Douglas and Agua Prieta both, they were hunting for the two men, in the towns and out in the chaparral. The Mexican and American police on the border would help each other out, I knew that.

Then Concha said, "But don't you worry, you just stay with Concha. We can just stay in bed and they'll never find you."

She wasn't stupid, and of course she had figured out by now that I was the contrabandista that had slugged the marshal. I told her maybe I would stay with her until I found out about Long Tom Mundt. But Concha's neighbors knew I was there, and if there was a reward posted—well they weren't friends of the gringo friend of their little puta neighbor.

I had to plan what I was going to do, but I hadn't had a thing to eat since that ham and egg breakfast, and I was so hungry I couldn't think.

We risked going to the Restaurante Sonorense, again.

Concha looked inside. It was pretty dark in there, but she said she didn't see any police, or any gringos.

We went in, and the first two or three minutes it was like sticking your head in a sack of soot, because there were only two smoked-up kerosene lamps way in the back and a candle stuck in a bottle on every table.

We no sooner sat down when a ragged little kid came in trying to sell me the paper from Ciudad Juarez, three days old. I said, "No," and he said, *"Mugriento cabrón gringo!"* and I tried to slap him but he dodged and ran out. Concha said, "I think he followed us since we left my place."

I said, "Well, he has to sell his papers, and us gringos are all suckers, true?"

"Don't call yourself gringo!" she said.

It's a real insult when a Mexican calls you that. Yanqui and norteamericano are all right, but not gringo.

And about that kid, I never thought a thing.

I ordered stewed goat meat a la Mexicana, that means seasoned hot as hell, and three cheese enchiladas, and it would be served with about a pint of refried beans with melted cheese over them. There were four army officers at a table in back, and four Rurales splitting a bottle of mescal near them, and the rest were ranchers and business men.

In Mexico, they heat your dinner plate in the oven, and the waiter has to use a thick napkin, and if you're yanqui, they usually warn you not to touch the plate. And the hot sauce is in a bowl with a spoon in it, so you can put on as much as you dare. It's a wonder the spoon doesn't go up in a puff of smoke, like you had stuck it in sulphuric acid. That sauce will actually put blisters on the hands of the women that make it, and you'd better not get any in your eyes.

So the waiter brought Concha's order, and my plate, blistering hot, and I ladled on the hot sauce, because I love the stuff.

The screen door opened and a kid held it back and said, *"Ahi 'sta el gringo hideputa!"* It was that newsboy, and he was pointing at me, and right behind him was Cassie Greenfield, dirty and his clothes ripped by thorns, and his hair all tangled, and the side of his head bloody where Marshal Mundt whacked him with the pistol. He looked like he just broke out of a lunatic asylum.

He had that dead deputy's double-barrel shotgun, and he was going to kill me.

Only the damn fool had to make a speech about it, first.

He swung the scattergun to bear on my belly, and the whole restaurant was quiet as a mouse. I got to my feet. Cassie said, "Kel, don't you move!"

I had both hands braced on the table, and I didn't move an eyelash. Those two eight-gauge bores looked like stove pipes. I slid my right hand half an inch under my folded napkin on the table, and he didn't see it.

His eyes kind of glittered in the candle light. "Kel, boy," he said, "you really think you could deal yourself in, there in front of the hotel, and I wouldn't catch up with you? You really think you could pull that gun on me and stop me and give that deputy time to get there? You really think you could do that, Kel, boy? Hold me off while that deputy cut my brother in half?"

I slid my hand with the napkin over it under the edge of my plate. The cheese on the enchiladas and the beans was still so hot it was bubbling.

Cassie waggled the shotgun. "Because," he said, "it wouldn't have happened, only for you."

He took a step closer. Concha was whimpering, and that was the only sound. And I got my right hand a little bit under the plate with the hot sauce all over the meat and enchiladas, and Cassie said, "You hadn't no call to horn in between us and Old Man Mundt. It wasn't none of your look-in. And if you hadn't of done what you did, why our mother wouldn't be in jail. Oh, yeah, Kel! Didn't know I knew that, did you! The boy, there, I give him a dollar to find you for me. I laid out there behind the shack where he lives, and he came back and told me about mama. And he found old Kel for Cassie, too, didn't he!"

He wasn't quite through with his speech, yet. He was staring into my eyes, and I had to take my chances. I got my hand all the way under my plate, palm up. The napkin got pushed off, and my hand was burning.

And he said, "Kel, you know you're gonna get blowed in half with this same shotgun, like my brother Polly? Because if you hadn't of done what you did, that marshal, he'd be dead, all fair and square. But Polly wouldn't be dead."

I didn't dare throw the plate, because his fingers were on both triggers, and those twin bores were a foot from my belly.

Then two Mexican police shoved the kid out of the doorway and stuck their heads in. Cassie jerked his head around and one of them said, "There's both of them!"

I could have thrown it then, but I had to make sure I got him square in the face and eyes. I don't know how I held still, with the palm of my hand blistering under the plate.

Then Cassie turned his head back, quick, and I heaved the plate in his face and jumped sideways.

He screeched and tripped backward over his spurs, and jerked off both barrels while he was falling.

The blast of those eight-gauge barrels blew most of the candles out, and people were trampling around in the half dark, knocking over tables and chairs. In the back, a man was screaming. My ears were ringing, but I could hear that!

I got up and dragged Concha toward the door, and by then I had the Bisley in my hand, and cocked. People began yelling and swearing.

I looked back and I could barely make Cassie out, down on his knees, clawing at that blistering food all over his face and in his eyes.

Then one of the police shoved in between me and Concha, and the other grabbed my left arm and said, "Gringo, you are arrest! We always givin' *cooperación* to Douglas *policía!*"

He hadn't seen the gun in my hand, and I rammed it into his belly and asked him in Spanish if cooperating with the Douglas police went so far as getting his spine shot in half.

He had the nerve to grin at me. He stepped back and said I had a strong argument there in my hand.

Then men jumped on Cassie and flattened him out on his belly, and were swearing and grunting and clawing at him, and the two police went to untangle them. In the back, one of the army officers yelled for a light and a waiter brought a lamp. They picked up an army officer from the floor. He must have taken most of the buckshot. He was limp as a rag, and his head just flopped around, and the whole of him was red with blood.

I pulled Concha outside and we ran down the street, then I pulled her down to a walk so we wouldn't attract attention. She was crying and hanging onto my arm, and I said, "Hey, it's over! No use to cry, now."

"He was going to kill you," she said.

"The police have him," I said, "so it's all right."

And when I said "police," it made me remember, and I

said, "They were after me, too! Remember, they said, 'There's both of them'?"

At the restaurant, a block back, a crowd was collecting. More police came, and in the light from the doorway, we saw them drag Cassie out. He was screeching at them, and one of them hit him in the face with a pistol, and he slumped down and they hauled him away. Probably in a few minutes, Cassie would be up against a wall, for killing the officer. I was surprised they didn't shoot him right there.

Concha and I stood in a doorway till things quieted down. That's when I made up my mind I better not go back across the line for a couple of months, anyway.

So I told Concha she'd been a real good friend, and maybe I'd see her again sometime. Well, she began to blubber that she loved me, and I couldn't leave her.

I said, "Shut up! You want people to come see what's wrong, and catch me?" I looked back, and a man I hadn't seen, leaning against the front of the restaurant, straightened up and started after us.

I swore, and Concha saw him, too. She said, "He's after you!" and tried to run. I pulled her back and said, "Just act like we didn't see him."

We walked to the next street and turned the corner and I pulled her into the doorway of an empty patio. If the man went on down the street, all right. But if he turned the corner after us, I was ready, with the gun in my hand.

He came hurrying around the corner, and didn't see us in the doorway. I stepped out behind him and got my left arm around his neck and bent him backward, and shoved the Bisley into his kidneys.

He gasped and said, "No shoot! Señor, no shoot!" Believe me, he was scared.

I said in Spanish, "You could get hurt, following a man like this."

I got his revolver out of a shoulder holster, and backed away from him and waited.

It was too dark to see what he looked like. He said, "You speak Spanish, that's what I had to find out. Señor, let me lower my hands."

"You can put them down," I said, and he did, and I said, "Go ahead. Talk."

He said, "I saw it all, when the marshal tried to take your

gun, and when one of the twins was killed and the other shot the deputy. I tried to follow you but you got away." He wiped his face on his coat sleeve.

He went on, "Then I looked for you here in Agua Priesta, thinking here is where a fugitive would come. And I saw you and the . . . this lady . . . go into the Restaurante Sonorense, so I went in. And I saw you subdue the twin with the shotgun, and I saw you dominate the police officer."

He was talking *castellano* and lisping all the z's and some of the c's, but I understood him all right. I said, "Are you an agent of the police?"

"I am Hector Estrada Palacios y Garza," he said, real proud, like I ought to know him and get down on my knees.

When I only said, "So you are Hector Estrada Palacios y Garza," he said, "of Los Cerritos," like it ought to mean something to me.

I didn't say anything, and he said, "The ranch of the fighting bulls, near Nuevo Casas Grandes in Chihuahua. Why, man, anyone who loves the *corrida de toros*. . . !"

I broke in, "What do you want? Hurry it up!"

"I need a bodyguard," he said. "A man I can trust. Why, I can't trust my own *peones* these days! With this revolution going on and their minds warped and their loyalties twisted, and forgetting their obligation to me, and the place of their birth which provides them with food and work and homes!"

"Come on, Concha," I said, "this man is a windbag." And I said to him, "I'll keep the pistol to remember you by, Don Hector Estrada Palacios y Garza."

Today I had found out for the first time what kind of power a man has with a gun in his hand, and even a vicious son of a bitch like Cassie Greenfield, with his own gun in his hand and his miserable brother to side him, will back down from you, and Mexican policemen get real polite, and Don Hector Estrada Palacios y Garza that owns a big bull ranch, will treat you nice. This was a new feeling to me, and it felt good.

Palacios said, "Señor! Please! You are wanted, and you need a place to stay. And I need a man with no interest in the politics of my country, who will not betray me, if I pay him well. Why, two weeks ago one of my own trusted guards whom I paid well, tried to assassinate me! Because as he said, spitting at me even as we stood him against the wall, he considered me a plunderer of the people, a bloodsucker, and his only regret in dying was that he had failed to take me with him, for the good of the revolution."

"About that pay," I said, "what would it amount to?"

He was right, I didn't have any place to go. And getting paid just to pack a gun sounded like a pretty good living.

"A hundred pesos a month, gold," he said. "And good clothing and a good horse, your own quarters."

I said I would take the job.

"Let's go back to the corner, where there is more light," he said, "and I will give you a note for my daughter. I must go on to Cananéa and then to Tucson and perhaps to Phoenix before I return home."

We walked back to the corner, and he wrote something on the back of his business card with a little pencil that gleamed gold in the dim light from the restaurant down the street.

"What is your name?" he wanted to know.

I couldn't see any reason not to tell him. Most likely he had already heard it in Douglas, anyway. So I told him how to spell it, and then asked him, "What did you write on the card?"

He said, "You have only to show it to anyone in Chihuahua, to trainmen, soldiers and Rurales. It is to my daughter. It reads, 'Lidia, this introduces my new man, Kelly Adams. He will take the place of Andrés. Furnish him with whatever he requires. Your father'."

"I'm not your man," I told him.

"Just a manner of speaking," he said. "If you wish, I will change it to 'my employee'."

"Never mind," I said. Then I asked him for the loan of one of his cards and his pencil, and I wrote a note to Uncle Frank, saying Rancho Los Cerritos near Nuevo Casas Grandes, Chihuahua, would be my address, and for him to pick up Brownie and get my gear from the Gadsden Hotel.

I gave the card to Concha and told her to give it to Andy Henning in the livery barn so he could give it to Uncle Frank when he came to town.

Then I asked Palacios how to get to Los Cerritos.

"Take the Mexican North Western from Ciudad Juárez," he said. "Get off at Nuevo Casas Grandes, about two hundred and fifty kilometers. My ganadería, Los Cerritos, is only five kilometers from the town."

I could make out his face, now, in the light from the restaurant. He was a big man, in a business suit and a narrow-brimmed Stetson. He had a thin black mustache and a little black goatee and a lot of black hair and thick eyebrows. He was maybe forty-five, and beginning to run to belly and jowls.

Concha began to bawl because I was going away. I jabbed her with my elbow, and she quieted down.

I said to Palacios, "What about the revolution? Is there any fighting around Nuevo Casas Grandes?"

"Oh, no," he said. "Nothing. Just a little guerrilla activity. You will have no trouble. The right people hold Chihuahua."

"Who are the right people?" I asked him.

"Why, the Federal forces!" he said, like I was a stupid kid that ought to know better. "Fortunately for decent people, the Rurales transferred their loyalty to Madero after Porfirio Díaz resigned. They have dealt with the insurrection in our area, and General Huerta is whipping that dog Pascual Orozco from pillar to post. Here," he said, "you'll need funds for expenses," and he flipped me a gold coin, like I was his servant.

I didn't like him very much. I figured he was what the Mexicans call a *gachupin,* a Spaniard. Mostly, they hate the Spaniards, and gachupin is as bad an insult as calling an American a gringo.

I gave him back his pistol. Then I looked at the gold piece, and it was fifty pesos. I imitated his castellano way of talking, and said to Concha, "You will need funds for expenses," and I flipped the gold piece to her the way he did to me.

She caught it and quit sniffling, and began to grin.

He said, "Then, Adams, just wait at Los Cerritos for me. Have my *caporal* show you around. I may be gone another month." He didn't shake hands, just walked away.

I turned to give Concha a hug and say goodbye, but she was trotting after Palacios, saying, "Señor Palacios! Psssst! Señor Palacios! Where are you going to spend the night?"

First I was mad, and I was going to catch her and get my fifty pesos back—then it struck me funny, and I let her go.

The moon was up, and I didn't have any trouble getting out of Agua Prieta and through the brush and the international fence, and walking the ties of the El Paso Southwestern until I came to a water tank, just east of Douglas. I took off my coat and rolled it up for a pillow, and laid on the ground. It was a nice warm night, and I settled down to wait for an eastbound freight.

CHAPTER 7

I was so tired I went to sleep, in spite of all I had to think about. It was real early in the morning when a freight woke me up. I stood in the shadow of a telegraph pole while they took on water, and then I climbed into an empty box-car before they picked up speed. There was some straw on the deck, and I pulled it together and laid there watching the country roll past, by moonlight.

We rambled along pretty fast. I recognized Antelope Pass in the Peloncillos, and we went through Animas and Rodeo without stopping. About daylight, we stopped in Hachita to pick up some freight. I was about starved, but I stayed in the boxcar and nobody bothered me.

I'd been to El Paso by train, and I knew it was only forty-five miles farther, from Hachita to Colombus, New Mexico, on the border. I thought maybe the brakeman or conductor had seen me, and might know about the trouble in Douglas and would telegraph ahead to El Paso, or even hunt up the law in Columbus, so when we slowed down outside the town, I dropped off. The brakeman was going along the top of the train setting up the brakes, and the conductor was leaning out from the far side of the caboose platform, and they didn't see me.

I got me a drink at a railroad water tank and went into the brush and went to sleep, because I was so tired I was ready to drop.

When I woke up I decided to play it as safe as I could, and stay off the railroad and the roads. From what Palacios said, I thought his bull ranch might not be too far south of the border. Maybe I could head into Mexico from right here.

About nine, I got up and brushed the sticks and sand off

47

me and walked in to Columbus. Nobody on the streets paid me any attention, and I had ham and eggs and fried potatoes in a Chinese restaurant, and then went into Ravel Brothers Mercantile and there weren't any other customers there, and only one clerk. I asked him about getting to Nuevo Casas Grandes.

He said I was crazy to go into Chihuahua with a revolution going on, but, anyway, there was a road south from Columbus, through Las Palomas and Las Bajadas, La Ascención, then Janos, and next was Nuevo Casas Grandes, about a hundred and fifty miles.

He sold me a canvas warbag, a razor and soap, four big cans of tomatoes and two boxes of crackers to put in it. I got two boxes of .450 cartridges for the Bisley.

The clerk told me how to find the livery stable, and I bought a ten-dollar horse for twenty dollars, a roughed-up old McClellan saddle for two dollars, a single-ear headstall with a rusty half-breed bit for three, and a pair of Mex spurs for two-fifty. The livery man threw in an old army blanket for free, and told me to go south past the depot, then past the Thirteenth Cavalry army post, and just ride through the gate in the international fence.

My little roan horse was one of them that was twelve years old and never got any older, no matter how many times he was sold, over the last twenty years. But he was a cow pony, and he reined good.

A guard at the army post entrance said, "Hold on there, mister! Where you think you're goin'?"

I just kept going, and he hollered louder, but I didn't speed up or slow down or look back. At the border fence, the gate was open, and there was another guard. The one behind me was yelling, and this one stepped into the middle of the gateway with his carbine ready, yammering at me to halt. I didn't think he'd shoot me in the back without any more reason than he had, so I just kept going.

If he hadn't stepped back at the last second, my horse would have stepped on him. But he did, and it didn't, and he was swearing worse than any muleskinner when I hit a lope into Mexico.

That was May thirteenth, 1912, and if anyone had told me on my birthday that in less than a week I'd be across the border, on the run, and not knowing whether or not I killed a man, I'd've said they were crazy.

I didn't know, then, how everybody in Mexico was a rebel of one kind or another, and fighting each other and the government, or they were for the government and fighting everybody else, and you couldn't trust anybody but your family and friends, and maybe not them, either.

That was awful poor country, and I don't know how anybody made a living. It was mostly sandy, with stunted mesquite bushes and creosote bush and yucca and a lot of salt bush, but not a tree in sight, except miles away on the mountains. The Sierra Madre Occidental, to the west, blue and far away and just piled up higher and higher into the sky the farther south they went.

Toward dark each day, I started looking for water or a windmill, but there wasn't any. Two afternoons, I split a can of tomatoes with Old Timer—that's what I named my horse —and he sure didn't turn up his nose at it.

I didn't stay over in Las Bajadas or La Ascención at night, because people sure weren't friendly, and Old Timer and me, we just got a meal and a drink, then slept out in the sand hills, away from the road.

It was the third day, about ten in the morning, and we were getting near Janos, and five Rurales rode out of the chaparral. Four of them had carbines pointed at me, the shortest carbines I ever saw, fastened to a swivel on a leather sling over the left shoulder. The other one was an officer, and he had a converted Remington six-gun on his hip. He told me to hand over my gun.

I said, "I have a pass from Don Hector Palacios of Hacienda Los Cerritos."

He said, "Read it for me. I don't know how, and my men are even stupider." They all laughed, and I thought he was joking, but he wasn't.

So I read what Palacios wrote—"Lidia: this introduces my new man, Kelly Adams. Put him with Narciso and see that he has what he needs until I return." The signature was just a scrawl, all loops and curlicues, that they called a rubric.

The officer took the card and looked at it, then he said, "Yes it is his rubric. I have seen it before, so I accept you as authentic. We'll ride to Janos with you. I am Salvador Cano, Chief of Rurales at Nuevo Casas Grandes, at your service.

Let me compliment you on your Spanish. For a yanqui, there is almost no accent."

I thought he'd ask what my work would be for Don Hector, and I didn't want to say *pistolero* because that word has a kind of bad meaning. But I guess he knew. Anyway, he didn't ask.

The *Guardia Rural* uniforms were big felt sombreros, wrinkled white shirts with big clumsy red neckties, short gray coats with rounded skirts and four big silver buttons, vests with a whole string of small silver buttons, and those wrinkled charro pants coming down over the short boots, and big spurs. They had badges on their rifle slings—the cactus with the eagle and snake—and machetes slung on the nigh side of their saddle horns, and the saddles were those Mexican trees with the oversize roping horns and the white rawhide covering, and a mochila over the whole thing, with huge saddlebags built right onto the saddle skirts.

We rode along together talking, and outside of Janos there was an old building with a broken down adobe wall around it, and a row of buzzards flopping and squawking on the wall, and the whole place buzzing with flies, and there was an awful stink.

Three peones were leaning on shovels beside a short trench, watching us ride up. I stopped right in the middle of something I was saying, and I must've looked pretty foolish, because Salvador Cano laughed and said, "They were very bad boys, Señor Adams. Two of them shot a Rural, and the others wouldn't tell us who the two were until we questioned them for more than an hour."

There were dead men piled head to foot in the trench, dirty and bloody, with their mouths open, I don't know how many. It made my stomach queasy.

When we rode into Janos, women and kids got off the street, and men stopped talking and watched us ride past. And I thought my friends were pretty watchful, too, and maybe a little nervous. Salvador Cano invited me to have a beer, and we tied our horses in front of the cantina. The owner set chairs around a table under an arched gallery, and he was bowing and grinning—but he was nervous and scared. I was nervous, too, and still sort of numb from seeing those dead men in the trench.

The man brought us our beer, and the officer, Salvador Cano, said they were riding on to Nuevo Casas Grandes, about fifty kilometers. He said I'd never make it before midnight, on Old Timer, and I'd be better off to stay in Janos overnight. I said that's what I'd do.

I wasn't sorry to say goodbye to him and his four Rurales.

Later, when the man brought my supper, I asked him what Nuevo Casas Grandes meant—New Big Houses—because none of the houses I'd seen yet were new, or big either.

He said there was a very small town, a real old one, about five kilometers south of Nuevo Casas Grandes, and next to it was a hundred acres of ancient, prehistoric ruins—the "big houses"—pyramids all grown over now with grass, and adobe buildings as much as six stories high, all falling to pieces. People found a lot of beads made from small sea shells, and beautiful pieces of pottery. The people that built the place so long ago were the Paquimé, but I couldn't figure out how anybody knew that, if they were all dead a thousand years ago, because who would you ask? Anyway, I thought I'd go see it the first chance I got.

I slept in a real bed that night, in the back of the *cantina*, and got an early start in the morning. We made the thirty miles to Nuevo Casas Grandes in good time, with only one stop at a patch of grass near a little spring. We were following the river, the Río de Santa María, and there were rounded, grassy hills, now, and a few trees.

Then we were going between apple and peach orchards in bloom, just about the prettiest sight I'd seen since I left the Turkey Track Ranch, and I had an empty feeling in my belly, real homesick, even though I didn't have anybody to be homesick for except Uncle Frank, and I really didn't miss him very bad. Then the river turned and a little road branched off the main road, and I saw a sign *Hacienda Los Cerritos 5 kilometers*. I turned Old Timer to follow it.

Five kilometers is only about three miles, and it was the middle of the afternoon when I turned Old Timer in under the archway of a big, double, plank gate that had both wings swung partly open, and started him down a lane that ran between high stone walls. The arch had Los Cerritos, 1824 carved on the keystone.

That's when I met Ángel. He stepped out behind me from in back of one of the gate wings and asked me politely to put my hands up, and let him take my gun.

I pulled Old Timer up short, but I didn't look around. I knew if I didn't make a stand, right here, didn't kind of de-

clare myself, I'd be off to a bad start. I put my hands on the
saddle horn, one over the other, and said in my politest Spanish, "It is against my strongest principles to give anyone my
gun. If I ride ahead of you, you can kill me as easily as if my
hands were tied. I hope this will satisfy you, because you
must decide before we move on, or before one of us moves
on. Because you have no idea how stubborn I am, nor how
fast I may be with my pistol, nor how many slugs I will put
into your belly if your first shot doesn't stop me dead. What
I'm saying is that I won't give you my gun. Besides, I have
business at Los Cerritos."

I looked around then. He had a Marlin carbine pointed at
me. His lean, brown face was screwed up like he was thinking hard, and his mouth was clamped tight shut under his
stubbly mustache. A clump of iron gray hair came down to
his eyebrows. He was a vaquero, and I knew, the real thing—
with a heavy straw sombrero and an old blue shirt and tight-
fitting old charro pants, and flat-heeled boots with big six-
point rowels on his spurs. He had a cartridge belt across his
chest.

He said, "Señor, you surprise me, with such good Spanish,
but obviously norteamericano. Ride ahead, and for your own
sake, be careful. Right now, keep looking down the lane."

He had a horse behind the gate, and I heard the stirrup
leather creak when he got on.

"Will you read a note from Don Hector to his daughter?"
I asked, and he said, "You must show it to someone who can
read. Have the kindness to lead the way."

The wide lane ran half a mile to a huge, sprawling house
with a red tile roof and a long, shaded gallery behind brick
arches. I could see, through another arched gateway at the
end of the lane, the big paved patio with flower beds against
the walls, and men working on them. The river ran behind
the house and a dozen other adobe buildings, and a half mile
away was a little village of shacks.

Acequías full of water were laid out to irrigate corn and
wheat fields as far as I could see, and in a big field that must
have spread forty acres, eight different ox teams were pulling
clumsy wooden plows.

The lane ended at the other high, arch gateway, and Ángel
said, "We will stop here. You'd better get down."

I did, and he got down too, and yelled, "Narciso!"

A monstrous big mongrel came charging out from behind

the swung-back gate, pulling on a chain so hard it was choking—and snarling and showing a row of teeth like a shark.
Holding it back was a short, thickset man, dressed *charro*
fashion and packing, of all things, a big Bisley Colt on his
hip.

He pretended he wasn't looking at me, but he let that God
damn dog lunge to within a foot of me, and it took just everything I had to stand still.

"Ángel," the man said, "why haven't you taken this
gringo's pistol? Have you lost the little intelligence you were
born with?"

Ángel told him, "Narciso, I just look out for Doña Lidia
when the *patrón* is away. But you are the big bully boy,
snorting fire and pawing the ground, and guarding us all
from revolutionary assassins and strangers carrying big pistols like yours. So I wouldn't for anything cut in on your job.
You take his gun!"

And like with Ángel, I knew I had to get off on the right
foot with this Narciso, the bodyguard Don Hector had told
me about, or I just wouldn't make the grade.

He said, still not paying attention to me, "No one, not
even friends of the household, is to approach the house
armed! And as for strangers, pistoleros like this gringo . . ."

I broke in, then. I said, "Narciso, three things I will bring
to your attention. First, I have a note from your patrón to
his daughter. Second, don't call me gringo again! Third, if
the dog makes one more jump at me, I'll use my gun."

He looked at me then, and laughed with just his mouth,
not his eyes. He said, "You must be fast as lightning if you
can draw it before Tigre has you by the throat." But he
didn't call me gringo.

I said, "I'll put my arm across my throat, and while he's
chewing on that, I'll plug you before I kill him. Now have we
got it all straight?"

He really wasn't scared of me—he was a tough boy, that
one—but anyway, he held the dog back and said something
to it, and it didn't jump at me any more.

Then a girl said, real mad, "Narciso! Chain that beast to
the wall! Who is that . . . that person? And why is he
armed?"

She came out from the shadow of the archway and into
the sunlight.

CHAPTER 8

It seemed like everyone was going to talk about me and at the same time pretend I didn't exist. Because she kept looking back and forth between Ángel and Narciso for answers to her questions, without looking at me. That made me mad, or I wouldn't have been rude and stared at her like I did, to show her I wasn't some *mozo* that didn't dare look her in the eye. She was worth staring at, and I wouldn't ever forget how she looked if I never saw her again.

She was little, about the size of Concha, but on the lean side, with high cheekbones, and her jaw firm, but round, too. She was dark, what the Mexicans call *canela*—and that means two things, cinnamon colored, or something very beautiful. And if I thought my own eyes were black, well, they weren't, compared to hers. Her face was beautiful, that's the only word for it, smooth skinned, straight nosed, full lipped, thick eyebrows black as midnight, and straight hair so black it had a blue shine to it, done up in a big bun on the back of her neck.

Ángel said, "Señorita, this person claims to have a message from Don Hector."

I got sore, I said, "Let's all get this straight . . . I haven't come begging to your door. I offered to show this peon here," and I nodded my head toward Ángel, "the note. And if he wasn't so ignorant he could tell you if I am lying." Then I jerked my head sideways toward Narciso, and said, "And this brave boy, instead of examining my message, turns his dog on me. No doubt he is as stupid as this other mozo. And you, Lidia," and that was kind of an insult too, using her first name, without any doña or señorita in front of it, "why

54

don't you ask to see the message, and then have me whipped off the ranch when you find out I am lying?"

Narciso took a step toward me and growled, "Show respect for the señorita, gringo, or I will . . ." and he put his hand on his gun butt. That got me really mad, and rash the way I always get when I'm that mad. I swung around on him and said, "I told you about that gringo stuff! I'll bend my gun over your thick skull."

I don't know what he would have done, but she said, real sharp, "Narciso!" and his eyes sort of flickered, and he backed away and snapped the dog's chain to a ring bolt in the gate column.

Then she said to Ángel, "Why was it you who met him at the other gate? Narciso is paid to guard us."

"Señorita," he said, "it is not Narciso's fault. Salvador Cano and four Rurales stopped to tell me that this norteamericano would appear, and I feel a personal responsibility when the patrón is away, and, well . . ."

He sort of trailed off, and she smiled at him. She said, "Is it that you don't have entire confidence in our brave Narciso?"

I picked up Old Timer's reins and swung up into the saddle. When I turned him around and started him back down the lane, she came running after me.

She grabbed the reins and said, "Please, Señor! Wait! It is I who am rude! Let me see the note."

I said, "You could have seen it ten minutes ago, without all the chatter. Well, if you will call off your three dogs . . ."

Ángel said, "Señor, if I am called dog, I will . . ."

I said, "I'm sick of your talking. Shut up!"

She said, "Ángel, keep quiet! Narciso, go away! Go chase Rosita or Azucena, as usual, if you are not too tired."

Narciso glared at her and then at me, and unsnapped the dog's chain and walked away. Ángel didn't leave me alone with her, not for a second—but at least, he kept his mouth shut.

Then Lidia said, "Please, Señor! Get down!"

So I dismounted. I really couldn't blame any of them. I was norteamericano, and I hadn't shaved in several days, my clothes were wrinkled and dirty, and I was packing a big iron on my hip.

She read the note on her father's card, and said, "Ángel,

take Señor Adams to the kitchen and see that he is fed. He is to be well treated, so you will take him to the *tienda de raya* and let him select clothing, and whatever he needs to look presentable and to carry out his duties. Tomorrow, choose a good mount for him, if he is capable."

Then she said to me, "Señor Adams, the tienda de raya is the store which we maintain for the benefit of the peones and the salaried employees. You understand that it is not free, it goes on an account in your name."

"No, it doesn't," I said. "Not clothes. I pay cash for my clothes. Nor will a horse, nor cartridges be charged to me. My agreement with Don Hector is that all necessary equipment is furnished."

Ángel spoke up again, "Well, we'll see when the patrón returns."

I said, "Ángel, you will see to nothing concerning me. So no more suggestions. No orders. Unless, of course, you want to argue the point."

He surprised me by grinning at me. "What a rooster of a man!" he said. "Perhaps, later, we will be friends. For now, I will tolerate no disrespect to our *patrona*. In spite of your note from the patrón, we don't know you. At present, you have the appearance of a low grade bum. But let us not fight over things of little importance."

How could I not grin back at him? I said, "Well, man, let's go warily and get this gear for me, and a good horse."

He turned to Lidia and said, "With your permission, Señorita?"

Lidia said, "First let me ask a question, Señor Adams. All norteamericanos are wealthy, and I wonder why you have come into Mexico to be the servant of a Mexican, for the small pay such jobs command. Could it be that you are a wanted man?" She said it like there could only be one answer.

I said, "It pleases you to be sarcastic. Very few norteamericanos are wealthy, as we both know. My salary will be almost as much as I have ever earned. And as for my being a wanted man, I don't know whether I am or not. I understand there are thousands of wanted men in Mexico, wanted by one side or the other. Are they all criminals?"

She smiled at me, then, for the first time. "No, of course not," she said. "How did you learn Spanish so well?"

"Guadalupe, from Lagos del Moreno, brought me up from

the age of three," I said. "Really my stepmother, but a real mother to me."

Then they both smiled at me, and Lidia said, "Ángel, Señor Adams is to have Andrés' quarters." Then she said to me, "I hope you are not going to follow in Andrés' footsteps."

I said, "I have no plans to assassinate my employer, nor to die in front of a wall."

"One thing I admired about Andrés," she said, "even though he tried to kill my father, he had the courage to die for his principles."

"That wasn't proven," I said. "He was caught. And if you're caught, you may just as well die a hero, because you're going to die, anyway. But you needn't worry, I'm a yanqui, and everyone knows yanquis have no principles."

"Everything you said is true!" she said, and went into the big house.

On the way to the ranch store, we passed a blacksmith shop and a wagon shed that had not only work wagons but a beautiful shiny coach, a heavy Concord like they still used in parts of Arizona, even with automobiles coming into use. Ángel said it was used to bring high-toned guests from Nuevo Casas Grandes when a *tienta* was held at Los Cerritos. A tienta is the testing for bravery of young heifers that will be bred to get bull ring bulls, and of every young fighting bull when he's about two years old. They let the young bulls charge a picador and take the lance in the shoulder a couple of times, just to see if they *will* take it, or if they quit. And the heifers, they let them charge the picador till they quit, and Ángel said some of them will charge over twenty times, driving in onto the lance with their shoulders all mangled and bloody. But if they're quitters, they go to the slaughterhouse. He said the ranch had its own bull ring, for the tientas.

I saw the stone corrals with the feeding troughs where the bulls are fattened up, six of them, with maybe a couple of extras in case of accident, before they go in the bull ring.

Hacienda Los Cerritos had its own church, a fancy little chapel with a statue of the Virgin of Guadalupe and a lot of carving covered with real gold leaf. There was even a priest living on the hacienda, Padre Arrellaga. The *cuadrilla*—the headquarters, that is—was a little city. Ángel told me he didn't know exactly, but thought the hacienda was about fifteen by twenty-five kilometers.

At the tienda de raya, I got a couple of white shirts and some underwear, and a charro outfit, and a heavy, felt sombrero.

It was sundown, and ox drivers were bringing in their teams, and *vaqueros* were riding in by twos and threes, and Ángel took me to my quarters and said Narciso would show me where to come for supper.

My room was in a little U-shaped adobe house, one of three rooms with separate doorways opening onto a paved patio. There was a table and one chair, and a dresser, and a double bed with a busted cotton mattress and two wool blankets and no pillow. The one window had shutters but no glass, just some mesquite sticks set into the adobe for window bars. There was a good Mexican saddle on a rack in the corner, and a braided horsehair headstall with a spade bit, and braided reins with a romal quirt with a leather popper. In the big saddlebags they called cantinas, built right onto the saddle skirts, was a rawhide *reata* as slick as a snake, and at least eighty-five feet long.

Narciso lived in the room to the left of mine, and the other was empty. When Ángel brought me there, Narciso was leaning in his doorway rolling a corn husk cigarette, and that damn monster dog was chained to the wall. It snarled and charged me and near choked to death when it hit the end of the chain.

Narciso just went on rolling his smoke, and Ángel didn't do anything, so I just asked which room was mine, and Ángel showed me and went away.

There was a basin and a pitcher of water on my dresser, and I washed up and shaved and got into my new clothes, and when I went out, Narciso was gone. The dog was still there, though, still chained up, and it near went crazy trying to get at me. I came within a whisker of shooting it.

It was dark then, with lights all around, in the big house and the shack village where the campesinos lived, and there was that wonderful smell of charcoal fires. I asked a man where Don Ángel had his dinner, and he went with me to show me. The kitchen of the big house was a separate building with a dog trot in between, and Ángel and Narciso and three men in suits and shirts and neckties were eating at two tables. I sat down by Ángel, and he announced to the room in general that I was Kelly, a new guard for the patrón. They all looked me over like I was something nasty that had just crawled out of the refried beans. Ángel told me the fancy dressed ones were a bookkeeper and a secretary and the storekeeper.

Narciso was across the table from me. He smiled at me for the first time, and said, "How was Tigre when you left?"

"Tigre," I said. "Is that the dog?"

"That's right," he said.

"You didn't hear the shot when I killed it?" I said.

He swore and shoved his chair back, and I began to laugh. Then his face flushed dark as mahogany, and he got up and went out.

Ángel said, "Man, you'll go too far! He's a tough boy!"

Everybody stopped chewing and drinking and waited, and I said, "I'm not hunting trouble, but if I back away, what do you suppose happens to me? I have another question for you," and I looked all around the tables before I went on—"Why do you think Don Hector hired me? Because I turn tail when somebody says 'Boo'?"

I didn't feel as tough as I talked, but I needed the job, and I couldn't let anybody bluff me. And besides, I was just mule-headed enough so I couldn't stand being pushed around.

Ángel and I sat a while talking after the others left. He told me he was foreman of the vaqueros that took care of the fighting bulls, and it was a big job.

Then we said buenas noches, and I found my way back to my quarters. The dog growled, but it was behind Narciso's closed door. I thought I wouldn't get to sleep, with so much to think over, and in strange quarters, but I did, right away.

It was barely daylight when roosters and fighting cocks and burros and mules and a couple of lovesick bulls all sounded off at once. Already people were moving around, and I heard the talk and laughter, and a couple of women in a battle of words. I got dressed and went out, and it was a fine morning, the air like velvet, not a cloud in the sky. The dog growled from inside Narciso's room when I crossed our little patio on the way to the kitchen.

Ángel was just getting up from the table, and Narciso was eating, and three dudes came in and sat down. Ángel said he had to get his vaqueros lined out for the day, and after that he would come for me and we would choose a horse for me.

He went out, and Narciso cleared his throat and looked across at me, and everybody else stopped eating. He said, "Señor Yanqui, as you know, it is my responsibility to protect the life and property of my patrón. Now, if the patrón were here, I could ask him about your degree of ability—but I must know to what extent I can depend upon you as my assistant in case of need."

I said, "I wasn't hired as your assistant, Narciso, but if it's a shooting match, why let's go." I knew I'd have to prove myself, sooner or later, and I had an itch to know how good he was.

I had my breakfast, and when we went out, the secretaries and bookkeeper followed and word got around somehow, and it was surprising how many vaqueros and household servants and ox drivers and kids and dogs happened to find themselves hanging around an old section of adobe wall at the edge of a plowed field, when Narciso led the way there.

I was nervous and sweating. I hadn't figured on an audience like that, but Uncle Frank was a good teacher, and I thought if I stayed calm I'd probably be all right.

That old wall was bullet-scarred like the one I saw behind that awful trench outside of Janos, and Narciso said, "Andrés went bad, like a locoed horse. This is where we shot him."

"That must have been good fun," I said, "with his hands tied. Was he blindfolded, too? What are we going to shoot at?"

He snarled a dirty word, then called for somebody to set up some bottles, and to hang one on a string, from a pole that stuck out over the wall. A couple of vaqueros set up four tequila bottles and tied one on the string.

Narciso pulled his hat off and bowed to me like I was the crown prince of somewhere, and said, "Now, Señor, show me how to shoot."

I said, "You first! I want to see what I'm up against." He smiled and put his hat on and bowed to the crowd and loosened the Bisley in the holster.

Well, he was faster than me. But like Cassie and Polly he gave up accuracy for speed. His trigger was tied down, and he just cocked the hammer with his thumb and slipped it. You can get off a lot of shots fast, that way. He drew good and fast and let all five off in about three seconds. He broke two bottles on the ground and cut the string just above the hanging one.

The crowd was exclaiming and Narciso was bowing at the

compliments. The two vaqueros started tying the bottle onto the string again and I said, "Wait a minute, please."

Narciso said, real nasty, "Oh, but surely, señor, you are not going to deprive us. You have chosen not to demonstrate?"

I said, "Has anybody got something that will make a mark on that wall?"

"Oh!" Narciso said. "The norteamericano prefers a target with the rings numbered one to ten so we can keep score, and thus figure out who would have killed who in a gun duel?"

People laughed, and a man handed me a chunk of white plaster and I walked up to the wall and drew the dog. It was a pretty bad dog, but it was the right size, and good enough so everybody knew what I was getting at. I guess everybody on the ranch had heard of Narciso's dog and me.

I walked back to our line, about fifteen yards from the wall, and when I got there I didn't wait. I swung around and pulled the Bisley as I turned, and took aim and hit the dog picture right in the heart. I kept on shooting, cocking the hammer every time. I was a lot slower than Narciso, but my next three shots knocked chips from the wall within a hands breadth of my first one, and my last one got the dog in the head.

I reloaded the Bisley and turned around and walked through the crowd, and they weren't saying a thing as they made way for me. And if Narciso hadn't moved back, I would've rammed into him, because I wasn't going a step out of my way to miss him.

When I got back to my quarters, I took my chair out into the patio and leaned against the wall and waited for Narciso. The dog was snarling inside his room, and sniffing along the bottom of the door. And pretty soon Narciso came and didn't look at me, and went to his door.

I said, "Just a minute."

He turned around and scowled at me and said, "What is it?"

"Two things." I said. "You cut out the smart remarks, and I will. And that dog, Narciso . . . I'll shoot him."

"All right," he said. "I'll keep him chained at the main gate, and the mozo can take care of him."

Ángel came into the patio. He said, "Come on, Señor

Adams, bring Andrés' saddle and bridle, and his leggings, too, unless you're afraid there's a ghost in them." He made a cross with his left thumb and forefinger, and kissed it, and said, "May he rest in peace."

I got the gear, and he had a wonderful horse tied to the rack outside our patio archway—what the Mexicans call an *alazan ruano*, a roan sorrel, if there is such a thing, with white mane and tail. He had Old Timer there, too, and my little old cowpony nickered when I scratched his chin. I wouldn't put that spade bit in *his* mouth, but I tied the halter rope like reins and saddled him and got on. I hung Andrés' bridle over the saddle horn.

Ángel showed his horse off a little, turning him right or left with just a touch of his heel, making him rear and spin on his hind legs by raising his hand beside its head, and things like that.

We rode a long ways to a big, circular, stone corral, and people we passed were polite and said, "Buenos dias, Señores!" and bobbed their heads—women and naked little kids and young sprouts practicing roping, and brown young Indian girls that giggled when Ángel made bawdy remarks to them.

The corral had about forty horses in it, real good ones, and Ángel got his rawhide reata from under the big saddlebag onto his saddle skirt, and we got off by the pole gate and tied our horses.

There were horses of all colors and markings in there, all fine saddle stock, and I began to talk about horses, to let Ángel know I wasn't any greenhorn, and he listened politely. Then suddenly I said to myself, you damn fool, just shut up and watch and listen, because I got a hunch you don't know nothing!

Ángel smiled politely and said, "One sees that you will not need advice. Come inside and show me which animal you want," and we climbed over the bars into the corral. Of course, when those critters saw the reata, they got as far from him as they could. That gutline of his was smooth as a snake, and all of eighty feet long, and he built a loop big enough to rope a stage coach. We went to the snubbing post in the center of the big corral, with horses dodging and charging past us and shying away and raising a big dust.

He stood there patiently with the loop spread on the ground to his right, and a little back, and I watched those beautiful animals circling us, trying to crowd to the outside. They all looked great to me, but one specially, about sixteen hands, and I pointed him out and said, "How about that big *grullo?*"

He said, "Well, all right, if that's what you want," but he was muttering to himself and I barely heard it, with all those hoofs pounding around us—*"Ni grullo ni grulla, ni mujer que arguya"*—"Not a grullo, nor a woman that argues." Then he said, "Señor, you sure you want that grullo?"

So I got wise. I said, "Do me the favor. You pick my horse."

"Well, if you insist," he said, and watched a small, line-back, bay gelding that knew it had been picked, the way it tried to keep behind the rest of them. Old Ángel, he turned slow, waiting for a clear shot, then swung that loop just once around his head, and let it sail. The big loop stood straight up, and I swear it changed direction in the air, and it was over the bay's head, then it snapped down flat and pulled tight around his neck. The bay sat on his rump to put on the brakes.

"He's rope broke," Ángel said, which was plain as the big nose on his face, and we walked over to the bay and Ángel petted him and talked to him, and led him to the gate. I let the bars down, and put them up again behind us.

I was a grass rope, tie fast man like Uncle Frank taught me, and what Ángel did with that gutline looked like a miracle to me.

I asked him, "Tell me why you picked this *bayo?*"

"You should say it right, because there are more than ten colors of bay horse," Ángel said. "This one is a *bayo mapano*, a yellow bay with the same color mane and tail. He is charro trained . . . three years of training. Try him out, and you'll see why I picked him. But if you haven't used the spade bit, remember, no force, no pressure. It's like sending a telegram, just twitch your finger under the rein, or touch his neck with it."

The little gelding almost reached for the bit, and while I was pulling the saddle off Old Timer and cinching it onto the bay, I said, "Has he got a name?"

His name was *Gato Montés*—Bobcat—and Lidia had named him when he was a little colt because he had little dark spots under his yellow coat, like a bobcat's skin.

Ángel put Old Timer in the corral. He said, "Circle around

a little. He knows all the *ayudas,* the squeeze with the knees to turn on the speed, the tap with the heel to make him swing his rump one way or the other, the move of the hand beside his head to make him turn on his hind legs, and all the others. You are not used to them, but Gato will teach you a lot."

He was more horse than I'd ever sat on before, or even seen. I could've reined him with a silk ribbon. We walked a while, then Ángel leaned forward, and I didn't see any signal, but his sorrel squatted down and went away from there like a jack rabbit, with old Ángel giving out with that long Mexican coyote yell. I squeezed with my knees and was going to swat Gato with the *romal,* and he almost left me sitting alone, five feet off the ground. I grabbed the horn and hauled myself back into the saddle, and in three hundred yards, he had his nose almost against the sorrel's tail, and we were sailing over walls and in and out of ravines and skidding on the turns, and finally slowed and walked side by side along a wall of piled up rocks that ran for miles.

I asked Ángel if Los Cerritos raised any beef, and he said the beef herd was way over on the other side of the rancho, and the only cattle near the home ranch were the bulls that his vaqueros took care of, managing the breeding, running the tientas, branding the little bull calves with great care so their horn buds wouldn't be damaged in wrestling them around, fattening up the four-year-olds that were ready for the bull ring, and one man always watching each herd sire in the separate breeding pastures, keeping track of which cows they mounted, so the records could be kept straight. He said fighting bulls were different from beef bulls or dairy bulls, and would attack anything that moved, from a mouse to a locomotive.

After while we got off and loosened the cinches and slipped the bridles, and let the horses nose around for grass while we sat and held the *mecates.* Ángel rolled a cornhusk cigarette and offered me the makings, but I couldn't make the cornhusk stick with spit, like a cigarette paper, and he said you have to hold them together.

He asked me what I thought of the revolution.

I said, "I don't know. It just seems like a lot of fighting and killing, and most norteamericanos don't know who's fighting who."

He blew smoke through his nose and said, "It is a terrible thing, my poor country torn in two. When Madero won the rebellion, we thought he would do what he promised and kick out the rich from government positions, and the foreigners, and break up the big haciendas and give land to the peones. That is what Pancho Villa and Zapata were fighting for. But he hasn't done it, and people are saying that he is under the thumb of those who rob Mexico and bleed her for their own pockets. And now his own generals are turning against him, Zapata in Morelos, and Pascual Orozco and others."

I said, "Orozco got badly beaten by General Huerta. I read it in the El Paso paper."

"Yes, we heard," he said. "But they will never overthrow Madero, not while Pancho Villa lives. Madero is a god to Pancho Villa, no matter what he does. Well, he used to be, to all of us. Why, it was only last November he made a triumphant journey the length of Mexico to take the presidency. I could have touched him when he rode down the *Paseo de la Reforma* in that open carriage, and six hundred thousand people roaring his name. And Lidia was crying with happiness. And already . . . already it is all lost, and all the fighting to be done again."

"Lidia!" I said. "She went to see the inauguration?"

"Oh, yes," Angel said. "Her father wouldn't give her money, and said she was a sentimental fool who knew nothing of practical politics—but she went. And she asked me to go with her, and I did, I and Mateo and Lucas, to watch out for her. When we returned, he was going to have us whipped but Lidia said she would leave home, and it would be a scandal. And he saw that in spite of Narciso and Andrés with their hands on their pistols, we would not allow ourselves to be whipped. But he told us that Madero was a weakling and a fool and had deceived half of Mexico. And it appears that he was right."

He stepped on his cigarette and said, "Well, a man must talk sometimes, let off the pressure of things on his mind. Would you like to have a look at the bulls?"

After what he said about locomotives, I didn't particularly want to hobnob with any fighting bulls, but I couldn't admit that.

While we were tightening the *latigos,* he said, "The worst are the Rurales. When he became president, he should have driven them all into the sea. They are the creation of Porfirio Díaz, whom he fought and drove out—and then, when they professed loyalty to him, he accepted those murdering bastards! Spawned in the prisons and slums, felons, rapists, assassins, given reprieves from the firing squad in exchange for absolute loyalty to their bloody officers. And our trusting Madero, our beloved little man in the president's chair, he kept them and trusts them! And no man is safe from the firing squad, unless he is a gachupin or an *hidalgo* like Don Hector!"

We rode a while, then opened a pole gate in a stone wall, and closed it behind us, and went toward a stand of low trees. And there they were, about thirty of them, with the curving, white horns with the black tips, the great humps of muscle on their necks, the flopping dewlaps, the long, sway-backed bodies black as midnight, and the dangling tails almost brushing the ground. They watched us, and Ángel held his hand out to stop me, and gently stopped his horse.

"We won't talk," he said in a whisper. "As long as they're together, there's little danger, but get one alone and he is an assassin. If one should charge, don't wait for me. Give Gato the spur and put him over the nearest wall."

I would just as soon have been somewhere else. A bull took four slow steps toward us, and Ángel whispered, "Don't move!" and the bull backed up two steps and moaned deep in its throat and threw sand over its back.

"That's Conquistador," Ángel whispered. "Isn't he beautiful! Four years old, and ready, and no *corrida* for him because of the revolution. What a waste! Well, let's go."

By then I had shivers up my spine. I lifted the reins and squeezed with one knee, and Gato turned and walked away. I watched over my shoulder in case we had to run for it.

We pulled up for the gate, and I told Ángel, "Do me a favor. Don't ever let me get within a mile of one of those again!"

We walked the horses back to the cuadrilla, and Ángel told me there was a shed with stalls, and a small corral, behind where I lived, for Narciso's horse and mine. He said, "A boy will bring hay and a little grain every day, and clean out the stalls. Ride Gato every day, for the good of both of you. Remember, *lo peor para caballo, descansar y engrasar.*" (The worst for a horse is too much rest and too much fat.)

He'd been spouting wise proverbs at me all day, and I said, "Do you just invent proverbs to fit the occasion?"

"No," he said, "I think they're out of the Bible, but I can't

read it. I'll ask Padre Arrellaga. Well, put up your horse and
come to dinner. But don't get a paunch on you like Narciso.
Remember, *el que quiera ser buen charro, poco plato y
menos jarro*," and he rode off, still laughing. What he said
was, "For him that wants to be a good cowboy, little plate
and less jug."

CHAPTER 9

In the afternoon, I saddled Gato again and rode
around to the patio of the big house, hoping to get a look at
Lidia. Narciso was half asleep on a bench by the big gate.
His dog snarled and charged to the end of the chain, but
Narciso hauled it back and beat it on the head with his fist
and swore at it, and it shut up. He said I was crazy to be riding around in *siesta* time, and that everyone but the peones
would be taking a nap till about three. He acted so decent for
a change, I said if he wanted a siesta, I'd watch the gate till
he came back. He was so surprised, he even said thanks. He
yelled and a mozo came and got the dog. Narciso got his
horse from where it was tied under a *ramada*—that's a shade
of poles and branches—and rode away. I tied Gato under the
ramada, then sat on a bench in the shade of the wall and almost went to sleep myself.

It was more than an hour when Lidia came out and stood
under the portal, stretching and yawning like any common
moza, and I was struck all over again with how beautiful she
was. Then she hauled her skirt way up and started pulling
her stockings up, and suddenly stopped and looked around
and saw me.

I thought she would jerk her skirt down, but she didn't.
She stared right at me kind of contemptuous and took her
time straightening her stocking, but her face flushed darker.

She said, "Are you enjoying the view, Señor pistolero?"

"Very nice," I said. "But what are you sore about? I didn't haul your skirt up!"

She grinned then, and said, "You'll have to forgive me. I get careless when nobody is in the house except the servants —well, Padre Arrellaga, but he doesn't count, either. I shouldn't snap at you like El Tigre just because you are a pistolero, and a yanqui."

"Señorita," I said, "I can handle my pistol, but I am not a gunfighter. I have never shot a man. Your father offered me this job and I need it. As for being yanqui, I had no choice. But don't expect me to apologize—I'm proud of it."

She came and sat on the bench. "Yanquis are bleeding Mexico," she said. "They have the oil fields around Tampico in their dirty clutches, and the railroads, and the mines, in Guanajuato and Saltillo. They own ranches in Chihuahua ten times the size of Los Cerritos, that Colonel Greene and the Hearst woman, while my people are starving." Her chin stuck out and her fists were clenched.

I said, "*I* don't have any oil wells in *my* clutches! *I* don't run any railroads! *I* didn't steal any gold mines!" I got mad, too. I said, "I went through the *poblada* this morning, where your *campesinos* live. The shacks are made of broken boards and pieces of rusty corrugated iron, and adobe walls falling to pieces. And naked kids with sore eyes wallowing in the dirt, with more flies on them than the pigs have. You're sure kind and generous to your campesinos! But I forgot! You're not Mexican, you're Spanish, a *gachupina*."

She was so mad she stuttered. She said, "I am not a gachupina! I am Mexican! I did not choose my Spanish father any more than you chose to be born yanqui!" She looked away, then, and there were tears in her eyes. She said, "I get mad because what you said is true, and nobody likes to hear the truth about himself. I know that all yanquis are not the same, just as all Mexicans are not. Now tell me, where is my fine Narciso?"

"All morning," I said, "I was riding around enjoying myself. And here was Narciso working his heart out guarding you from harm, and my conscience hurt me. So I took his place to give him a rest."

"I heard you also shot El Tigre this morning," she said.

"Oh, no!" I said. "Somebody lied to you!"

She laughed, then, and said, "The Tigre you drew on the wall. Hortensio told me Narciso has cooled down somewhat. Now, tell me, did you choose my little Gato Montés for yourself? You must know horseflesh."

"It's Ángel who knows the horseflesh," I said. "I was going to take a big *grullo*."

"Well," she said, "he would have given you the *grullo* if he thought you were not worthy of Gato."

Somebody coughed under the arcade, and the priest came over to us in his long black gown with the white rope knotted around the waist. He wasn't much older than me, with a sharp, pale face and white, soft hands. When he spoke, I knew he was Spanish, not Mexican. "Daughter," he said, "I have not had the privilege of an introduction to this . . . this . . ." It sounded like he didn't know whether to call me a gringo or a bum, or what.

Lidia said, "Señor Adams, Padre. My father's guard, to take the place of Andrés. Padre Arrellaga takes care of our souls, Señor Adams."

I said, "How do you do, Padre," but he didn't look at my hand when I held it out. Like everybody yesterday, he was going to pretend I wasn't there. He said, "Let us hope he will be more faithful to his patrón than was Andrés. And of course he is a good Catholic?"

Lidia looked at me, and I said, "She doesn't know, Father. You could ask me."

He looked at me then, staring down his long, thin nose. He said, "I will not tolerate insolence!" and turned and walked back to the house.

When he went in, Lidia said, "Well, are you?"

I said, "When Don Hector returns, I will ask him if he requires a good Catholic, or a good man with a pistol."

"Really," she said, "I don't care if you are Catholic!" Then she calmed down and said, "But Señor Adams, don't think all priests are like Padre Arrellaga. He feels his importance, and he is Spanish. Father Guzmán who was here before was gentle and strong, and loved everyone. The Rurales jailed him, and after that, we don't know any more. They have been very hard on the priests and nuns, seizing their property, jailing them, some have even been shot. It is true that many priests and even bishops have forgotten Christ, and are grasping and money hungry and the church is very rich.

They say our new constitution prohibits any priest from own-
ing more property than he can carry on his back—because
the church was so wealthy, and the people so poor."

I didn't want to argue religion with her—I didn't know
how, because I never was a churchgoer. Uncle Frank used to
read the Bible, and I had read a lot of it—and it seemed like
she didn't know which side she was on.

So I was glad when Narciso came back and tied his horse
under the ramada. He swept off his sombrero and bowed to
Lidia and said, "Buenas tardes, Patrona."

So while they were both there, I asked Lidia if Ángel was
right to tell me I could spend time with him, looking the
ranch over, until Don Hector returned.

"Oh, yes," she said. "Don Hector would want you to be fa-
miliar with Los Cerritos. Besides, with my father away, there
is little for you to do, and Narciso would much rather just sit
here in the shade and think about Rosita and Azucena than
show you around, because he is tired from chasing them all
the time."

I thought Narciso would be embarrassed by her sarcasm,
but he said solemnly, "Oh, Señorita, it is not necessary to
chase them! They pursue!"

So then I thought she would be mad at his insolence, but
she grinned at him and said, "This, I cannot imagine. Run
past the house some time, so I may watch this chase."

"Doña Lidia," he said, "they would catch me long before
I could get here for refuge. They always do."

They both laughed, and she went into the house. I got on
Gato and went home. I put him in the corral, and the mozo
stripped him and got a sack and rubbed him down. When I
went into my room, a little Indian girl was coming out with a
bucket. She had filled my pitcher, and there were my dress-up
clothes, all washed and ironed.

I said, "Thank you, *chulita!*" and gave her ten centavos.
Her dark little face went red, but she took the ten centavos
and I said, "Wait a moment. Are you Rosita? Or perhaps
Azucena?"

She said, *"Sí, Señor.* I am Azucena."

I asked her if she was a good runner.

She said, real proud, "I am Tarahumara. The Tarahumara
are the greatest runners in the world!"

She left and I stripped and had a bath, and then had a siesta.
When I woke up, it was dusk, and I got dressed and had

my supper with Ángel and the secretary and bookkeeper and storekeeper. When we were finished, Ángel asked, "Are you coming with us tomorrow? My boys are going to ride fences and look at gates and acequías and tanks, mostly to exercise the horses, because there is so little to do, with this revolution stopping the bullfighting. So we all ride together, for company."

I said, in English, "You bet!"

Ángel said, "Eh? What's that?"

So I said, *"Sí! Por supuesto! Con todo gusto!* What time do we start?"

He said, *"A quién madruga, Dios le ayuda,"* and that means, "God helps him that gets up early."

I groaned. I said, "I suppose that means at daylight."

"You bet!" Ángel said.

I came awake when the roosters were crowing, and there was just a pale yellow streak in the east, and stars still shining in the west. I lit my candle and got dressed and put on the leggings I inherited from Andrés. Gato was glad to see me, and I rode to the dining room and tied him.

There was just Ángel and me, and Josefa, the fat old cook, who gave us a fine breakfast; ham, *chorizo* and four eggs and fresh tortillas and strong black coffee, and of course, refried beans.

We rode to a big circular stone corral, where a few vaqueros were roping out their mounts from a big remuda. Most of them, about fifteen, had already saddled up, and some were walking their horses around, and one or two were putting on a few halfhearted crow hops. Of course, there are plenty of salty horses in Mexico—that's where we get the word 'bronc'—but with such fine stock as these on Los Cerritos, there wouldn't be any cold-jaws or hammerheads. Mexicans respect a good horse, and bring him along real slow when they break them.

The riders were tipping their hats and saying good morning real polite, and Ángel said, "Lucas! Tomás! Saddle Moro for Doña Lidia. We will meet you in the patio at the big house."

Starting out beside Ángel, I said, "She's coming with us?"

"Yes," he said. "There hasn't been a real inspection since Don Hector left, and she likes to get out of the house and onto a horse. We will look at boundary markers and springs and acequías, and she will ask the people whether they are all right. They need everything, and there isn't much she can do, but it makes them feel a little better."

He told me the names of the vaqueros, and it sounded like a roll call of the apostles, out of the Bible, not to mention two Jesuses nicknamed Chuy and Chucho to tell them apart. There was Matéo, Marcos, Lucas, and Juan. Then Pedro, Jaime, Pablo, Bartoloméo, Tomás and Tadéo. Andrés had died in front of that wall.

Tomás and Lucas brought Lidia's horse to the patio, a beautiful big black, wearing a sidesaddle, that clumsy rig with the leather hooks for the knees, that women rode so they wouldn't have to wear pants or straddle a horse. Lidia came out and said hello to everybody, and she sure looked fine. She had on a long, black skirt that almost covered her hand-carved boots and the one silver spur on her left heel. She wore a short leather jacket over a white shirtwaist, and a flat-crowned black hat with a chin string, and a broad leather belt with a small pistol in a holster.

She rode between me and Ángel, explaining to me about the hacienda and what they grew and where they sold it—because it wasn't only a *ganadería* for raising fighting bulls weren't the whole thing, though they were what everyone was proudest of, from Don Hector and her right down to the lowest peon.

There was lots of water, brought from the Rio de Santa Maria in miles of acequias, for the big orchards—apples and peaches—and there were tobacco fields, and mile-wide fields of giant *maguey* that they used for about everything. You could cook and eat the leaves, and the thorns were as hard as nails, and the fibers made rough cloth and cord, and those hard, tough lassos. Then the juice made *pulque*. And you distill the pulque and get *tequila*, or *mescal*, depending on what kind of maguey, or agave, you've got.

The big thing was corn. You just couldn't see the end of some of those corn fields, they ran right past the horizon.

There was work going on wherever we passed—men mending walls, pruning the orchards, and plowing with oxen. There were a few little villages, too, with maybe half a dozen miserable adobe shacks, and we rode to every one of them, and I could hardly believe it, in all that misery and poverty, they were, most of them, glad to see Lidia. Or maybe they didn't dare look like they weren't. Anyway, they came out to say hello, and she picked up filthy babies, and went into the shacks. She passed out medicine, and needles and thread from her saddlebag. Some of the vaqueros had blankets, bundles of them rolled up like their serapes behind their cantles, and she passed those out, too.

There were goats and mangy dogs and skinny pigs in those little villages, all rolling in the dirt with the naked kids. I wondered how they kept warm in winter, because there weren't any windows, just openings with a steer hide across them, and the roofs just logs and brush covered with dirt. The women were cooking outside on pieces of sheet iron over charcoal fires.

I got to not liking Lidia very much, because I couldn't help thinking how she was getting her clothes and her soft hands dirty, picking up those smelly little kids and going into those shacks—but in a little while she'd be back home, taking a hot bath, with some Indian girl lathering her back for her, and laying out clean clothes for her, and others cooking her dinner for her, and probably that priest pouring wine for her. She could damn well afford to be the great lady, and pass out a few miserable bottles of cough syrup and a couple of sleazy blankets.

We had our lunch under a stand of oaks. The vaqueros poured water from a canteen for her to wash her hands. She was sitting by me and Ángel, and pretty soon she said, "Well, Señor Adams, what do you think of all our happy little peones living the simple life in the midst of plenty, like Adam and Eve?"

Maybe she was being sarcastic, but I thought she was making fun of those poor devils, and I said, "Excuse me," and got up and moved twenty feet and sat down by myself.

Ángel came after me and said, "Señor, you will apologize to Doña Lidia!" and I said, "It will be a cold day when I do!"

He reached to grab my shoulder, and I came to my feet and said, "Don't lay a hand on me!"

The vaqueros all got up and were muttering around. I was nervous, but when I get mad enough, I just don't give a damn.

Lidia said, real sharp, "*Ángel!* All of you. Sit down!"

I threw down my tortilla and meat and walked over to

Gato and tightened his cinch and slipped on his bridle, and
untied him from the tree, and nobody said a word when I got
on and nudged him into a trot over the hill and down the
slope.

CHAPTER 10

I was still boiling, and it was a while before I noticed that Gato had his ears pricked up and was interested in
something off to our right, in the tall grass on the bank of an
acequía. Then a man popped up out of the grass and ran toward us, then stopped and dived back into the grass.

I reined Gato over and squeezed with my knees, and he
didn't lose any time covering that hundred yards. When I
pulled him up I had the Bisley Colt cocked in my hand. I
don't know what I was afraid of—but Andrés had tried to
murder Don Hector, and maybe someone hated Don Hector's daughter.

It was a miserable peón, so scared he was grovelling on
the ground. I said, "Man, what's going on here?"

He got to his knees and said, "I thought you were one of
the vaqueros. Then I didn't know you, and I thought you
were one of them!"

"What's the matter?" I asked him.

He said, "I saw her and Ángel and the rest of them ride
over the hill, and I was going to tell him that . . ."

His eyes rolled white in his brown face. He was soaking
with sweat like he had run ten miles. I said, "Damn you,
speak up!"

"They killed Patricio!" he yelled at me. "And they wounded Paco, and they're still hunting for him, in the fields and in
the houses."

"Who?" I yelled. "Who shot them?"

"Rurales!" he said. "Salvador Cano and eight Rurales!"

Ángel and his vaqueros were coming down full gallop, and out in front was Lidia, quirting her big black horse. They'd heard us yelling at one another.

They slid to a stop around us and nobody could see anyone else in the dust. Then the man ran to Ángel and grabbed his knee. He stood there with tears running down his face.

Lidia said, "Who is he? What's the matter?"

Ángel said, "He's Diosdado, one of your field hands." He ruffled the man's hair with his hand and said, "What is it, man?"

The peon said, "Patricio! They killed him! And Paco is shot, hurt bad, and . . ."

"Where is Paco?" Lidia said.

Then Ángel said, "Careful!" and raised his eyebrows and looked at me, and then back to her.

I said, "He says it's the Rurales, Salvador Cano and his men."

Ángel squinted at me. He said, "How do you happen to know Salvador Cano?"

I said, "Why, you damn fool, this man told me it was Cano! And when I came through Janos . . ."

But he wasn't listening. He jerked his head toward me, and Tomás and Lucas pushed their horses up on each side of me. Lucas had his hand on the machete slung from his saddlehorn. He said, "You want his pistol, Ángel?"

I gave a light tug on the reins, and Gato backed up, and I had the two of them in front of me. Others were all around us, but I paid no attention to them. The Bisley was still in my hand, and I pointed it straight up, ready to chop it down, and said to Ángel, "Well, answer the man! Do you want it?"

Then Lidia said, "We're wasting time, Ángel. Señor Adams, I would like you to see me home. You and Tomás and Lucas. Come, now! Nothing will be done until you leave."

I said, "Goddamn you, what do you think I am! You're wasting time! Tell that fool Ángel to go and help the man!"

I touched Gato with my spurs, and he slammed into Lucas's horse and knocked Tomas's off balance, and we were clear of the bunch. I pulled him down to a trot, and didn't turn around, and Lidia, Tomás, and Lucas caught up with me.

The two *vaqueros* pulled in on both sides of me, and I

took a backhand swing with the gun, and Lucas almost fell off, dodging it. I said, "You two *cabrones* keep your distance." Calling a man a goat is fighting talk in Mexico, and a dirty word, to boot, but I didn't care.

Tomás said, "You watch your dirty tongue around the señorita!" He had his machete in his hand.

I said, "Just shut your face, cabrón!"

Lidia said, "Boys, quit being brave! We can keep an eye on him without getting you shot!"

Then we saw the Rurales—Salvador Cano, and eight others, and they were leading a horse with a body slung over it face down.

They turned to cut our path. Lucas and Tomás closed in on me again, and Lucas said, "Don't you say one word, Señor!"

I told him, "Stay clear of me, you stupid fool! How do *I* know where Paco's hiding any more than *you* do?"

When we met them, everybody stopped. Cano said, "How pleasant to meet you, Doña Lidia! And the yanqui pistolero, is it not?" He was grinning like a shark.

Lidia said, "You are on private property. With whose permission?"

He grinned even wider, "Why, that of President Francisco Madero, of course, and whoever is commander in Chihuahua since Pascual Orozco turned traitor. And we always have the permission of your esteemed father, a loyal Maderista if ever a man was."

Her dark face had gone almost pale, and she didn't look at the body on the horse, but said, "Who is the dead man?"

"One of your vaqueros, Señorita. We trapped him and another in the hills, with four pack horses loaded with Winchesters. We killed this one, and we will catch the other, because he has a bullet or two in him, and his blood trail led to a gate in the wall of your cuadrilla. So Señorita, you must lead us to the wounded man if you know where he is, so we may question him about the source of those rifles."

After a moment, Lidia said, "I'm afraid he will be too well hidden, by now. There are still other rebels on the hacienda, and a thousand hiding places. I have no authority when my father is away. He leaves his orders with the caporal of vaqueros. So I cannot invite you and your men to stay. You will have to leave. But that is a Los Cerritos horse, and the dead man is one of ours. So you will turn both over to us. We will see to the burial."

Cano said, "I'm going to hang him in your main gateway as an example to others."

"No," she said. "I'll arm twenty vaqueros and turn then loose on you."

Still grinning, Cano said, "Is it possible there are also female rebels on Los Cerritos? All right, you can have him. But, Señorita, we can't leave until we have found the wounded man and questioned him. As you well know, your father, being a loyal citizen, keeps the barracks building east of the cuadrilla for the convenience of the Guardia Rural. I would regret to report to him any lack of cooperation."

"Then go there," she said, and told Tomás to take the horse.

"You deprive me of the pleasure of your company!" Cano said. "Very well. Warn your people to stay indoors tonight. We will be searching for the wounded man, and in such hostile surroundings, we shoot before asking questions of anyone prowling around. *Vaya con Dios,* Señorita."

We rode the rest of the way without any talk, until we were almost back to the cuadrilla. Then Lidia said, "Patricio had no family, is that right, Tomás?"

"No parents," Tomás said. "And his brother is in the army, somewhere. He had only Camila who cooked for him."

She said, "Then bring him to that shed behind the big house. And send Camila. We will wash him and lay him out. Tell everyone that Padre Arrellaga will say a requiem mass tomorrow afternoon."

"Doña Lidia," Lucas said, "this is not a thing for you. We will lay him out."

"No," she said. "This is for women."

When we went into the cuadrilla, the women and children began to follow us, and the crying started, and one young woman fainted and others carried her into a hut.

Lucas said, "That Camila! She won't be much help to you, Doña Lidia."

Then I spoke up, "Señorita, I didn't know him. Let me fix him up. It won't bother me the way it will you or his friends."

She just said, "No." So I left them and went to my quarters and put Gato in the corral.

Narciso's horse was gone, and I supposed Narciso was standing guard at the gate.

I took off my boots and jacket and laid down for a while. I thought about all that had happened in three weeks. It took me a while to count back to my birthday, but this must be May twenty-first, a Tuesday, and I wondered what Uncle Frank would think if he could see me now, a hired gun on a big Mexican ranch, not sure that I was going to be loyal to my boss, and disgusted with his daughter for pretending to be like a sweet little mother to the peones that kept her living in luxury while they lived like animals—and half in love with her, too, after only two days. And me starting to hate those bloody Rurales, like the town people and the farmers and the vaqueros—and the farmers and vaqueros suspecting me of being a spy. And a kind of a truce between me and Narciso, who I knew was completely loyal to Don Hector, and jealous of me, the new gringo gunman. And I wondered how Uncle Frank was making out alone, and whether Concha had got Don Hector to sleep with her that night, and whether the Mexican police had shot Cassie and sent him to hell to join his twin brother—and whether *I* was no better than them, but a killer too, even if I had been lucky enough to get away after I slugged Long Tom Mundt.

I got up after while and went to the dining room and had supper. Ángel was there, but he pretended I wasn't. So I thought, well, the hell with you, old man! But I felt bad about it, because I thought he ought to know-I'm no informer, even though there wasn't any reason why he'd know it. Narciso came in, but we both pretended the other wasn't there.

Back at our quarters, I rolled a smoke and brought my chair out to the patio and sat there watching the stars. After while Narciso came and went into his room. When he came out he had a carbine, and I said, "Going snipe hunting?" But I guess he didn't know that old joke. He said, "At night? No, I'm going to help the Rurales find that wounded man."

I said, "Maybe Ángel and his vaqueros aren't going to like you so well!"

"Who cares?" he said. "They are only peones." I think he was stupid enough not to be afraid of them.

He rode away, and after while I saw lights moving around up by the peones' village. Salvador Cano and Narciso and the Rurales looking for the wounded Paco, I supposed. And the thought hit me—Narciso watches at the gate all day, but he quits at supper time, so who guards the house? Who's watching out for Lidia, just the servants? I didn't like the idea, with Cano and those Rurales on the prowl, and remembering what somebody told me, Concha or somebody, that they recruited a lot of them from felons and murderers, giving them the choice of joining up or going against the wall.

So I saddled Gato and rode to the big house.

That horse had eyes like a cat for the dark, and we rounded the corner of the big house and moved onto the cobblestoned front patio, and somebody a few feet to my left, whispered, "Get your hands up, quick!" Believe me, I did! To my right under the arcade, somebody said, "It's the yanqui."

Then there were four of them around me, and I could see the glint of starshine on their carbines. So others had been worrying about Doña Lidia, too, and I recognized Tomás's voice when he said, "What are you doing here, gringo?"

I said, "I came to see if the señorita is all right. Don't you fools know the Rurales ordered everybody to stay indoors so they won't get shot, and they're searching the whole place for Paco?"

Then the priest spoke up, under the arcade. His robe didn't show in the dark, and he looked like a face floating a few feet off the ground, like a ghost. He said, "What is this disturbance?"

Tomás said, "We have caught the gringo sneaking around."

Padre Arrellaga said, "Who are you? What are you doing here? You are not Rurales! You are not official! Go to your quarters."

Tomás reached up to grab my arm, and said, "Come on, gringo! We've got some questions. About how the Rurales knew where to ambush Patricio and Paco."

I kicked his elbow, hard, and he grunted, and I said, "Padre, I am Kel Adams, Don Hector's bodyguard. I came to see if I could be of help to Doña Lidia."

"Oh, yes," he said. "It's high time sombody came to help her! Alone in the shed back there with that body! That is no task for a highborn young woman!"

And I thought, why the hell aren't you back there helping her?

I thought the vaqueros wouldn't do anything as long as I was with the priest, so I said, "I don't think she should be without a guard."

"She's got guards," Tomás said. "Four of us! We didn't know she was back there in the shed."

Padre Arrellaga said, this time in a real shrill tone, "I order you to go to your quarters! And you, Adams, this way. Come through the house."

I got down and tied Gato to a portal pillar. Those boys didn't like it, but I guess a priest still had some authority. Anyway, they didn't try to stop me.

That was the first time I was in the big house, but I couldn't see much. There were a couple of kerosene lamps with round globe shades in a long, tiled hallway, with stiff looking chairs, and some paintings of people on the walls, and over the door at the back end was a huge, stuffed head of a fighting bull staring down at me. Padre Arrellaga led me through a big dining room and down another hall and out under an arcade in the back, and there was another wide patio, and light leaking around a door in a small building on the far side.

"Over there," he said, and went back in the house.

I hurried across the patio, and a man stepped out of the shadows with a carbine half raised, and said, "Who is it? Tomás? Lucas?"

I said, "It's me, Ángel. The yanqui."

The door opened a crack, and Lidia said, "Who is it, Ángel?" She sounded scared.

Ángel pushed me inside the shed and shut the door. There were candles stuck here and there, and Lidia stood there, and her eyes were very big and scared. Her sleeves were rolled up, and there was blood on her hands and arms, and bloody rags and a basin of water on the floor and a smell of carbolic, and behind her on some planks on a couple of sawhorses, covered with sheets that hung down to the floor all around, was Patricio's dead body. At least, I figured it had to be Patricio. He looked almost peaceful, wearing an old-fashioned suit and a white shirt and a wing collar and a necktie, and with his arms crossed on his chest. They had tied his jaw shut with a cloth. His big mustache was very black, and he hadn't shaved for a week or so, but the whiskers didn't hide the bullet hole in his right cheekbone.

Lidia said, "What do you want here?"

I said, "For the love of God, what's the matter with everybody? Am I a leper or something? All I came for was to be sure you are all right."

"Well," she said, "as you see, I'm not alone. So you are not needed." I thought I saw the sheet move, the one hanging down from the trestle, but maybe it was only a shadow from the candles.

I said, "Well that's a fact! You sure aren't alone! Half the vaqueros are in the front patio, stumbling over one another and waving guns around."

Ángel swore, and said, "I told the fools! I gave orders, stay in your *jacales,* because these murdering Rurales are out looking for Paco, and for any excuse to shoot somebody else."

He made a move like he was going to charge out the door and eat some of them alive, Lidia said, *"Ángel!* Don't leave me!"

He said, "I've got to send those fools home before Cano catches them!" but he didn't go out.

"Narciso is with Cano, too," I said, "and they're hunting through the shacks in the *poblada.*"

Then I damn near jumped through the roof, because somebody groaned under that trestle, and a bloody hand came flopping out onto the floor from behind the sheets.

We stood there staring at one another, and Lidia's eyes filled with tears. She held her hands out to me like a beggar, and said, "Señor, Paco is so badly hurt! Please! Please you won't tell them?"

And something hurt me, too, like a knife in my guts, and I said, "What kind of a monster do you take me for?"

Ángel said, "I'll lay you dead beside Patricio before I'll let you out of here!"

There was no use to try to hide the wounded man from me. Lidia squatted down and pulled the sheets aside. He was lying on a blanket, on the dirt floor. They had him bandaged from armpits to hips, and the bandage was leaking blood over his stomach. He mumbled something, and he was breathing harsh and loud.

Then we heard the back door of the house open, across the patio, and the priest was saying, ". . . only Doña Lidia and the gringo pistolero, in the shed laying out the dead man."

Still squatting there, Lidia looked up at Ángel, then at me. She pushed Paco's limp hand back out of sight and pulled the sheet back in place and stood up.

In the patio, Narciso said, "Many of the vaqueros are not in their shacks. Have you seen them?"

Padre Arrellaga told him, "Four or five of them were in the front patio a while ago."

Then Salvador Cano said, "Narciso, go tell the men to search around the corrals and feeding pens and in the granaries. That bastard has to be somewhere! Maybe they even brought him here, those men Padre Arrellaga saw."

I whispered to Ángel, "Get under there with Paco! Hurry it up!"

He got a stubborn look on his face and started to swing the carbine to bear on me. But I was too close to him. I grabbed the muzzle and pushed it aside and pulled the Bisley. I held it down beside my leg and let go of Ángel's carbine and kicked the door open. As I stepped out, Ángel called me a filthy name, and I heard Lidia gasp.

Salvador Cano whirled to face me, and Narciso scowled, trying to see me against the candle light. I didn't pay any attention to the priest.

Cano grinned, and his gold teeth were shiny in the light. He said, "Well, now! The norteamericano! You know, Señor, I'm getting a little annoyed with you. I thought I gave orders for you to stay in your quarters. Perhaps my memory is failing, eh?"

I imitated his tone of voice, like talking to a two-year-old kid. I said, "Well, now! That must be it! And another thing you have forgotten—you don't give me orders, eh? I'm getting a little annoyed with you! So you talk polite to me, or keep your fat mouth shut, eh?"

He said, "Step aside, so we may see what is in there, behind the Señorita?"

He took a step toward me, and Narciso started sliding to one side, out of the light from the doorway. Cano said, "We are two to one, Señor, and you are not so foolish. We are going in to see if that is the man we killed this morning, or maybe the one we're searching for."

Ángel must have been standing out of sight in the shed, because they both jumped when he stepped out beside me with the carbine ready. He said, "Count again, Cano! Then get away from here, the two of you!"

They took his advice. As they walked around the house, Narciso said, "Chief, we forgot about the dog! El Tigre will smell him out!" Then we heard their horses moving off.

Padre Arrellaga cleared his throat and said, "Ángel, you must tell me, your confessor, where the wounded man is hidden, so we may learn where the contraband rifles are coming from, and who is . . ."

Ángel said, "Padre, I don't want to be rude to you, so go into the house." And the priest turned and marched into the house, insulted and mad, like a kid sent to his room.

We went back into the shed and closed the door, and I put the Bisley in the holster. Lidia took both my hands in hers, and wouldn't look up at me, but hung her head, and said, "Can you forgive me? Can you ever forgive me?"

I said, "It's all right," and Ángel started to say something, then didn't, but held out his hand. I hesitated, because I was still sore, then I took his hand.

Lidia bent down and pulled the sheet aside. Then she let it fall back, and stood up. She brushed her hair back with the back of her hand, then made the sign of the cross. She sighed like she was exhausted, and said, "He's gone, too. May he rest in peace. I'll find some clothing for him. Bring more water, and clean rags."

Ángel said, "At least, Señorita, they can't question him now, and beat out of him where the rifles come from. Hurt as he was, he couldn't have held out against them."

Lidia began to cry, and leaned her head on Ángel's shoulder, and he cuddled her like a child.

Lidia, and Patricio's Camila, and Paco's woman weren't the only ones that cried that night. After I helped Lidia and Angel clean Paco up and lay him beside Patricio, I rode Gato home and put him in the corral, and went to my room—and as I stepped through the arch into the little patio, there was Narciso sitting on the cobblestones with his back against the wall, cradling that monster of a dog in his arms. Its tongue hung out, and it was dead. He looked up at me, his face in the starlight wet with tears. He said, "They hanged him! In the arch, there! With a reata. Why would they want to kill him?"

CHAPTER 11

I expected there would be a lot of weeping and screaming.

At the double funeral the next afternoon, only Camila, Patricio's housekeeper, or whatever you want to call her, was bawling and yelling and they had to hold her back from throwing herself on his body, in the pine coffin beside Paco's. There was only room inside the chapel for her, and Paco's woman and his four kids and Lidia and Ángel. There must have been two hundred outside, though, all peones that worked at the headquarters ranch, and the vaqueros, quiet and hard faced.

The service was in Latin, and Padre Arrellaga hurried through it like he had to catch the last fiery chariot for heaven. Then they nailed the lids on the coffins, and we all walked to a cemetery on a hill, just mounds of dirt and weeds, and a few wooden crosses.

Everything went a lot better for me after that. Ángel and I were friends, and because he trusted me, the rest of them did, too. They told me what the revolution was all about, and there sure wasn't any doubt in my mind about whose side I was on.

I had a general idea about the trouble President Madero was having since he ran old Porfirio Díaz out and got elected president, himself—how Zapata was fighting him and getting stronger in the south, and generals that had fought with Madero against Díaz had turned against him, General Reyes and a General José Salazar that was backing a man named Vázquez Gómez for president. And when Madero ordered

84

General Pascual Orozco to put down the Vázquez revolt, Orozco turned traitor and backed Vázquez.

But what I hadn't heard before was the terrible condition of the peones. Every new leader and general promised them land, the only thing they wanted, and every one of the leaders and generals took it away from them for their own private property, and all the timber lands, so the campesinos couldn't even cut firewood or graze their miserable goats. They could only be tenant farmers on the huge haciendas. They could be arrested or put into the army or even shot for running away. They never got out of debt to the hacendado for their food and clothes, and Rurales would shoot a man for stealing a sack of meal to feed his family. One governor of Sonora paid a bounty for Yaqui scalps, and scalp hunters poisoned them like coyotes. The Díaz government wanted the rich Yaqui land in Sonora and Sinaloa to give to rich Mexicans and foreigners, and Yaquis were shipped to Yucatan to work in the *henequén* plantations, and they never came home, they died there by the hundreds.

The worst, though, was the Rurales. Not all, but a good many of them, were taken out of condemned cells in the big cities and given uniforms and good horses and good pay. But they had to obey any order without question, no matter how cruel, or they'd be the next to be shot. With that obey or die order, there was nothing, absolutely nothing a *Rural* wouldn't do if they ordered him to.

So what it amounted to now—my boss and the Rurales were on one side, and I was on the other, with Ángel, the vaqueros, and every peasant in Mexico. Narciso and Salvador Cano knew I had sided Ángel when they were looking for Paco. Don Hector wasn't going to get a very good report on me.

The one I really couldn't figure out was Lidia. Here she was, the daughter of a big hacendado, living like most Mexicans couldn't even imagine, and on the face of it, every bit as much a bloodsucker as Don Hector. But it seemed like every peon at Los Cerritos would go jump off a cliff if she told them to.

She had changed toward me, and she trusted me, now, all the way.

It was her that told me Hacienda Los Cerritos was a distribution point for guns smuggled from the U.S. for the rebels.

Most of them came from that hardware merchant in Columbus, New Mexico. There was a contrabandista, Lobo Barrera, that had smuggled guns by the hundred for the Maderistas, and now he was doing the same for the revolt against Madero. Lidia had spent all the money she could pry out of her father to buy guns, and a few wealthy ranchers that thought the rebels were going to win, gave money for guns.

Ángel's vaqueros took the money to Barrera in the mountains, and brought guns back to Los Cerritos and delivered them to the rebels.

The vaqueros didn't go armed around the hacienda because peones weren't ever allowed to have guns. Ángel armed them with smuggled guns only when they were on smugglers' business. And of course, he'd hand out carbines if real trouble broke out at home.

She said no rebels had come for guns and cartridges since I arrived, and only a few rifles had been sent to the rebels or guerrillas because the fighting was so mixed up and scattered. There was a pretty good stock on hand, hidden in different places.

Lidia said her father wasn't so stupid he didn't have a good idea what was going on, but he was stupid enough to think it wouldn't affect him in the end, and that he could just go on raising the bulls he loved and taking trips to Tucson, Arizona, to visit some woman. He scolded Lidia for sympathizing with the rebels, but treated her like she was some schoolgirl that would get over all this foolishness.

Lidia said the danger was Narciso, because he was completely loyal to her father and the Madero government, and knew the hacienda was a hotbed of smugglers. But the worst danger was Salvador Cano and his *Rurales*.

I could feel trouble coming between me and Narciso, and I didn't want him checking when I came and went. I knew he was after my scalp since Ángel and I chased him and Salvador Cano away from Lidia and Paco, that night, so I told Ángel I needed a new home. He said I could bunk in his room in another small house where he lived alone. So I moved in with him and slept on a mattress on the floor, and kept Gato handy in a small corral, with Ángel's sorrel roan.

I was getting nervous about what would happen when Don Hector got home, because I knew Narciso was going to mess it up for me. I'd have gone to Texas or some place, and taken my chances on being arrested over Long Tom Mundt, except for Lidia. Because over the three weeks or so before Don Hector got back, I got to know her pretty good, and it got so I couldn't stand the thought of being anywhere where she wasn't.

Narciso had taken to prying around all over the hacienda, trying to scare people into telling him about the gunrunning, and he didn't bother at all about guarding the house. I jumped him about it, and he said, "You do it! Earn your keep for a change! I am hired by Don Hector, not his daughter, and my responsibility is to him."

So I took over guarding the gate, and Lidia got to coming out to sit and talk with me. The priest told her I was a heretic and she should keep away from me. But she had lost respect for him, and for the church in general—and this bothered her a great deal, because she was religious. She said the church had become infested with priests and bishops that were greedier than any common person, and their position and the respect, almost worship, the peones gave them made it possible for them to pile up personal property and wealth. Many of them were hypocrites, she said, and they told the peones that God put them in their misery in this life, and they had to accept it, and their reward would be in heaven. She said a great many people didn't trust them any more and wouldn't go to Mass—but they loved God and Jesus and the brown Virgin of Guadalupe, right along with their old heathen gods. Some would travel miles on their knees to certain shrines, to do penance.

Then she would talk about Padre Guzmán that had been the priest at Los Cerritos before Padre Arrellaga, how he didn't own anything but the robe on his back, and he spoke the Indian lingo and would walk miles to give medicine to the campesinos, and would sit all night with a sick man, and comfort the women whose husbands never came back from the fighting. And he even had the nerve to tell Don Hector he was selfish and sinful. The Rurales came and took him away and she never knew why, but he was probably mixed up in the Madero revolution.

Well, I hadn't ever been in love, but I was falling in love with Lidia, and that was a box canyon with no way out. Because no daughter of a *hidalgo*, proud of his Spanish blood, could ever have any serious thoughts about a hired gunfighter, and a yanqui at that. And if she got a little fond of him, and her father found out, they'd find the yanqui gunslinger in a ditch some morning, leaking blood at every pore. Maybe that was the reason she let herself go and got so friendly, because she knew it was too impossible to even think about, that anything serious could ever happen with me and her.

One afternoon, she said, "Kel, Ángel said he tells you of the terrible trouble my people are in, and that you are very *simpático*. Maybe you will help us. You would have, the night Paco died . . . I know that."

"I would have fought for you." I said. "Doña Lidia, I'm confused. You're Spanish, and the daughter of a *hacendado,* and the hacendados own the country. Aren't you fighting your own people?"

She got mad. She said, "I am not Spanish! I'm Mexican! My ancestry is nobler than my father's! I'm descended from Malinche!"

So I had to ask her who was Malinche, and she said I was stupid like all yanquis. "Malinche was the woman of Cortés," she said, "who interpreted for him and advised him and knew the weakness of the Aztecs, and had a son by him. Without her the Spaniards would have been slaughtered on the beach at Vera Cruz. Many Mexicans say she was a traitor to her people, but she fought for the countries enslaved by the Aztecs, who were no different then than the rich people and foreigners now, bleeding Mexico for their own profit! And Malinche used Cortés, and his horses, cannon, and steel armor, to free Mexico from Montezuma. I will give my life for Mexico. And I will fight even my own father, because he is a greedy gachupin without a conscience, as Hernán Cortés was."

She said old Porfirio Díaz had fought the French, and then he had fought against the great hero, Benito Juárez, because Juárez was about to be reelected president, which just gave a president more time to loot the country—even though everyone knew Juárez was a real patriot. Anyway, after coming out for no reelection, ever, Díaz got himself elected ten times! And he ruled Mexico for thirty-five years, and got more and more cruel, and cheated the Indians and *mestizos,* and helped rich Mexicans and foreigners keep them in slavery.

And for over thirty years, business was humming in Mexico, and the rich got richer and *peones* were treated worse and worse. Díaz favored the foreigners that had money for bribes. And the land of Mexico was still ninety-eight percent in the hands of only two percent of people like her own father. The English and Americans owned the railroads and the mines and the logging operations. The French had the textile mills and the fruit production. Even the Mormons had big orchards just north of Nuevo Casas Grandes. The Spaniards owned the business houses and the banks, and the Germans owned the breweries.

She said the rich Mexicans themselves were the worst, because their own people on the haciendas were slaves. The Terrazas family owned about half of the whole state of Chihuahua, and when someone asked General Terrazas one time, "Are you of the State of Chihuahua?" the way they put it in Spanish, he said, "No. Chihuahua is the estate of the Terrazas."

Another day she talked about how terrible it was to have to fight, now, against Madero. "We loved him," she said, "every Mexican that hated Porfirio Díaz. But he has made such awful mistakes, keeping the Porfirista army, and even worse, the Rurales, and so many cabinet officers and senators who are still Porfirista, and working against Madero. It is as bad as ever, the peonage and land thefts and the repression . . . and that is why his old comarades have turned against him, and even me, and it breaks my heart!" She was almost crying.

Up till then, I wasn't ever interested in anybody but myself, and I wouldn't have felt bad about all the injustice or done anything myself if it wasn't for her and Ángel. They were risking their lives (more than once) for their beloved people. And I even began to think like a *revolucionario* and act like one—but I doubt like hell that I'd've died like one.

So every time Lidia went riding around the place with Ángel, I went, too, because I kind of figured I was her bodyguard. We covered the hacienda, and rode in to Nuevo Casas Grandes, and to old Casas Grandes, because Lidia wanted people to see me with her so they'd trust me.

We went out to the prehistoric ruins, too, on a kind of picnic, just her and me and Ángel and Lucas. I'd seen a few ruins in the mountains around home but nothing like this— rammed adobe walls six feet thick, and what was left of six-story buildings, and a water system. There were long corridors like the hall in a hotel, with low doors opening off them into single rooms, dozens of rooms. And there were pens where they'd kept the sacred parrots.

Heading home, we cut across the fields, and I noticed that Ángel and Lucas kept looking at a field of maguey a mile away, forty acres or more, with the big gray-green plants laid out row after row like any orchard.

If you never saw a maguey, why you might think of an enormous dandelion plant, the way the leaves all spring out from the same root, and the same kind of saw-toothed edge to them, except the leaves on the maguey will run six feet long, and a foot broad and a couple of inches thick and feel like stiff leather. And every saw tooth has a thorn so stiff and tough you can actually drive them into wood with a hammer. And the thorn on the end of each leaf is a spike a quarter of an inch thick and maybe four inches long, and sharper than a needle.

There was a flock of buzzards circling above the maguey rows. Ángel jerked his head sideways, and Lucas turned his horse and headed over for a look.

Lucas got smaller and smaller, and stopped at the edge of the maguey field and stood in his stirrups, looking this way and that between the rows.

Then he waved his arm, and the three of us went into a gallop. When we pulled up, I got a good look at what had been thrown up onto the terrible spikes on the ends of several maguey leaves. It was the vaquero, Tomás, stripped naked, and hanging there. It couldn't have been done very long before, because he wasn't dead yet. He was bleeding, and his mouth opening and closing like he was gasping for air. Maybe whoever did it figured we might ride home this way, and see the buzzards.

Ángel said, "Doña Lidia, ride fast! Send a wagon, and, you know, water and bandages and a blanket. Yanqui, you go with her. Lucas, get down! How are we going to get him off of there?"

Lidia got off her horse. She said, "He can send the wagon. I'll stay here."

I started to protest, but she said "*Vete!*" and the way she said it, she meant, "Get the hell out of here!"

I hit Gato a lick with the *romal,* and he really "uprooted himself," the way the Mexicans say it.

CHAPTER 12

We came into the cuadrilla across the big pasture, and jumped the wall, and I saw Marcos and Bartoloméo just riding into the big corral, and galloped over to them. I said, "Tomás is hurt bad, and we're going to get him with a wagon, and we don't want . . ."

Marcos interrupted me—"Roll out the spring wagon. I'll get the mules."

Bartoloméo said he would stay and get ready to help when we brought Tomás home.

In ten minutes, we were on our way, me and Gato loping beside the wagon, and Marcos standing up pouring the leather into the six-mule team, cutting across plowed fields with the wagon bouncing and rocking. When we were almost there, we saw Ángel riding toward us holding up his hand, and Marcos pulled in, and we knew we were too late. Ángel's shirt was torn and his hands were bleeding.

"He died," Ángel said. "He talked, just a little. It was Salvador Cano and his troop. They followed him to a meeting with Lobo Barrera in the sierra, but he spotted them before he met Barrera, and tried to lead them away. They caught him, though, and beat him with rifle butts, and the last he remembered, he hadn't told them anything. But he isn't sure he didn't, after. Maybe he did, and I've got to get word to Barrera."

He looked at me and said, "I chopped the leaves off with my machete and we eased him down, but we might as well not have hurt him, because he didn't last five minutes."

Lidia didn't say anything. Her hands and clothes were ripped by the thorns, like Ángel's. Lucas was as quiet as her.

91

We wiped off the blood and dirt and wrapped Tomás in the blankets we brought and lifted him into the wagon.

Marcos said, "There is news, Señorita. Orozco's army is badly defeated again, at Ojo Caliente de Santa Rosa, and refugees are scattered all over. And the Rurales at Nuevo Casas Grandes have been reinforced with ten new men. They say the government is determined to stop the gunrunning, and Cano is boasting that he will root us out like a nest of snakes."

I laced my fingers together to make a step for Lidia, and swung her up onto her big black. She reined him over to the wagon and leaned down and smoothed Tomás's hair. I saw how beaten and swollen his face was. She was crying, but not making any noise.

She said, "You three go ahead, Ángel. I'll ride with Kel."

Lucas said, "Not just the yanqui, Señorita! I'll ride with you, too."

Ángel said, "Come on, Lucas. She's as safe with him as with you."

The wagon rattled off, with Ángel and Lucas trotting their horses beside it, and we started at a walk. For a while we didn't say anything, and when she did talk, it wasn't about what had happened.

She talked about when she was a little girl. Her father and mother got married because their parents made the match, and her mother brought a huge dowry, and that's when her father bought his breeding stock, the wild black cows and the great fighting bulls. She said they were Miura stock, from Spain and had been bred to fight for three thousand years.

"We are all crazy," she said. "We all love the bulls, anyone with a drop of Spanish blood. There is nothing like the feeling that clutches your heart when the trumpet blows *La Vírgen de la Macarena* and the great black beast comes bawling out of the gate, and the little man waits for him with only a cape in his hands to ward off death . . . to prove something, only nobody knows what he is trying to prove, really. And even though I know it is useless, a waste of life, and terribly costly . . . while the crowd roars like a great beast, itself, and then the little man struts around the ring holding up the ear of a bull, if he is lucky and very brave, I am shaken to the marrow of my bones, like lying with a lover."

When she said that, I had a wild, hot flash of jealousy that shook me, too.

She went on, "But it is criminal, maybe ten thousand pesos for six bulls and thousands more for the matador and picador and banderillero and sword handler, and all for a couple of hours of excitement for fat, bored people, while the peones starve, or die fighting for bare justice."

We rode a while in silence while the moon came up like a big, bright gold coin from behind the mountains a hundred miles to the east. Then she said, "Did you know a bull killed my mother, Kel? He scrambled over the wall of a feed pen, and he was hot, and my father whipped up the buggy horse, trying to get through the gate into the patio, but the bull threw the buggy end over end and killed my mother and the horse, and by that time Ángel was there. My father lay stunned, and Ángel played the bull in the narrow lane with only his serape, until the guard shot it.

"My father really didn't care. He never loved her, just her dowry, because she was Mexican, not Spanish. But she had a large fortune, and half of it, she willed to me, but I have only a few pesos for spending money and clothes when we go to Chihuahua or Durango. My father says I will have it when I marry, or when I am twenty-one, and that will be two years yet.

"I have a dream, Kel. If ever Los Cerritos becomes mine, I'm going to make it an *ejido,* a great cooperative ranch, for the benefit of the hungry peones on Los Cerritos, and for others, many others."

Again she was silent while we rode a quarter mile. Then she said, "Well, a foolish dream, isn't it! Because the fighting and the killing and the slavery go on and on, as they have for four hundred years."

When we got back, I dismounted in the patio in front of the big house, and she said, "Help me down, Kel."

She slid off the sidesaddle and I caught her with my hands around her waist. I wanted to pull her tight against me, but I set her on her feet, and in the moonlight I saw the track of tears down her face. She said, "I'm glad you came to Los Cerritos—but you are going to regret it, one day."

I did grab her then, just my hands on her waist, and all I could say was, "Lidia . . . Lidia . . ."

She said, "Take care of Moro for me, will you?" and pushed lightly against my chest, and I let her go.

From the dark under the arcade, Padre Arrellaga said, sharply, "Lidia! Explain to me . . ."

She said, "I am Doña Lidia! I may confess my sins to you, but I explain only to God and my conscience. So be quiet!"

In the middle of the night, somebody tossed gravel through the window bars into our room, and before I was clear awake, Ángel was at the window, naked, with a carbine in his hands. He whispered to somebody, then unbarred the door and let a man in. We put our heads together, and the man whispered, "A bunch of Orozco's soldiers, from the defeat at Ojo Caliente de Santa Rosa, four of them wounded badly, and most of them hurt. Federal soldiers and a few Rurales have followed them as far as the field by the bull pasture."

"Where are the soldiers?" Ángel said.

The man said, "We put them in the granary, behind the sacks of corn."

"They're not safe, there," Ángel said. Then he turned to me. "Kel, this isn't your trouble, but . . ."

"I'm in it already," I said, "what do you want?"

He said, "We need time to take these people to a safer place. Saddle up. I'll have Lucas and Barto meet you at the big corral. Find those Federales and Rurales and let them chase you around for a while, but not toward old Casas Grandes."

Lucas led me and Barto up a grassy arroyo that topped out near the bull pasture, and there were bulls-eye lanterns flashing, and men stumbling around looking for tracks, and across the wall the fighting bulls were stirred up and moaning. The searchers couldn't do much in the dark, but they would sure come to the cuadrilla and turn everything upside down.

Lucas said, "It's a shame to shoot thin air instead of some stinking Rural or Federal, but now is no time to stir up more trouble. We'll put a few over their heads. Then we scatter."

We walked our horses on the grass to the corner of the wall, a hundred yards from where the Federales were milling around.

An officer down there said, "We lost them. Mount up and we'll go ask a few questions of the caporal. And I hear there's the daughter of the patrón, whose loyalty is questionable and the patrón is absent. I will have to question her . . . looking straight down into her lovely eyes, if you understand what I mean." He laughed.

I said, "Lucas, lend me your carbine will you? I can nail that son of a bitch even by moonlight."

"I regret," he said. "Maybe later. Are you set?"

He raised the carbine and shot over their heads, and I cut loose twice with the Bisley. Barto shot, too, with a carbine, and they were all milling around slamming into one another and swearing when we went down the hill at a trot. A couple of shots followed us, but not close. Then they got organized and cut out after us, about twenty of them.

At the bottom of the hill, the three of us went three different directions, and they split up and came charging after us. I let Gato out a notch then, and we went turning and twisting in and out among trees and shadows and moonlight. There were four of them after me, and they kept banging away like damn fools. They weren't close enough, and shooting off a running horse nothing but a lucky shot would touch me.

I heard distant shooting, too, and none of it in the direction of old Casas Grandes, which was what Ángel wanted.

Then I made a sweep into open country and let them see me, and I touched Gato with the side of my spurs, and he opened out another notch. The four of them were bunched together, and I let them close in to about fifty yards, and we were going full out down an arroyo that got narrower and deeper, and now I was scared, because their shooting was really damn good, and a couple of ricochets went whining past so close I could almost feel the breeze.

That arroyo opened out through a cutbank right on the edge of that huge field of maguey where we had found Tomás hung on the thorns. Just as we broke out of the *arroyo,* I twitched Gato's rein, and he slid on his rump, and I kneed him into a left hand turn, and we pounded along under the cutbank, only arms length from the maguey plants.

Four horses didn't make the turn, and plowed into those terrible stiff, spiked maguey leaves. The men were screaming, but the horses were worse—that terrible screaming and thrashing around. I was almost sick.

I found a break in the cutbank, and Gato scrambled up. The screaming stopped, and I heard the men coaxing the horses out of there, and calling on Jesus and the Virgin, and cursing me to hell.

There was a faint streak of light in the east, when I turned into the lane. I heard voices behind me. Ángel and Lidia and two vaqueros and three women on burros, and I called out.

Lidia rode up to me and put her hand on my arm. She said, "Thanks, Kel. Ángel told me."

She sounded bone tired. I said, "Are those men all right?"

"Yes," she said, "in a big room we fixed a long time ago, in the Casas Grandes ruins. A couple of men are watching till daylight and two women stayed to take care of the wounded."

Ángel said, "Señorita, I'll ride ahead, now. I've got to find out if the secretary and the bookkeeper know what happened last night, and I have to shut Narciso up. He's the real danger to us."

"No," she said. "I sent him an urgent message last night, right after the woman came for me, that Salvador Cano wanted him in Janos by daylight. He lost no time in saddling up and leaving. Our real trouble will begin when my father comes home, but we may still have a little time, because he has a blonde whore in Tucson, and can hardly bear to break away from her whenever he invents a business trip to there."

We were all up before daylight, expecting trouble. The Rurales and Federales had caught four poor devils we couldn't do anything about. The chief asked for breakfast, and Lidia ordered them fed. Four of them were all bandaged up. They had run into a maguey field in the dark, chasing a rebel soldier. They'd had to shoot one of their horses. The whole bunch ate in a hurry and rode out, and it looked like they thought they'd caught all the fugitives, but maybe they were nervous about all the vaqueros hanging around staring at them.

The villagers buried Tomás that morning, a hurried-up job. Lidia went, and me and Ángel, and all the vaqueros.

Other fugitives straggled in and told us about more in the hills that needed medicine and food and a place to hide. Lidia told the vaqueros to bring all of them they could find to the granary after dark. She said to bring in thirty or forty loose horses, too. When they rode out carrying food and skins of water, she said Ángel, me and her better talk things over, and I said my old room was safe, with Narciso gone.

When we got there, I put a chair in the patio for her. She told us, "We can't hide what we're doing much longer. Almost everybody knows about it, but Salvador Cano just hasn't caught us yet."

Ángel said, "If we could just hang on, somehow, till Orozco wins . . . and maybe Zapata will take Mexico City again and chase all those Porfirista generals and deputies."

"I think we can keep on operating until my father gets back," Lidia said, "and maybe even after that. But we've got to do something about the secretary and the storekeeper."

"And the bookkeeper," Ángel said. "Señorita, we're in a rough game. You know it. So . . ." and he made the motion of cutting his throat.

She drew in her breath and looked away from him. "No," she said. "I couldn't order *that!*"

"I can order it," Ángel said, "or do it myself. What else is there?"

She said, "The bookkeeper is in love with me. No trouble with him so long as I remember to let him kiss my hand every week or so. Now, I'll fire the secretary for forging a check. He signs many things for my father, and I will forge a crude forgery of his forgery. Let him yell. Who will take his word against mine? And Calzadíaz, in the store, I will only have to exaggerate what he has already done—a few bolts of cloth missing, a few *arrobas* of corn not accounted for. I'll tell him if he doesn't keep his mouth shut, I'll fix up his accounts. That will scare him half to death, because father is ruthless to anyone who steals from him."

"So that leaves Padre Arrellaga," Ángel said. "A fanatic for the government—but who would threaten a priest?"

Nobody said anything for a while.

Finally I said, "What would he do if a yanqui heretic with a big pistol told him to keep his mouth shut?"

Suddenly Ángel grinned. "Why, I think he would keep his mouth shut. At least until Don Hector comes home."

Lidia looked a little scared. "You are awful, the two of you!" she said. Then she grinned, too, and said, "Padre Arrellaga is God's representative on earth. Do you think you can scare God?"

Ángel went to see what could be done about the refugees his boys would be bringing to the granary that night, and Lidia went to threaten the secretary and the storekeeper. I had a queer feeling about threatening a priest, even though I wasn't very religious.

I found him under the arcade, where no servants were

around. He was taking his siesta, snoring in a net hammock. I sat down on a bench and rocked him gently with my foot, and he snorted and gargled, and woke up.

He said, "Explain this intrusion, you . . . you . . ." I guess he couldn't think of any word for me that wasn't a swear word.

I pulled the Bisley and scratched my cheek with the front sight, and his mouth snapped shut and his eyes snapped open. I said, "People are saying they hear and see some funny things going on around here, nights. Clearly, nothing could be going on with me and Narciso on guard, could it? Except Narciso has gone away somewhere, hasn't he? So if, for instance, Salvador Cano could happen to ask about any such reports, or the patrón when he returns, you would be in a position to say that nothing has been happening . . . no shooting . . . no voices in the night."

He couldn't take his eyes off the pistol. He gulped and said, "Why, yes! No! I mean . . . I certainly haven't been aware of . . ." He was very scared, and I was ashamed of myself, and I got up and left.

Lidia had about the same results when she talked to the bookkeeper and the storekeeper. Of course, this didn't make us safe, it just gave us a breather. Maybe they wouldn't risk running to Salvador Cano, but they'd sure talk when the chance came. But the breather was a godsend, because the Rurales and Federales didn't come back, not then.

And for ten days, fifteen—I don't know *how* long—none of us had any rest. Night and day we hunted for refugees and tended the wounded and gave horses to those that could ride, and hid wounded and desperate men in the ruins of Casas Grandes, and little by little got them away to the mountains, or buried the ones that died on us, until the wreckage of Pascual Orozco's defeat disappeared. And all the time we prayed that no one would betray us to the Rurales and that Don Hector would stay with his blonde in Tucson. We slept only when we couldn't stay on our feet another minute, and we didn't take time to wash or get out of our clothes.

Lidia's eyes seemed to get bigger and bigger as the days went by. She had on a dirty shirtwaist and a short leather jacket and a riding skirt—a real wide pair of pants that you couldn't tell wasn't a skirt. She apologized to me for wearing it, because pants of any kind were very unladylike. They let her ride astride, which was the reason she wore them.

And finally, the last wounded man was put in a wagon, under the stars, and the last fifteen sound ones left for the mountains, escorted by a half dozen vaqueros swaying in their saddles from exhaustion, and each with a tired soldier up behind him, and the last peon and his woman set out for Los Cerritos, and Lidia and me were left alone in that big underground room in the ruins at Casas Grandes. It was just the way those old Paquimé left it a thousand years ago, with the fire pit, and the smoke hole between the heavy *vigas* that held the roof up, with its two feet of packed earth—just the same except for a couple of bottles of water and some scraps of tortilla and a stack of dirty blankets and pieces of bloody bandages.

It will show how used we got to each other from being together night and day all that time, and how exhausted she was, so tired she just didn't care—she took off her shirtwaist and poured a little water into a bucket and scrubbed at her face and hands, and she didn't care that her shoulders were bare except for the straps of her underwear, or that I could see down her front when she bent over.

And I was so tired I hardly bothered to look at her, with her dark hair like a cloud around her bare shoulders and her beautiful face shining with the water, in the candle light. I sat on the blankets and managed to pull my boots off, and just fell backward, sound asleep.

Then it was daylight, and a shaft of sunlight was pouring down through the smoke hole. When I tried to roll onto my side, my left arm was so numb I couldn't feel anything. And there was Lidia pushed up against me with her head on my arm, flat on her back and snoring. Her hair tickled my nose, and I sneezed hard enough to tear my head off.

She slowly opened her eyes and blinked at the sunlight, then without turning her head, she rolled her eyes and looked at me, and shut her eyes.

She rolled away from me and pushed up to her hands and knees, staring at me like I was a rattler coiled to strike. I grabbed her wrist and tried to pull her back to me, and she jerked and yanked, biting her lip and not making a sound.

I said, "Whatever the hell is the matter with you, it's too late! What are you scared of? If you were a virgin last night, you're still one this morning."

She quit jerking to free her wrist, but I held on. She said,

"How did I get here, in bed with you?" like I had tricked her into it.

I said, "How do I know! I was asleep! You were washing your face, and I went to sleep!"

She put her free hand on her bare shoulder and ran it down her arm, and twisted to try and reach her shirtwaist where she'd thrown it down, but I was afraid she'd get away, so I held on and she couldn't reach it.

She relaxed then, and laid beside me again and said, "You can let go. I'm so tired I think I'll die. Will you be good to me? Will you just let me sleep?"

"Sure I will," I said. "I'll have a look at the horses."

The horses were all right, where we'd penned them in a thousand-year-old patio in the shade of high, crumbling adobe walls, and some vaquero had left them a wooden tub of water and some hay.

I went back to Lidia. She had put her shirtwaist on, and she was already asleep, curled up like a baby. When I laid down beside her, she smiled without opening her eyes, and took my hand. Then she raised her head and pulled my arm under her neck and settled back, her head snuggled down on my shoulder.

And even if I had wanted to try anything with her, I was too tired to know what I wanted and what I didn't want, and too tired to do anything if I wanted to. But suddenly I remembered something, and I pushed up on my elbow and said, "When you were talking about the bullfights, you said they made you feel like you were lying with your lover. You mean you've got one, and you've been doing that?"

She mumbled something, and fell sound asleep.

I was welcome at the big house, now, even if Padre Arrellaga scowled at me and wouldn't talk to me. I spent a lot of time in the shade of the front arcade, enjoying being with Lidia. But not just that. I was hired to protect her and the household, and if anything happened to her, I couldn't stand it. I was that sure by then.

Narciso was a damn fool. When he came back, two days after we got the last refugee started for the mountains, he was sore as a boil over being sent on that wild goose chase to see Salvador Cano in Janos.

Lidia and me and the priest, were sitting there that afternoon when Narciso came riding down the lane, and he dismounted and stood by the steps, and didn't even take his hat off. It looked like he'd been getting madder every mile he rode from Janos. It was that fake message Lidia sent him, that night the first batch of refugees came in. I wondered where he'd been for nearly two weeks.

"Salvador Cano was not there!" he said. "He hadn't been in Janos for a week! He was up in the mountains with twenty men, after that gunrunner—that Lobo Barrera. I went to find him, because I had things to report . . . a few little suspicions, Doña Lidia . . . that we will discuss later."

Padre Arrellaga muttered some excuse and went into the house. He sure didn't like to be around anything that might turn into trouble. I was glad, because he might not be so scared of me, with Narciso back. But it didn't matter much, because he would sure talk to Narciso and Cano when he got the chance. Only I would rather have Ángel and a few of his men around when the going got rough.

Narciso said, "One of your peones has talked, Señorita, and I was fortunate to be with Salvador Cano when he used the information to set the trap in the mountain pass and cut Lobo Barrera's band to pieces. Barrera, himself, ran, and left his men to die—but we will get him."

"Who is this 'we'?" I said. "Since when are you an informer for the Guardia Rural, and not just a bodyguard for Don Hector?"

"Don Hector is not here," he said. "I do my duty. I cooperate with the lawful authorities."

Then he turned to Lidia—"Salvador Cano has given me authority to act, and I demand that you stay here. Don't go away!"

She laughed. "You demand!" she said. "Anyway, where would I go if I wanted to run away?"

He marched back to his horse and rode away, heading toward his quarters.

Lidia said, "Poor Tomás. He was so beaten he didn't remember, but he talked!"

"That had to be it," I said. "Poor devil. I'll find Ángel. He'll want to get in touch with Lobo Barrera."

She took my hands and looked up into my face. She said, "Oh, Kel, how I wish . . ." and suddenly her face flushed dark, and she twisted away when I reached for her, and ran into the house.

I found Ángel, Lucas, and Juan working with a couple of

horses in the corral and told them about Narciso coming back, and what he said about the gunrunner, Lobo Barrera. Ángel swore, and said, "Tomás should have died before he talked! Juan, you leave tonight, find Barrera. He'll be at that cave way up past Huerigos. Find out what he needs and where he wants me to meet him. Tell him I'll send all the help I can, but if Don Hector comes back, then I can't go myself. It looks like trouble for us, too, Kel. It was bound to come. Stick with her."

"I'm not enough!" I said. "Not just me alone!"

"Well," he said, "you're a tough boy. You've got that big pistol, just like his. I wouldn't worry," and he turned and walked away. I began to get scared. It wasn't like him to leave the trouble to somebody else—but then, so far, I'd only seen him in action after trouble happened, not face to face with it. And I had no proof, only his talk, that Lidia really meant anything to him. She was the patrón's daughter and, as Narciso said, Ángel was a peón.

After supper, I hung around the patio of the big house, but she didn't come out. Nobody did. So after dark I rode to my quarters and got a blanket and came back. I slept in a damn hammock, only I hardly slept at all.

She found me there in the morning, and laughed at me for being a worrier, but she laced her fingers with mine when she led me into the house and showed me a bathroom. I washed my face, and wished I'd had a chance to shave. She got my breakfast, herself, then we went out and sat on the bench under the arcade. She had a house mozo lead Gato away from under the ramada where I'd tied him, to feed and water him.

It wasn't long before Narciso came. He was afoot, and he had Camila with him, the girl that had lived with Patricio. And I guess it was because I was gawking at her, wondering why he'd brought her along, that he caught me flat-footed. Lidia had stood up, like me, when they came up to the steps, and now she grabbed my arm and kind of gasped, and I looked at Narciso, and I was looking right down the bore of his Bisley.

He said, "Adams, you are not foolish. The señorita might get hurt."

I wouldn't have gone for my gun for anything, not with

her there beside me. He knew it, too, because he just strolled up and took it, and walked back and stood beside Camila again.

He said, "Doña Lidia, I will hold Adams here as a guarantee. Have somebody hitch a team to the surrey and bring it here, while you get ready. You both are coming to Janos. I have the evidence and this witness. If you were a peasant, you would be shot without trial, because you are a traitor."

Lidia looked like she was going to spit on him, and he said, "Tell them, Camila!"

Camila did spit at Lidia. She called her a slut and a murderess and said Lidia had sent her man to his death, and many others, so she could make a profit selling contraband guns. She said she would tell the Rurales that Lidia and I and Ángel hid Paco from Salvador Cano the night he died, and that Lidia was a bloodsucker, a leech like her father, a monster, fattening on the blood of the people, and that we would all die, the gachupines and the foreigners. She went on, saying that Patricio had told her all about the gunrunning and she was glad she had told Narciso where the Rurales could ambush Lobo Barrera and his band—and that Lidia, rich and greedy, with the blood of the people on her hands, would be tried in public before they hung her, and this was the day she had lived for—and she went on and on, spitting and fuming —until the carbines began to fire.

That awful, ear-aching blast of carbines firing, and white smoke rolling from behind the ramada and over the patio wall, and Lidia with her hands over her ears, screaming, and Narciso driven backward by the lead smashing into him, and falling, twisted and crumpled and bloody . . .

The firing stopped, and Camila stood staring down at him, until suddenly she turned and ran down the long lane between the stone walls. A carbine fired, raising gray dust behind her flying feet, and fired again, and she spun around and fell and lay still.

Then it was too quiet, nobody running to see what happened, Lidia and me staring through the drifting white smoke at the two bodies.

Then we heard feet running in the house, and a scream from the doorway, and servant girls looking out, and Padre Arrellaga came pushing past them, his face white as flour. He

was saying, "What? What is it?" When he saw them lying
there, he grabbed his throat with both hands, and actually
staggered like somebody hit him.

Then he screeched into my face, "Beast! Murdering beast!"

I shoved him away. I said, "You are a fool! Narciso took
my pistol before they shot him!"

I hauled him down the two steps and made him bend over.
"Pick them up!" I said. "Both pistols! His and mine! Tell me
if they have been fired!"

He was shaking and looked like he was going to be sick. "I
can't!" he squawked. "I don't know how!"

"Then watch," I told him, and picked up my pistol and
punched the five cartridges out onto the ground, then did the
same with Narciso's. I said, "See? No empty shells. When
you are asked, what are you going to tell them?"

He said, "Oh, yes! I will! I will tell you you didn't do it!
Please! Let me go now!"

He went stumbling back into the house, and people were
coming, now—servants and cooks and field hands, and the
bookkeeper and secretary and four or five of the vaqueros,
galloping up and sliding their horses to a stop.

Lidia had got hold of herself. She said, "So Tomás didn't
talk. And now, Camila can't, nor Narciso. But Salvador
Cano knows all about us."

"He knew a long time ago," I said. "He just never found
out who was bringing the guns from Columbus, or what trail
Lobo Barrera was using. He hasn't got his witness, now, but
he can get others easy enough. It's just luck he couldn't come
himself, with a troop of Rurales."

Well, at least, I had two Bisley Colts, now. Just for insur-
ance, you might say, I hid the one I inherited from Narciso
under the tiles of the eaves of Ángel's house.

CHAPTER 13

For about a week, the dust sort of settled. Nobody went to Narciso's funeral except his two little loves, Rosita and Azucena. Camila's family wouldn't let her be buried at the same ceremony, so the priest had to go through it twice.

So far as I knew, nobody asked any questions about how they died. But we were on edge, Lidia and Ángel and me and the vaqueros, expecting Salvador Cano to come riding in with his whole troop, but it turned out they were still blundering around in the foothills trying to catch Lobo Barrera. The word went around the hacienda that anybody that had anything to say to the *Rurales* better just shoot themselves, first.

We all rode out to the bull pastures one day where the vaqueros were going to turn four little bull calves into oxen because their mothers weren't brave enough at the last tienta. Lidia wouldn't watch, of course, but Ángel had to be there, and she wanted to get out, and we wouldn't leave her unguarded at the house.

On the way back, Ángel said, "As soon as Cano gets tired of chasing Lobo Barrera, he'll pay us a visit. And my men won't submit to arrest. Maybe we'll take to the sierra and join Barrera."

"No," Lidia said. "Los Cerritos is as much mine as my father's . . . maybe not yet, under the law, but by right and justice, and I won't abandon it. The house is built for defense, with stone walls and tile roofs, and there are canned food and dried meat and beans, and a cistern of water under the kitchen floor."

Even while Lobo Barrera was being chased around the foothills by Salvador Cano, Ángel had already got in touch with him and they had set up a new place to bring guns across the border—to Ojo Agua Blanca and then by a very bad trail through Coyote and Gran Morelos and Ojo Frío.

Something was bound to happen to me when Don Hector came home, so I wrote to Uncle Frank, to see if it would ever be safe for me to go back. I told him where I was and that I was probably in for some trouble when my boss got home, and I had to know if Long Tom Mundt died. I asked him, too, what happened to Letty Greenfield Kelly, and if he had heard about the Mexican police shooting Cassie.

Ángel said he would pass my letter on to Lobo Barrera, and he would mail it for me (in El Paso or Columbus), but not to expect any answer for a long time, the way conditions were. And he said to tell Uncle Frank to use a Mexican name when he wrote back, and address it to Ojo Agua Blanca, so Barrera could pick it up for me if it ever got there.

Then one morning, the secretary packed his bag and Ángel drove him to Nuevo Casas Grandes to take the train. Lidia's threat to accuse him of forgery worked fine. Then the storekeeper got the same idea, and he left. So what we still had to worry about was the bookkeeper and Padre Arrellaga and whatever peones might hate Lidia like Camila had. There was bound to be some of them.

Pascual Orozco's army finally took such a beating from Victoriano Huerta, at Bachimba, that Orozco pulled out of the state entirely, and Huerta put Madero's governor, Abrahan Gonzales, back in office. Huerta had the reputation of a cruel, diseased drunk, but he was a damn good general. All that happened the first week in July, and I had lost track of time and could hardly believe it when I read it in the Juárez paper that Ángel got in Nuevo Casas Grandes. It was sure July weather, hot as hell, and thunder storms every afternoon, and the corn tassels turning brown and the *peones* harvesting the beans and peppers.

Stragglers kept coming in from Orozco's army, and we passed them on to some place where they could get back to their families. Lidia and me took care of most of them, and the more I was with her, the more I knew there wouldn't ever be anyone but her for me. She liked me, too. Maybe more than liked me—but it was still hopeless for me, the yanqui pistolero and the daughter of a Spaniard that owned a 240,000-acre hacienda.

But we had that peaceful time together, long rides and long talks, and I told her all about the twins and Letty and Uncle Frank, and how I didn't know if I had killed old Long Tom Mundt. And all the time, it was like hearing thunder so far off you kind of felt it in your bones instead of hearing it, but you knew it was getting close, and the lightning had to strike somewhere.

Then Don Hector Estrada Palacios y Garza came home.

There was the hell of a racket in the lane, and Lidia and me jumped up off the bench under the arcade, and Padre Arrellaga came bustling out trying to look like he wasn't hurrying.

Down the lane came a beautiful brand new 1912 Simplex, all red lacquer and brass radiator and big brass headlights, big wide mudguards, and two spare tires beside the gear shift lever and the hand brake, and varnished wooden wheels, and the touring top folded down. In the passenger seat on the left was Don Hector, smiling and waving. The driver was a little, ugly, dark man in a linen duster and goggles.

Even if people might hate the patrón, they had to pretend this was the happiest thing that could happen, and everybody crowded around smiling and making polite remarks. Old Ángel was there, grinning and bowing with his hat off. A lot of miserable peones actually got down on their knees and were saying prayers of thanks for the patrón's safe return.

The two of them got down and the ugly little man took off his cap and goggles, and they plowed through the crowd toward Lidia and me and Padre Arrellaga. His face was pockmarked, and he had a white scar in place of most of his right eyebrow. Lidia stepped up to her father and held her face up and he kissed her cheek and said, "My dear!" He said hello to the priest, and it was just like the first day I came to Los Cerritos—everybody pretended like I wasn't there.

Don Hector got a big smile on his face with his gold teeth shining, and pulled the little man up beside him and said, "Lidia, my dear, allow me to present Don Fructuoso Urrutía!"

Lidia sure wasn't impressed. She bowed about a sixteenth of an inch and said, *"Mucho gusto, Señor Urrutía."*

She didn't hold out her hand, but he grabbed it anyway, and actually kissed it. And he said, *"Doña Lidia! Servidor de usted, que besa sus piés!"*

You don't say, "Your servant, who kisses your *feet!*" unless you're a lover, or engaged. Lidia's face looked like it was carved out of wood, and she pulled her hand loose. Then Don Hector said, "Yes! Don Fructuoso Urrutía, *El Niño de Burgos!* The Kid from Burgos!"

There was a gasp from everybody there, almost, and Lidia's face lit up and she grabbed the little monster's hand and said, "We are deeply honored, Señor Urrutía!"

He grinned like a stunted shark and said, "Please, Señorita! My friends just call me Kid!"

I stood behind Lidia ready to shake hands with Don Hector and be introduced to that little bugger. But the three of them walked past me like I didn't exist.

I untied Gato from the ramada post and swung in beside Ángel when the crowd broke up. I said, "Who in hell is that monkey?"

Ángel said, "My God, how can a man be so ignorant! That's the Burgos Kid!"

"I know! I know!" I said. "Who's the Burgos Kid?"

"Only the greatest matador since *El Carnicerito,*" he said. "He is a lecher and has chronic gonorrhea like all *toreros,* and is half crippled with horn wounds, and he has guts of a kind you wouldn't know about. He can only write X for his name and he is stupid and arrogant, and I would die happy tomorrow if I could see him and Conquistador in the arena together."

I said, "I didn't know you were childish, too. I thought only the Spaniards have chronic bull fever."

"Who says I have no Spanish blood?" he said, grinning. "Clearly I am quite a mixture. I may be a mestizo, because I never knew who my father was."

For two days I didn't see Don Hector nor Lidia, either. Then he sent for me to come to his office on the second floor of the big house. He didn't say "Hello, I hope you like it here," or anything, just, "Move into the house, now that I am back. One of the mozos will show you your room. Be ready for my orders twenty-four hours a day. Understood?"

The way he talked to me got me sore, like the first time I saw him. I said, "Nothing's understood until I get paid. Two months at a hundred pesos a month, less that fifty pesos in Agua Prieta."

He said, "Later. Later. Now tell me, how did Narciso die?" He didn't mention Camila.

I said, "Later. After you pay me."

He swung around in his swivel chair then and stared in my eyes. "You had better learn your place," he told me.

"I know my place," I said. "I also know what we agreed."

He pulled out a wallet and offered me some bills, and I shook my head.

He swore, and went into a closet and closed the door, and came out and gave me three fifty-peso gold pieces.

I put them in my poke and folded it and put it in my pocket. "He got shot," I said.

"I know he was shot, you fool!" he said. "I asked . . ."

I wouldn't have been so sharp, but I figured I wasn't going to last around there, not after Padre Arrellaga and Salvador Cano got to talking to him. I said, "Four or five carbines cut him down right in front of Lidia . . . I mean, Doña Lidia, and me."

He said, "Adams, I am not blind. I am aware that certain activities are carried on here. I don't think for a moment that you are blind, either. Don't forget what you are buying and what you are selling for a hundred pesos a month . . . my silence concerning the interest of Arizona authorities in your whereabouts, and your complete loyalty to me."

Well, my conscience hurt me then, because I did take his money, and I sure hadn't been very loyal to him, so far.

I moved my gear into a little room on the ground floor near the kitchen and handy to the box stall and small corral, behind that wood shed where Lidia laid out the dead Patricio, and where Paco died.

Then all I did was hang around the patio gate bored to death, and went on a couple of long rides to see the bulls, with Don Hector and the bullfighter, but as far as they were concerned, I wasn't there any more than their horses. The only time I saw Lidia was when some fancy people and Army officers would come from Nuevo Casas Grandes for dinner and she met them at the door—and once when she came out to go for a ride up and down the lane with that pockmarked little bastard in his fancy automobile. Of course, she wouldn't go out of sight of the house, because the Simplex didn't have any room for a chaperon.

Oh, she'd smile at me when she went past, but there was never a word, and I had to hear him giving her those outlandish, flowery compliments. And I wanted to slap her, and kick his ass good for him. And she'd smile and look away, or say, "Oh, Niño! Don't say things like that!", or give him a little push and pretend to look mad. Of course, she couldn't stop and gossip with the hired help—not with her father home again. And of course, I really didn't understand, not then, or ever, how fighting bulls and everything about the *corrida de toros* made anybody with a drop of Spanish blood kind of crazy. They seem to think that a really brave matador is the next thing to God, Himself.

I couldn't move around like before and see what was going on, but ever since El Niño arrived, there seemed to be a kind of excitement in the air, and I asked Ángel about it, and he told me about the bullfight . . .

"When it comes to the bulls," he said, "everybody is crazy, and nobody worse than a bull breeder. He is prouder of them when they are brave in the arena than is the *matador* that kills them. The breeder is the wildest *aficionado* of any."

That word aficionado, it's supposed to mean just somebody that likes something, but they use it to mean fanatic.

Ángel went on, "There have been only a few corridas de toros for two years, because of the revolution, but there was one in Juárez, and the patrón saw it just before he came home. The senior matador was El Niño de Burgos. And of course the world's best matador had to meet the breeder of the world's best bulls, and Don Hector invited him here.

"Well, Don Hector and Doña Lidia would no more have spoken to him than to a mangy dog, because they are aristocracy, and he is the lowest of the low. Except! Yes, except for one thing . . . he is a killer of *toros bravos,* and a great one, and that is why he is welcome in the house and can say things to Lidia with that sissy Spanish lisp that would get him whipped if he were not El Niño de Burgos."

"I'll break his ugly oversize head for him," I said.

Ángel gave me a crooked grin and invented another of his proverbs—*"Mas puntiagudo que colmillo de víbora es la envidia,"* jealousy is sharper than a snake's tooth. "If I were not constantly interrupted," he went on, "I could tell you how other aficionados told Don Hector that they would pay for two bulls if he would stage a small corrida, here, for El Niño de Burgos. Well, for all he is a pinchpenny, Don Hector's pride wouldn't permit anything but the best, and one of the bulls will be Conquistador! Now, as you know, always there are six toros and three matadores, but . . ."

"I don't know anything about bullfights, and I don't give a

damn about seeing the great Niño de Burgos fight, except maybe he'll take a horn up the *culo.*"

"Well, that has happened," Ángel said. "As I was saying, there will only be the two bulls and El Niño. The workers are painting the bull ring, and there will be aficionados from Juárez and Chihuahua, and even from Mexico, if the trains are running!"

For a week, the whole cuadrilla was in an uproar, with Lidia running the regular servants and a dozen others brought in from the poblado, cleaning, washing and ironing, polishing silver—and outside, workers fixing up the little bull ring, oiling harness and polishing the brass on the beautiful Concord coach. I even got dragged in on the housework—well, not really the work, but when Lidia needed an errand run or something carried somewhere when all the servants were busy. So I got to talk to her a little, and it was almost worse than not seeing her at all. Because she was all excited about the corrida de toros, and the fancy guests coming, and there wasn't much of the old closeness, like when we were hiding refugees together. Only once, in the upper hall, when I was going to get down a box of silverware from a closet shelf for her, she stopped talking and looked up at me, then took my hand and held it against her cheek.

She said, "This is a hard time for you, isn't it? Well, it won't last forever. It may be the last fun I'll have for a long time, Kel, so don't begrudge it to me."

I reached for her there in the dark hallway, when that Goddamn gypsy bull fighter yelled from his room down the hall, "Doña Lidia! Are you there? Can you have somebody bring my sword case?"

She jumped away from me, and called back, "I'll have it sent up!" then said to me, "Will you take it to him? All the mozos are busy."

I carried the silverware chest to the kitchen for her, and she showed me his sword case, in the luggage room. It looked a little like a guitar case, only slimmer, and it was expensive leather, carved and stamped.

When I went into his room with it, he was standing there naked, looking at a suit spread out on the bed—knee breeches with silver tassels, and a jacket, and a pleated shirt. The suit was blue silk with silver and black embroidery a half-inch thick all over it—what they called the *traje de luces,* the suit of lights. But I hardly looked at it because I couldn't keep my eyes off his scars.

He said "This one was in the *Plaza de Toros* in Madrid," and he showed me a huge, knotted scar in his left buttock. "And this," and he pointed to a half-circle of white scar under his left arm that must have almost taken it off, "was in my own town, Burgos, from a great bull. And I killed very well after he gave me this, and I cut both ears and the tail."

Well, he sure wasn't any shrinking violet, and I hated his guts because of Lidia, but Ángel was right, I didn't know anything about his kind of courage. There was a knot of scar on his right calf, and a blue one eight inches long and an inch deep on the inside of his left thigh, and others.

The guests began to arrive and in three days we made six trips to the railroad station with that coach and its beautiful six-up team. It held nine people inside and two up beside the driver, and three more on a seat on the front of the roof, and the rest of the roof and the rear boot carried the luggage. Besides the driver and Don Hector, that was thirteen people each trip. Altogether about eighty people came, all hacendados or army officers or rich city business men. There were four wives and they each had a maid with them. The aficionados had brought a *picador,* too, a fat Spaniard with his special iron stirrup to protect his right leg, and an apprentice *torero* to do some of the cape work for El Niño. I rode escort to the coach, with half a dozen vaqueros.

For a week there was a *fiesta* every night with the guests at tables under the arcade, and the vaqueros furnishing the music in the patio that was hung with paper lanterns. I saw it all, from my guard station at the patio gate. The vaqueros had a guitar and a *vihuela* and a harp, and a big oversize guitar they called a *guitarrón,* and they danced for the guests, wild dances like the *Jarabe Tapatío,* and *La Bamba.* Lucas sang one just for Lidia, and it was very beautiful. I guess everybody knew Lidia was descended from the famous Malinche, and the song was *"La Llorona,"* The Weeper, because an old legend said that Malinche's ghost roamed the streets of Mexico City at night, and never stopped crying, because she was a traitor to her people. There were many different versions of the song, and they weren't all sad, and the one Lucas sang was like it was meant for me and Lidia. One verse went, *"Eres como aquel chile verde, Llorona, picante*

pero muy sabrosa"—You're like the green chile, Llorona,
sharp and stinging, but very sweet. And another one went,
"Aunque la vida me cueste, Llorona, no dejaré de quererte"
—Even if it costs my life, Llorona, I'll never stop loving you.
For me, they were both true, and the last one was almost a
prophecy, like Letty Greenfield's horoscopes.

CHAPTER 14

The day before the corrida de toros, I went with
Don Hector and El Niño and almost all the guests, when the
vaqueros brought Conquistador and the brindle bull down
from the pasture and put them in the *toril*, or bullpen under
the grandstand. The bulls hardly ever went on the prod while
they were with others, so they use tame oxen to herd them
along in the middle of the bunch.

Late the next afternoon, everybody went to the bull ring,
and Ángel and I sat behind Don Hector and Lidia and an
army general and his wife, to guard them. There were plenty of other guards in the crowd, vaqueros dressed in their
best, because that collection of hacendados and Federal officers would be a big temptation to any band of revolu-
tionaries.

El Niño and the other torero stood behind the *barrera*, the
circular wooden wall that makes a six-foot-wide alley between the seats and the ring, with openings in it so the bull
fighters can jump in there when they get in trouble. The
openings had little sections of wall in front of them called
burladeros, that didn't leave enough room for a bull to get
through. There wasn't any waiting room under the stands for
the bullfighters to march out of, so El Niño and the other
one just stood there when the band—four seedy looking bums
from the town with a guitar and a violin and a big, dented

tuba, and one with a trumpet played *La Virgen de la Macarena.* And when it came to the solo trumpet part, that unshaven bum made you want to yell and cry, all at the same time. I never heard any music like that. Then he played the signal for the *tercio de las varas,* the 'third' of the lances, and mozos swung open the gate, and when the bull came out, a vaquero leaned down from above and planted a barbed rosette in his shoulder, the colors of Hacienda Los Cerritos. The bull charged into the middle of the ring and stood there throwing sand and bawling, and the cape man ran out with a big cape and let the bull charge him. The bull went for the cape every charge, and the man finally ran across the ring trailing the cape in the sand, with the bull following and hooking at it, and jumped behind the burladero. Ángel said this was to let El Niño study how the bull charged, and if it favored one horn over the other.

Then El Niño stepped out with the big yellow and purple cape and the bull charged him half a dozen times, and he swung the cape easy and people began to yell *"Olé!"*, and the bull followed the cape like its nose was tied to it, and it didn't look dangerous to me. While this was going on, the big fat picador rode in on a skinny horse that had a kind of a mattress affair hung on it, and its right eye was blindfolded. El Niño trotted toward where the picador stopped the horse against the barrera, and kind of pointed the bull at it and got out of the way.

The bull bellowed, and slammed into that horse and almost lifted it off the ground, and kept pushing in, hooking, until El Niño and the apprentice flapped capes in its face and tolled it away. The picador had tried to plant his lance in the big hump of muscle on the neck. Well, he missed, and the lance point just slid off.

The horse was staggering and bleeding, and the bull wheeled and charged again, and this time the picador got the lance planted, good, and the bull backed off. It charged again, and when it hit the lance point, it backed off again, and the people began to groan and yell insults, and El Niño was swearing.

Lidia said, "Why, he's a coward! Oh, this is awful!" and Don Hector told the general, "I am disgraced!"

The trumpeter played the signal for the tercio of the *banderillas.* Banderillas are sticks a couple of feet long decorated with crepe paper, and they have sharp barbed points.

El Niño didn't want to fool around with *that* bull, and he handed a pair of banderillas to the cape man. He ran out into the middle of the ring, calling, *"Ah-ha! Torito! Vente, querido!"* The bull stood there throwing sand over its back and the man ran toward it, and finally it charged. The man ran across its path and the bull hooked at him when they passed, and the man went up on his toes and jabbed the two darts down into its shoulder hump. The bull squalled and ran around trying to hook the banderillas off, but it couldn't reach them. The cape man planted another pair, and then had to work real hard to make it charge again, and stick the other pair in.

Then the trumpet blew for the *tercio* of the death. El Niño de Burgos turned around, down in the alleyway, and gave Don Hector a dirty look, then beckoned to the cape man and said, "Here, *chico,* you do it!" and gave him the muleta and the sword.

The *muleta* is a red flannel cloth, almost round, and the torero holds it in his left hand, folded over a stick with a nail in the end, to stretch it out. The bull's big neck muscle is supposed to be so tired, with the jabs from the lance, and those six banderillas clattering and jerking that he will lower his head far enough when he charges to let a man spear him between the shoulder blades with the sword. Well, that brindle bull wasn't that tired, because the lance hadn't done much to him, so his head was still pretty high, and he was tormented by those banderillas gouging him, and that cape man got scared, and Ángel said he didn't get close enough when he went in over the horn to stick the bull. So he got hooked in the chest and thrown into the air—but not hurt bad. You just don't ever quit in the bull ring, or you're through forever. So he stabbed the bull eight or nine times, and kept hitting bone, and it was a bloody mess. And by the time the bull laid down to die, people were throwing bottles and cushions into the ring. The poor man finally had to give it the *descabello,* the mercy stab with a dagger, at the base of the skull. When he walked away, he was bleeding and limping, and almost crying. Mozos brought in a span of mules and dragged the dead bull out, and then dragged a plank around to smooth the arena.

I said, "This is supposed to be a sport? Why, for five thousand pesos, I'd do it every day if my stomach could stand it."

Ángel felt disgraced by that miserable bull, too. He just said, "There's another bull to come."

He was right, there was another bull—there was Conquistador.

El Niño dedicated Conquistador to Lidia, and tossed his *montera*—that's the little black hat they wear—into her lap. She stood up and bowed to the applause from everybody there but me, and blew him a kiss. When she sat down, she said, "If Conquistador is as bad as that other dog with horns, I will kill him myself."

Conquistador came walking out through the toril gate into the empty arena like a cat, and didn't even look around when the mozo planted the rosette in his shoulder. He stopped and looked the crowd over, and Don Hector said, "Jesus help us! Another one!"

Then from behind the barrera, El Niño flipped the corner of a cape into view, and Conquistador charged like a runaway freight train, and went right over the five-foot barrera and into the alleyway. El Niño and the cape man and vaqueros and mozos came boiling out through the burladero openings and over the barrera, and Conquistador was bawling and trampling around inside. The barrera was fixed so they could swing a hinged section into the alleyway and leave an opening back into the ring. And Conquistador charged out and the vaqueros and mozos ran for their lives, behind the burladeros. The crowd was up, howling, and El Niño yelled something at Don Hector, his ugy face shining with joy. And I thought, Great God Almighty! I wouldn't get into that ring with *that* brute for all the money in the world.

Well, that miserable cape man didn't lack for guts. He went out there with his cape and tried, but he couldn't get set for any fancy cape work, because Conquistador swarmed around like six bulls, and the poor man had to run for it, and the only way he got past the burladero alive was to throw his cape down and let Conquistador chop at it.

That bull got the picador's lance square into his shoulder hump and kept driving in and slammed the poor horse against the barrera, and it took El Niño and the cape man both to lure him away. And the second time, he did the same thing, and the third, he lifted horse and picador off the ground and slammed them down. He killed the horse and the picador got a broken leg. And I was on my feet like everybody else, yelling myself hoarse.

The crowd was going crazy, because that bull was something! He charged straight like they said, on rails, and wouldn't quit. El Niño planted those six banderillas in a little six-inch circle, outlining the target on the hump where he would ram the sword home.

When he went out with the sword and the muleta, it was quiet as a church, and I was sweating like it was me down there with that bull.

Then El Niño began the passes with the muleta, and he was talking to the bull, and Conquistador's tongue was out and his sides going like a bellows and painted red with blood from the banderillas and the vara, and he kept going for that little piece of red flannel. And every once in a while, after a cape pass, El Niño would turn sharp, and Conquistador would stop dead in his tracks, and the matador would walk away from him. Then El Niño spread his arms and motioned toward the bull, not asking applause for himself, but for such a great bull.

Don Hector said, "In Spain, he would cut both ears and the tail and four feet! This is the greatest bull and the greatest matador and the greatest tercio ever fought!"

Conquistador was almost dropping from exhaustion, but he still bawled a challenge and stepped toward El Niño. The matador got ready to aim the sword and sweep the muleta low from left to right in front of him and pull the bull after it, and lean over the horns and drive the sword home. And Conquistador caught him and threw him, spinning like a cartwheel, and when he hit the sand, the bull was there chopping at him. People screamed, and the cape man and Ángel and a half dozen vaqueros jumped into the ring and twisted the bull's tail and finally got it away from him. El Niño was all bloody down his front, and nobody knew if it was his blood, or all from the bull. One of his slippers was off and the sword was bent, and he stumbled when he walked to the barrera and a mozo handed him another sword. Everyone else got out of the ring, and Conquistador just stood there, head drooped and legs braced. El Niño picked up the muleta and began to limp toward him, and that beat down, worn out, half-dead, bloody bull bellowed and threw sand over his back and charged again! A clumsy, stumbling charge, but a real charge.

El Niño pulled him aside with a sweep of the muleta, and again got his feet set, and got the muleta in the right position, and sighted down the sword, then suddenly stepped back. He held out his arms like he was begging, and slowly turned all the way around. The bull took a step toward him, and bellowed again, and he let it charge once more, passing it with the muleta. It stumbled and went to its knees, then struggled up and turned to face him.

Lidia was the first to yell it—*"Indulto! Indulto!"* and she waved her handkerchief, and then they were all yelling it, and fluttering their handkerchiefs, and El Niño walked behind the barrera and left Conquistador standing alone.

Don Hector stood up, and the whole place went quiet.

He said, "In the absence of regular authorities of the Association, I take it upon myself. The indulto is granted."

Well, the place went wild, people yelling and crying and hugging each other, and the vaqueros drove a half-dozen oxen into the ring, and they got around Conquistador and took him out through the toril gate.

Going back to the house, behind Don Hector and the general and his wife, I asked Ángel, and he said, "It has happened very seldom in the history of bullfighting, at least so I have been told. But once in a great while, there is a bull so brave, so honest, and so perfect that people beg for his life. Do you think Conquistador earned it?"

"My God, yes!" I said. "And I take back anything I said about El Niño. With the guts he's got, every bull in the world should give him the indulto!"

Then somebody yelled to us to clear the way and the coach came slowly through the crowd. As it passed, I looked in, and El Niño had his head on Lidia's shoulder. He looked dead—at least, asleep—but she was grinning and waving her handkerchief out the window and people were crowding around trying to get a look at him.

Then I wished the bull had killed him.

CHAPTER 15

The next day, the guests left. We took them to the railroad station, and I went back to my job sitting on my butt at the gate waiting for something to happen. First chance, I was going to ask Don Hector when he was going to hire another guard, so I could get a little relief.

One day when Don Hector and that bullfighter went off in his car, I went with Ángel to the corral where Conquistador was retired. It was a round corral with a solid stone wall six feet high, and there was a stone shed opening into it, with a heavy plank door so they could shut him out while the peones cleaned up inside. The manger was in the shed, and they could put hay into it through a little open window. There was a water trough in the corral that could be filled from outside.

We climbed up on a box and looked over the gate and there he was, the flies black on the open wounds on his hump from the lance and the banderillas. Ángel said they were going to rope him and throw him and treat him for the screw worms, and grease the wounds.

Conquistador shook his horns at us and rumbled in his throat. He was ready to fight again, anything, any time. Ángel said, "I wish I had it as easy as you! Nothing to do but soak up the sun and mount all the pretty little heifers they bring you and make a lot of little Conquistadores."

When I went back to the house, Lidia came out. She was hurrying, and she looked back at the house door, and said, "That miserable priest! The only place I get any privacy is in my own room! Kel, I've got to talk to you!"

She looked scared and worried—but I was sore. I said,

119

"You sure you want to talk to me? With that famous bull-fighter chasing after you and . . ."

"Oh, Kel!" she said, almost crying. "Not now! Something has happened!"

And Padre Arrellaga coughed, under the arcade, and she said, "Oh, damn him!", and then we heard the car turning into the far end of the lane, and she grabbed my hand and squeezed it, quick, and went back into the house.

The next day Don Hector and that damn bullfighter drove off again in the Simplex, and I kept expecting Lidia to come and talk to me, but she didn't. Then after I had my dinner, about one in the afternoon, Lucas came around. He had his carbine, and he said, "I'll take over the gate. Ángel wants to see you, by the bull's corral."

When I got there, there was Ángel on his sorrel roan, holding Gato's reins. When I was mounted, he said, "She's in those trees up by the bull pasture. Don't be gone too long, or you'll get her in trouble. Come back here then, and I'll take Gato, and you can go back to your post."

When I got there she had her big black Moro tied, and was waiting for me under the trees, behind a fringe of brush, on a spot of grass. She was in that sidesaddle riding outfit, covered up from feet to neck with about ten yards of cloth.

When I got down she got her arms around my neck, without a word, and kissed me, long and hard!

She had to stop for breath, but she still hung onto me, and said, "Oh, Kel! What are we going to do!" and I said, "Well, for a starter, we can try that again," and I kissed her till she had to shove me away.

I tied Gato beside Moro, and sat on the grass with my back against a tree. Before I got settled, she was laying across my lap, kissing me again. She was pushed against me as close as she could get, and she took my hand and put it on her breast.

Then she said, "Salvador Cano came back to Nuevo Casas Grandes, and father is talking to him about hiring a couple of guards. Cano says he will find a couple of pisto-leros that father can trust. And that priest has talked to him about us, I know he has!"

I unbuttoned her coat and shirtwaist and got my hand inside and she didn't stop me.

She said, "I didn't want to love you! It's the worst thing

that could happen! I *tried* not to! And I was flattered by that little reptile, and I stayed with that Burgos Kid every minute I could manage, trying to push you out of my mind."

It was coming at me so fast I couldn't believe it, and all I would say was, "Lidia! Lidia!" over and over.

We stayed that way a long time, with her heart beating hard and her warm breast under my hand, and there was nothing else in the world—no revolution, no Don Hector, no ugly little bullfighter, no dead Patricio or Paco or Tomás or Narciso, nothing but her and me, there on the grass in the shade of the trees.

She said, "I can't believe he would do it. I can't! But he is such a fool over El Niño's corrida with Conquistador, and the *indulto* will make him famous all over Mexico . . . I think he might even try to make me marry El Niño!"

I came out of the dream then. I said, "He never will! I'll kill that gypsy!"

"That's the worst thing you could do," she said. "Kel, this is the last time I'll ever see you . . . but I swear I will kill him, or me, before I'll marry him."

I was shocked and scared. I said, "What do you mean, the last time?"

She said, "Father's going to discharge you as soon as he gets another guard, because he knows about us. He might even have you killed! You have to go, quick, and never come back! And, oh, Kel! I didn't know I loved you, really, until he said he was going to run you off the hacienda . . . and then . . . it will break my heart . . . and I love you! I love you forever! I don't want you to die!"

She wiped tears from her eyes with her sleeve and said, "You are American, and a fugitive, with no one to help you. And Salvador Cano suspects you. You have to go, Kel. And leave me. Leave me, just when I have found you!"

I held her close for a long time, with my face pressed against her black hair. And after while she said, "Kel . . ." and she kind of choked, and tried again, and said, "If you want to, Kel . . . because I can't bear to lose you and not have loved you."

So we got undressed and she spread her big skirt down, and when we laid down and I got her in my arms, and her face was hot against my neck and all of her slim brown body pushed up against me, I thought, this is all wrong. Like a couple of animals out in the woods . . . with her it's all wrong. And I wanted her very much, but not like Concha—not like I'd ever felt before.

Then she whispered, "This is the way it should be, the way I will remember, not in a hotel room somewhere like adulterers, or slyly under the roof of my father's house, but under God's sky, and God's trees, and God's breeze on us."

So I felt better about that part of it, but God's breeze wasn't cooling me! I found out, too, that what she said about making her feel like she was lying with a lover was just a way of talking, because she hadn't ever had a lover. I was afraid of hurting her. I did hurt her, and she didn't care. She was like Llorona in the song, hot, and very, very sweet, and she kept whispering, "I love you! I love you!" It was like we both caught fire. And when we were finished, and lying there quiet and sad in each other's arms, she said, "Now I have done what everyone says is a sin, but to me it is no sin because I love you, and you are my husband now, and the only one I will ever have."

I said, "Why can't we get married? What could he do?"

"He could have you killed," she said. "And the priest will never do it. But let's talk to my father, even though it is a waste of words."

So we got dressed, and I held her for a minute and then helped her up into the saddle. We rode straight to the house, and there was Padre Arrellaga looking at us from under the arcade.

Lidia said, "Is my father home yet?" and he said, "No."

Then we got down and went under the arcade, and she said, "Padre Arrellaga, I am going to marry Señor Adams, and we want you to pass up the formalities and do it right now."

He snarled at her, "You are insane! I would never ask for a dispensation, and the cardinal would never grant it! A foreigner! A heretic! A pistolero! Even if you have fornicated with this man, I still will never marry you to him and legalize your sin!"

She was shaking, and I took a step toward him. I don't know what I would have done to him, but she grabbed my arm and pulled me back.

She said, "I will live with him and be his wife, wherever he goes!"

The priest said, "Fool! Don't you know? Hasn't your father told you? When he hired this man in Agua Prieta, he was living with a whore!"

She jerked her hand away, and turned to stare at me. She looked like I had hit her between the eyes. She said, "He's lying, isn't he!"

"Listen!" I said. "I *wasn't* living with her! And I didn't even know you! How could I know I would ever find you! And why is it so bad? I'm not a priest with no balls!"

All the expression went out of her face, and she stepped around the priest and went into the hall.

I started after her, and he got in front of me. I knocked him sprawling with my shoulder, and ran and grabbed her arm. "What did you expect!" I yelled in her face. "Did you expect a virgin?"

She was prying at my fingers, and she said, so low I could barely hear her, "I was a virgin for you! And you have made me a whore. Go away!"

I let her go.

In the arcade the priest had got up and was brushing himself off. And when I rode to my quarters and got the old Mc-Clellan saddle, and then to the corral to get Old Timer, it's a good thing nobody else got in my way, because I would've rode down Ángel or Don Hector himself.

And when I went down the long lane, I hoped I would meet Don Hector and El Niño de Burgos coming home in that automobile, because I was sick inside, and spoiling for trouble. And all the time I hurt so bad inside I wanted to cry.

I rode into Nuevo Casas Grandes at about five in the afternoon. I knew there wouldn't be a train for Juárez till tomorrow, and I decided I would wait over in the hotel. It's a good thing the barracks of the Guardia Rural was outside the town a mile or so, because Salvador Cano and his troop had come back, and if any of them caught me alone, there'd sure be trouble, and the mood I was in I'd probably kill a couple of them before they shot me.

I tied Old Timer outside the first cantina I came to and went in and ordered tequila. A couple of townsmen came up to me, friendly, and looked around first, then said, "Señor, aren't you the yanqui guard from Los Cerritos? Because you are well known in Nuevo Casas Grandes, and we are all grateful for . . ."

I snarled at them like a mad dog. I said, "What if I am! What the hell do you want?"

Their faces got a wooden look on them, and they went out. The owner was a tough-looking man, and he said, "Señor, you better leave. In here, we don't want any . . ." and I broke in on him, too. I said, "Set the bottle out, and keep away from me!"

I was being a damn fool, and I knew it. I felt like a bear with a sore ear, ready to take a swipe at anyone that came in reach, and I didn't give a good Goddamn.

Nobody came near me, and it was getting dark when I went out and crossed the street to the restaurant. I took the first table, in a corner to the left of the door. I was feeling the drinks, but I wasn't stumbling. I ordered a double tequila, and the waiter didn't want me to have it, but I started to get out of my chair, and he brought it.

Some well-to-do townsmen came in, and three army officers, and sat where they had put two long tables together under a big chandelier with six kerosene lamps on it. On the wall behind the table was the stuffed head of a fighting bull with both ears gone, and under it was a crossed pair of banderillas with dried blood on the frilled crepe paper.

Pretty soon I heard that automobile stop outside, and Don Hector and El Niño de Burgos came in, and a dozen men that must have been waiting for them outside. One of them was Salvador Cano. They walked past my table without seeing me, and then everybody was giving each other the *abrazo,* and bowing to El Niño and saying how honored they were to meet him.

I sat there while they had supper—wine and the whole works—and you'd've thought El Niño was Jesus Christ in person. They kept telling him that no one had ever seen such bravery in the plaza de toros, such cape work, and what an honor it was to have him right here in Nuevo Casas Grandes. And that bull! Had anyone ever seen such a bull! And clearly no other breeder in the world could produce such a bull, only Don Hector Estrada Palacios y Garza! It was all pretty sickening, and while they were picking their teeth, and the waiters were bringing around brandy and cigars, I got up and stepped out where they could see me.

They all stared at me like I had just come up through the floor. El Niño began to grin, and Salvador Cano grinned too, and was the first one to say anything.

He said, "Well, Don Hector, he has saved us the trouble. I'll send for a few of my men."

I said, "Salvador, old boy, why don't you just take me in yourself? Old Narciso, he was going to do it, and he wasn't even a lousy Rural. Do you really need help?"

He called me something filthy, and I went on, "You people are a bunch of suckers. Don't you know the bull was drugged with peyote in his hay, and his horns were filed blunt? Why *anybody* could have handled the poor devil, let alone a miserable gachupín!"

I was about as nasty as a man can get, because I was just drunk enough, and I hated that bullfighter!

Two or three of them jumped up, and Salvador Cano had his pistol in his hand, but El Niño was smiling. He said, "No, hold on boys. Let's listen to this expert."

So I took another step ahead and said, "The poor bull could barely stand up after the picador jabbed him in the spine, and this great matador kept stumbling over his own feet! Didn't you see the bull throw him ten feet in the air, even when he was half dead and a child with a tin sword could have killed him?"

I couldn't seem to stop. It all came boiling out of me, the hate, the bitterness, the unfair things Lidia had said, the way that little gypsy and Don Hector had treated me like so much dirt—and I didn't give a damn what happened.

They were on their feet now, and there were guns out, and El Niño stopped them. He said, "I wonder if the gentleman would like to prove his point? Now there is the head of a bull on the wall there, and a pair of hooks. Suppose the gentleman plays the bull, and we will see if I can keep from being gored?"

They all began to laugh, and some sat down, and I knew I was caught. Because how could I back down? I never could, any time—and now that I'd been shooting my face off, I just couldn't bring myself to admit I was a fool, and would they please all forget it.

And I stood there like an ox while they got that stuffed head off the wall and pushed the tables back, and stood back around the walls. Don Hector and Salvador Cano and three army officers still sat behind the long table.

They gave the Kid the pair of banderillas, and he grinned and bowed at them all laughing and clapping their hands.

I almost ran out—but I was just too muleheaded. They gave me the bull's head, and it was lighter than I expected, just the skin stretched over a form of papier maché.

El Niño yelled, *"Ah-h-h-Hah! Toro!"* and made a curving run across the floor on his toes, with the banderillas ready to jab down. I just stood there holding that stuffed head in front of me, like a fool. And I thought, when he runs back, I'll smash the son of a bitch against the wall!

So when he ran back, I charged with my head down behind the bull's head, and that got in my way, and I felt something jab into my ribs on both sides, before I smashed into the wall. They were laughing so hard they were holding their bellies.

El Niño said, "Oh, well, another *manso.*" That's a tame bull.

And I thought I'd catch him by surprise, and I charged again with that damn clumsy stuffed head in front of me, and he danced sideways and jabbed me in the ass on both sides.

And while everybody was howling and wiping their eyes, he made a mistake. He turned the way he would have from a real bull when he had it "fixed"—stopped cold—and bowed to them, and I charged like a bull and caught him in the small of the back, and smashed him face down across the table and piled the whole thing, him and the table and dishes, bottles, silverware, food, on top of Don Hector and Salvador Cano and the officers.

I was sprawled out on the whole mess, and I got to my feet. El Niño was groaning and trying to push himself up and get to his feet, and everybody was yelling and Don Hector and the officers were trying to fight their way out of the wreckage, and I turned and walked across the floor toward the door.

And suddenly the yelling cut off and it was dead still, and I heard the click of a pistol hammer.

I whirled and dropped flat, and the Bisley was in my hand when I hit the floor. El Niño shot at me and missed, and while he was cocking the pistol, I shot him twice in the chest. He went down, and everybody was trying to flatten out on the floor or claw their way through the walls, and I rolled over and came to my feet, and ran outside. Shots splintered the door when I slammed it shut behind me.

I felt cold sober, now, and more scared than I'd ever been in my life. I ran down a side street toward the river.

There was a lot of hollering and horses running around, in the town, and I slipped into the river. It was waist deep, and I loaded the Bisley while I waded. I didn't get out of the

river till I'd gone a half mile, where it ran through a big
cornfield, with the stalks thicker than grass. I wormed my
way in, then figured out which direction it was to the ruins at
old Casas Grandes.

Once I had shot through the top of a privy over the heads
of Cassie and Polly, and I had knocked an old man down
with my pistol and maybe killed him, but not because I wanted to. And I had thrown a plateful of hot dinner into the face
of a man ready to blow my head off with a shotgun, and I
had fired over the heads of a bunch of Rurales and Federales, and tolled four men at full gallop into a maguey
field, and I had stood off Cano and Narciso with my gun in
my hand. And I had seen Polly Greenfield and a deputy marshal shot dead, and Patricio and Paco and Tomás after they
were murdered, and I had been a hired, professional gunman
—but I hadn't ever shot a man before. And now that I had, I
would have given anything, anything not to have done it.

But when he cocked that pistol, it was too late.

CHAPTER 16

I didn't have any trouble finding the Paquimé ruins
in the dark. I went to that big room, and the old pile of blankets was still there, where I held Lidia in my arms all night,
that time. I could feel her being there.

Getting drunk and starting that brawl with El Niño because I was jealous—and killing him—was the stupidest thing
I ever did in my life. It didn't really matter, though. Nothing
mattered. Because they'd track me here, easy, in the morning,
and without some kind of a miracle I'd never get ten feet
from the door before they chopped me down.

I tossed around on those blankets most of the night, trying

to make up my mind to start out for the mountains and find Lobo Barrera—but without a horse, it was hopeless.

At first daylight, I climbed a little hill that was really a ruin, because there was a piece of rammed adobe wall sticking out the top of it. I thought I'd see if they were coming after me, but what I saw was that miracle I needed—Ángel riding up from the river, leading Gato.

I slid down the hill, and when he rode up and dismounted, I tried to give him the abrazo, but he shoved me away.

He said, "If it wasn't for a few times you acted like a man, I wouldn't care if they hang you. I don't know what you did to Doña Lidia, but you murdered the greatest living matador!"

My stubborn streak flared up. I said, "Listen, viejo! All I did to her was try to marry her, and that's what she wanted, too! And as for . . ."

He broke in and said, "I would bet ten thousand pesos that isn't all you did to her! I ought to shoot you myself, and save Salvador Cano the trouble!"

"Then what are you doing here, with a horse for me?" I said.

He just grunted something, and I said, "What about Gato? Won't this get you in trouble?"

"Don Hector doesn't know one of his horses from another," he said, "even though he can name every bull on the hacienda. Lidia sent him for you. I brought your clothes, your razor and a few things in the saddlebags."

My heart began to pound. I said, "She has forgiven me! Could you bring her here and . . ."

"She despises you," he said, and I felt like he had kicked me in the stomach. "She just doesn't want to hear that you are dead, too. She says to go back where you belong. Now we'd better go."

All morning we rode in *arroyos* and *barrancas* and kept below the skyline and went west into the mountains. We were climbing, and we began to get into wide parks between growths of ash and oak and piñon pine. About two in the afternoon, we stopped and ate tortillas and goat meat and had a drink at a stream. When we were through and had a smoke, Ángel said, "We'll wait."

We didn't talk. The farther I went from Lidia, the more I was dead sure she was my whole world, and without her there was nothing, no joy, no laughter, no peace. And I needed her, because it seemed like the whole world was made up of nothing but people like Cassie and Polly Greenfield and Don Hector and Narciso and Salvador Cano—and even Ángel and the vaqueros that I loved like brothers were all killers. And I was right there with them. I was one of them. And whatever brought it about, my own stubborn meanness in that restaurant, or El Niño's pride that made him try to kill me—whatever excuses I kept trying to think up for myself—I had killed him.

A wild turkey gobbled in the pines, and Ángel said, "Come on," and slipped the bit into his roan's mouth and pulled the cinch tight.

I did the same with Gato, and we rode into the pines, and next thing I knew, there was a rider just behind me, and a little Indian in a big kind of a diaper and a long-tailed shirt, and with a red rag around his long hair, beside Ángel. He was on foot, and he had the strongest muscled legs I ever saw. There was a carbine slung over his shoulder by a thong.

I said to Ángel, "This must be the turkey," but he didn't answer.

He said to the Mexican, "This is the yanqui, Kel Adams."

The rider grinned at me. He was long and lanky, and he hadn't shaved in a week nor washed either, from the rank smell of him. He said, "Casimiro Valverde, at your service, Señor."

I was still sore at Ángel, because I didn't think he would turn against me the way he did. I said, "You forgot to tell him I killed the bullfighter that was always smelling around Lidia like she was a bitch in heat. Maybe he will despise me the way you and her do, and I won't be so welcome."

That stirred him up. He said, "If you talk about her like that again, I'll kill you!"

I said, "Another time you were going to take my gun away, remember? But you thought better about that, too, didn't you! I said nothing against her, and you know it!"

He swung his horse around and poked it with a spur, and went loping down our back trail. Then I wanted to yell after him and tell him . . . well, I don't know what. But I didn't want him to go like that, because we were friends.

Casimiro said, "So you shot the bullfighter? Well, that is one dirty gachupin less in the world. What is the sport in sticking banderillas into a bull, then killing it? Better to barbecue it."

We went at a fast trot whenever we crossed one of those wide mountain parks, and that little Indian kept up with the horses easy, and on narrow trails and steep climbs, he was always stopping to wait for us. Casimiro said he was a Tarahumara, and most of them lived in the deep canyons or up in the high peaks and kept away from people, but there were some that worked as guides and scouts for the revolucionarios or the Federales, whichever paid them best or bullied them the worst.

Late in the afternoon we got to a deserted Tarahumara village. Casimiro said the Indians went way back in the mountains when the Rurales were ramming around trying to find Lobo Barrera's band. What was left of the band lived in the cabins the Tarahumaras abandoned, ready to jump at the first sign of trouble, but the Rurales had gone back to Nuevo Casas Grandes.

"They caught us good," he said. "There's only five of us left. It was that girl did it, wasn't it? And your friend Narciso, eh? May their souls burn in hell!"

He told me about the ambush—the contrabandistas driving four mules loaded with rifles into the cave they used for headquarters then, and the ones that had stayed behind coming out to say hello to them, and the rifles opening up from three sides. And only him and Lobo Barrera and three others got away, and two wounded men that the Tarahumaras took care of.

That village was an interesting place—thirty or forty neat little cabins along trails among the trees, all made of handhewn pine planks. There were fenced cornfields and corrals, and corn cribs like big wooden tubs with thatched roofs, up on poles, with a notched log for a ladder. There was a kind of an altar, too—three wooden crosses stuck in the ground in front of a plank table at the edge of a cleared place where Casimiro said they danced, and sacrificed cows to some Indian god—because like all the Mexican Indians they were Christians, but they worshiped the old gods at the same time. The contrabandistas kept the rifles in a couple of the corn cribs covered up with corn, if they couldn't deliver them right away to Los Cerritos.

I could smell the meat cooking before we got to that dance plaza, and I was surprised to see only one man there.

It was Lobo Barrera, himself, and he gave me the big abrazo when I got down, scratching my cheeks with whiskers as stiff as a curry comb. He was a short, dark man, very broad in the chest, and his pot belly hung over his belt buckle. He had on wrinkled white peon clothes, filthy dirty, and flat, bullhide sandals.

He said, "Welcome, yanqui! We heard all about you. Here, something to wet your pipes!" and he handed me a bottle of mescal. "One good long drink . . . all we have till the boys get back!"

So I drank it down and had a hard time not to strangle, because it was so strong. My eyes were watering, and I suddenly remembered something about mescal—they always put a maguey worm in the bottle, a big fat grub, for some reason I never could understand, and it was an honor to your friend to give him the last drink, the one that had the maguey worm. I almost threw up, but I choked it down.

"How did you know we were coming, Ángel and me?" I said.

"We still have a few friends in the town and at Los Cerritos," he said, "and at certain hours we watch for signals. Heliograph. You know? Mirror flashes. So Chato was watching from our lookout on the cliff this morning, and he ran back to tell me, and I sent him and Casimiro to meet you."

Chato, the Tarahumara, took Gato and Casimiro's horse and fed and watered them in a corral where there was another good horse and three mules.

We ate tortillas and chilis and baked squash they got from the Indians, and sat around the fire, talking.

The sky turned orange and then purple, and the stars came out and the breeze stirred in the tall pines, and it was very quiet and peaceful, and I was sad, and sick in my heart thinking about Lidia.

After while Lobo Barrera got me a blanket and a couple of goatskins that stunk, and said I could sleep in one of the Tarahumara cabins—but I raked together a bed of pine needles and just wrapped in the blanket.

In the morning, we had coffee and tortillas. Then the Tarahumara picked up his carbine and trotted away, to go to the lookout, and I poured another cup of coffee and said to Lobo Barrera, "Did you get a chance to mail my letter?"

"Oh, yes," he said. "I mailed it in Columbus. Jorge, Moisés and Quintín have gone to Ojo Agua Blanca to pick up four mule loads of cartridges, and Quintín will go on to Columbus with money for more rifles. We can't bring them

from there any more, since that girl betrayed us, but it is still
our source of supply. He will ask for a letter addressed to
Rafael Gómez, is that right?"

"Yes," I said.

And right then was when I decided to leave Mexico, whatever I might hear from Uncle Frank. I really didn't want to
go back and just live with an old man and guide a hunting
party once in a while. But there was nothing in Mexico for
me now—less than nothing, because of Lidia. I'd go to California or Texas or Utah, and just start all over.

I said, "Lobo, I think I'll go with your boys the next trip.
Go home to the States."

He rolled a smoke, and Casimiro spit into the coals and
nobody said anything. Finally Lobo Barrera said, "Yanqui,
you are a good Mexican. A good revolucionario. Things will
not always be bad. Zapata is winning, now, in Morelos, and
Orozco is recruiting a new army. Me, I'll die a bandit, here in
these mountains . . . but there is much future for a young
man who has fought for Mexico . . . when the bloodsuckers
are all hung or shot. People know you, yanqui. They know
you have risked your life for Mexico when you didn't have
to."

Well, this made me feel even lower. I could have made a
good life in Mexico; but there was Lidia.

Lobo Barrera said, "But if you will go, it is easy enough. If
Quintín has made a deal for more carbines, we will be going
to pick them up. But you must wait and go with us because
Salvador Cano would be almost as happy to get you as me, I
think."

Late in the afternoon, we were dozing in the shade and
Casimiro hissed like a snake and snatched up his carbine and
faded into the trees. Lobo was right behind him, and me
right behind Lobo, and down the trail on the west side of the
village a mourning dove called. Lobo said, "It's all right,"
and we stepped into the open.

A little white-haired priest rode into the plaza on a mule.
There were a couple of Tarahumaras trotting beside him.

We walked over to him, and he got off the mule like all his
bones ached, and smiled at me. He said, "I heard you were
here. I'm Padre Guzmán. I used to be at Los Cerritos."

"Lidia talked about you," I said, and held out my hand,
and he took it and held it. He was bent over and wrinkled,

and his face was chubby and rosy, and his robe patched and threadbare.

He said, "She is very dear to me."

"Well," I said, "she isn't very fond of Padre Arrellaga, but she thinks *you* are very special."

"Padre Arrellaga is somewhat of a fool," he said. "I have been afraid to send word that I was here. I am a fugitive, more or less."

We had a long talk, him and Casimiro and Lobo Barrera and me. At first I was kind of shocked that a priest would be hobnobbing with bandits, but they told me how he had helped in the bad times of the Madero revolution, and given food and shelter to many a hunted and starving man, and believed more in the laws of Christ than in the way the church was interpreting them. And with his growing distrust of the church and the way it sided with the Porfirista government, he had got on the wrong side of the authorities. He didn't come right out and say he had been helping with the gunrunning, but I got the idea he had passed messages on, and things like that, and the Rurales arrested him.

"Yes," he said. "They put me in the prison of San Juan Tlaltelolco in Mexico, with other political prisoners. I think it was Lidia who got a message to President Madero, when she went to the inauguration. It was Madero himself who intervened and set me free. But he warned me against any more political activity. I had a very difficult journey, getting back, but I am now ministering to the Tarahumaras throughout the mountains. They are gentle people, most of them, asking only to be let alone, and the church has failed them. Well, my son, I must go. But I have heard of your unselfish aid to the downtrodden and repressed, and I had to come to tell you that people are grateful to you, God will bless you. Give my blessing to Doña Lidia, and tell her not to despair. Come and see me. Chato will guide you."

Casimiro and Lobo Barrera knelt for his blessing, and I walked with him to his mule.

I said, "Padre Guzmán, if Lidia had come to you and said she loved me, would you have married us?"

He looked at me a long time. Then he said, "I don't know. This is a very difficult question. Are you a good Christian? Would you take instruction toward becoming a Catholic, in good faith? You see, there are many obstacles. Of course, in an emergency, if you understand me—well, that would make a difference. Is this the case?"

I didn't answer his question. I just said, "Someone else will have to give her your message, because I'll never see her again."

When I got up the next morning, Chato had already gone to his lookout. Lobo Barrera was dealing three-card monte, and Casimiro was losing steadily—not actually money, but they were keeping an account, and Lobo said Casimiro owed him twelve hundred pesos. After I ate, I heated water in a clay pot and shaved.

About three in the afternoon, Chato came trotting in and said the other three contrabandistas were in sight. They got in before dark, Jorge, Moisés and Quintín, tired and hungry, and Lobo introduced me to them. The loads on the four pack mules looked small, a wooden packing case slung on each side of the sawbuck pack saddle, but they were heavy—.44-40 cartridges that would fit both the Winchester carbine and the Colt single-action pistol.

Quintín said to me, "Señor, I have a letter for you, from —just a moment!" and he got it out from under his shirt, dirty and crumpled and damp with sweat. He bobbed his head and grinned and said, "I'm sorry for its condition, but you know, if we had had to leave the horses and run into the timber, and it was in my saddlebag . . . let me see now . . . it is from . . ." and he obviously couldn't read the address.

"Is it from a Mr. Kelly and mailed from Douglas, Arizona?" I asked. "And addressed to a Rafael Gómez?"

"Yes!" he said. "When I asked for mail for Gómez, there in Columbus, the clerk gave it to me."

Uncle Frank wrote:

July 14th 1912

KEL, BOY

Your letter got here fast only six days.

Everything is fine here, and good news. I went and found Lupe she was living in Las Palomas think of that. And I am going to marry her and she sends you her love and says come on home. I guess first I should tell you what happent to Letty. She smugled a pistol to Polly in the county jail and he killed Long Tom Mundt and got out and nobody seen him sence. Becuse he didnt get killed that time by Mundts deputy he just got his left eye blind and his left elbow cripple so his arm is bent. But Letty she got shot and killed in the shoot out when she took the gun to Polly and him and the marshal shot it out. Polly got clean away and nobody seen him sence. And all that happent just last week. So you needent to worried about Long Tom because he was only in the company hospital two days when you knock him down with youre Bisley that time. You ask about Cassie no I never heard he got shot by the Mexicans. They caught him in a restrant over in Agua Prieta when he shot a army officer but nobody heard what happent to him after. So your worring was all for nothing and you can come home. Lupe and me have took over the house and you can have the cabin.

UNCLE FRANK

Of course that clinched it, and I was kind of glad I would be going. I knew what it was to love somebody, now, and it couldn't ever happen to me again, not like with her. But there was too much against us, right from the start. Maybe if she'd had just a little bit of Concha in her—not be a whore or anything like that, but not be so important to her that I slept with somebody else once. And then her being Catholic—not that I got anything against Catholics, but they really pound it into the little kids' heads what's right and wrong, in Mexico, and you wouldn't believe how strict a rich girl was brought up. What happened between us under the trees that day, why to her it was a terrible sin, and took an awful lot of courage to go against all she had been taught. It proved how much she loved me, but I couldn't understand why me not being a virgin was so important to her. I sure would have felt bad if she hadn't been one, but I wouldn't've stopped loving her, nor I wouldn't've quit her cold.

Well anyhow, I told Lobo Barrera if he would set me up with a little grub and draw me a map of the trails, I was going to leave in the morning.

The whole five of them tried to talk me out of it. They said that after the *Rurales* shot them up so bad they were real short-handed, and they needed me. Here was as tough a bunch as I'd ever seen, and they figured I was good enough to side them, and it meant all the more because I was a yanqui. But I said no—but I would never forget them and they were my *cuates*. That's a Mexican word, Aztec or something, and it means somebody even closer than a brother, like a twin.

Lobo said, "What will we tell Ángel to tell the pretty little señorita at Los Cerritos? Because we hear that there is more between you than just a little slap on the behind and a quick kiss in the dark."

I looked at him hard to see if he meant anything bad about her, but he didn't. So I said, "To tell the truth, Lobo, that is one reason I'm going. She decided she doesn't love me."

The Mexicans are very romantic, and they all shook their heads real sad and said they understood. Then Lobo said, "You can't go alone. You would never find the trail, and you might as well shoot yourself as show yourself on a public road. Specially since you killed that gachupín assassin of bulls. So Chato will go with you to the border. It's a long three days, on that trail."

It was still dark, but the birds were twittering when we got up. Casimiro had a fire going and the coffee boiling, and we ate tortillas and beans. When we left, they all gave me the abrazo and told me to come back when I got tired of the big cities.

Chato and me had only gone about two miles, but it was light enough to see, when he stopped and looked back, and when I asked him what was wrong, he put his finger across his lips.

A rifle fired back there, and then three or four together; Chato hiked up that diaper affair he wore instead of pants, and began to lope back along our trail.

"The hell with that!" I said, out loud. "I'm through with all that!" and I bumped Gato's ribs with the side of my heel. He started, and I'll never know why I did it, but I swung him around and for the first time ever I hit him with the spurs.

I had a hard time staying on him the way he went, ducking under limbs and skidding on the twisty trail, and I kept hearing the rifles, closer and closer.

Like a damn fool, I charged right out onto the plaza with the Bisley cocked in my hand, and Lobo Barrera was dead there, in a heap in front of the three crosses. Slugs were spouting dust under Gato's feet, and a Rural came out from behind a big pine working the lever of his carbine as fast as he could. The smoke was around him like fog, and I hit him twice and rode past. A man screamed up the hill under a corncrib, and I saw Casimiro rolling down the hill, arms and legs flying every which way. I pulled Gato up and slid off, and a Rural ran from behind a cabin and shot Casimiro again from about three feet away, and I cut him down and he fell across Casimiro.

Back in the timber, a carbine cut loose and another Rural came stumbling out into the opening, coughing, and fell on his face. Chato must have got that one.

I was reloading and looking around, and I saw Quintín lying dead in the corral, and two dead mules. I sort of came to my senses and sprinted for cover, and it seemed like fifty men were shooting at me, and something whacked me on the side of the head like a club.

I was groaning and rolling around on the ground, and I didn't know what happened or where I was.

I had fainted, and I came to because somebody was kicking me in the ribs and saying, "Get up, Kel, you son of a bitch!"

My head felt like it would explode, and I didn't realize at first he was talking English. I propped myself up on my elbows, and he rammed the butt of his carbine into my face and knocked me flat again. My head was splitting open and I was choking in the blood running from my smashed nose.

Somebody yelled in Spanish, "Don't do that! Don't hit that man again!" and it was Salvador Cano, chief of the Rurales.

The voice that had spoke English said in Spanish, "All right, Lieutenant. But I know this one. He's tricky, and I wanted to make sure of him."

I couldn't puzzle it out, not the way my head was acting up—because how could *he* be here? I opened one eye and looked at him for a second, till I had to close it because the light hurt it. He didn't look like himself, not in that wrinkled, dirty *Guardia Rural* uniform that hung on him like a blanket, and his hair cut short—and of course, it was because of that bullet crease above my left ear and that smash in the face from the carbine—but I thought he was Cassie Greenfield!

CHAPTER 17

My head cleared up a little. I still could hardly believe it was Cassie, but it was. He hauled me to my feet and headed me toward the corral, and every time I stumbled, he kicked me.

There were about fifteen of them, and they came out from behind the cabins and the timber, and two of them were dragging Moisés along. He was shot in the hand and bleeding bad. My left eye was swelled shut and I couldn't breathe through my nose. They didn't have Jorge or the little Tarahumara, and I hoped they got away, but there was no way of telling.

One of them said, "Salvador, we found four cases of cartridges in a corn crib, but that's all."

Salvador Cano said, "The next man that forgets I am now Lieutenant Cano Second Grade, and calls me anything but Lieutenant Cano will get the butt of my quirt in his teeth. I got the rank as a reward for the other ambush, and I will have the respect that goes with it. And Grinfeel,"—he meant Greenfield—"that goes specially for you. You are no longer a son of a bitch yanqui, you are a miserable insufferable enlisted man in the Guardia Rural, and you will regret any more breaches of discipline. Now load the cartridges on the mules. Load these two living dead men onto mules, too."

One of the Rurales said, "Salvador—pardon! Lieutenant Cano, what about the dead? Three of them and five of ours."

Cano said, "Put ours in one of the cabins. I will send peones from Nuevo Casas Grandes to bring them in. Just leave the others. Buzzards have a right to live."

So we waited while they dragged the five dead Rurales into a cabin and piled rocks against the door. Then they put Moisés and me on mules, bareback, and tied our ankles together under their bellies with some slack in the rope. They left our hands free so we could hang onto the manes, I guess. My mule had a backbone like a plank on edge and he damn near cut me in two. Cassie was leading him, and riding Gato.

My head ached like somebody hit it with a rock, every step the mule took, and the left side of my face was swelled up, but my head was fairly clear now, and I almost wished it wasn't. Because now it was all finished, no matter what. And I would never, ever again, see Lidia or hold her in my arms. I wondered why they hadn't shot us, already.

About an hour down the trail, Cano pointed to where a cliff fell away to the valley below. "See the buzzards, Señor Adams?" he said. "They have found your sentinel, as we did. Filthy smugglers are not the only ones who can hire Tarahumara scouts."

So that must be Jorge, over there. And if Lobo Barrera hadn't given me Chato to show me the trail that morning, Chato would've been on watch, and they wouldn't have got to him. I wondered how they got to Jorge, because we didn't hear a shot. Probably their Tarahumara got right up to him with a knife.

Cano said, "All we had to do was set a watch on Ángel, then put our Indian on his track. We let him go back. We can pick him up any time, and we didn't want any noise. So we just hid and waited for the smugglers to bring the rifles in. You are merely an extra dividend."

So we went sliding and jolting down the trail, and I tried to figure how in the world Cassie Greenfield was there leading me to a firing squad, but it just made my head ache worse, to try. My broken nose quit bleeding, but the bullet gouge over my ear was swelling and it began to feel hot. Behind me, with a Rural leading his mule, Moisés was groaning, with his smashed hand stuck in his shirt front.

It was late afternoon when we went through Nuevo Casas Grandes to the Guardia Rural barracks, and there weren't many people on the streets, just some soldiers that came out of the cantinas. But Don Hector and two pistoleros came out of the restaurant where I killed El Niño. They were his new bodyguards, I guess. He called out, "Looks like you made a fine haul, Lieutenant Cano. And you have rid us of the rabid gringo. My congratulations!"

The barracks was a long building, just a row of little rooms with separate doors. They shoved me and Moisés into a room that had some moldy straw in the corner, and that was all. After while a Rural brought us tortillas and a jug of water. We drank half the water and used the rest to clean up a little. I cleaned Moisés's hand up the best I could, and tore his shirt tail off for a bandage, and got the caked blood cleaned out of my nose and mouth, but I still couldn't breathe through my nose, it was so swollen.

I was so exhausted I went to sleep, and it was dark when Salvador Cano and Cassie Greenfield woke me up, arguing just outside.

Cassie said, "Lieutenant Cano, shoot the Mexican, but let me have Adams. It was me shot him, up there, and by rights he belongs to me. You're going to shoot him, anyway, as an example to the people!"

"We are going to shoot the Mexican in the plaza tomorrow morning," Cano said, "but the gringo is going to Chihuahua."

"Good God!" Cassie said. "What kind of stupidity is this?"

"Gringo murderer!" Cano said, "You have too much mouth! Maybe I will close it with my quirt!"

Cassie changed his tune. He said, "Lieutenant, please explain why that murderer goes to Chihuahua."

"Because he is gringo." Cano said. "Because he has stuck his nose into the affairs of Mexico, to plot with traitors, to murder a famous man, while the President of the United States himself winks at the smuggling of arms to traitors. So our Señor Adams will be sent to Chihuahua for interviews with the press, to expose the rotten meddling of the Colossus of the North. After that, they will shoot him."

Cassie said, "Lieutenant, this man has been my enemy since we were children. He caused the death of my twin brother. When I heard he was here, I asked for a transfer from Chihuahua to your troop, so I could find him. What does it matter to you? You can say he tried to escape and you shot him."

Cano said, "This is what it matters to me—I have had my commission ten days. If I am so careless as to have to shoot him, I become a private. Maybe I become a corpse full of bullet holes."

Cassie said, "I'll give you his horse and pistol. And I have three American twenty-dollar bills sewed into the lining of my boot. You can have that, too. Just let me have him."

It was kind of weird, laying there listening to them haggle over me. If Cassie got his hands on me, what him and Polly tried to do to that bitch coyote, back on the Turkey Track Ranch, would just be a starter.

Cano said, "Grinfeel, the horse and the pistol are mine, anyway." Then he hollered, "Guard!"

The guard was right there at the door of our room. He said, "Sir!"

Then I heard Cassie swear, and Cano said, "Grinfeel, if you move, I shoot. Guard, put him under guard. We don't want any accidents to our prisoners."

He was laughing when the guard took Cassie away, with Cassie calling him filthy names in English, and Cano called out, "Guard, bring me back his boots. And a sharp knife."

In the morning, Moisés and me just sat there waiting. I was feeling sorry for him, but it didn't matter much, because there wasn't anybody going to save me when it came my turn, either.

About eleven they routed us out, and Lieutenant Cano was riding Gato. They made us walk to the town, and Moisés could hardly stagger along. His smashed hand was swollen and there were red streaks running up the inside of his arm.

Myself, I was feeling better, but I still couldn't breathe through my nose or open my left eye.

I guess they routed out the town people to see Moisés shot, because they were standing all around the plaza by the depot. I found out that keeping on living meant a lot more to me than I thought it did. Because the firing squad lined up, and four Rurales shoved Moisés against the wall of the restaurant—and me with him. My heart was hammering and I couldn't get my breath, and Cassie yelled at me, "Sweet dreams, you son of a bitch!"

I got hold of myself a little, and Padre Arrellaga came out of the crowd and prayed with Moisés. I thought maybe Lidia might have come to town with the priest to see me one last time, but she wasn't there, and not even Ángel, and I didn't have a friend in the world.

Then Padre Arrellaga walked back into the crowd, and Lieutenant Cano yelled orders, and the firing squad took aim. I managed to stand up straight, but I shut my one good eye.

Cano yelled, "Fire!" and there was the hell of a crash and the white smoke rolled around me like a cloud, and I wasn't hurt!

I looked around, kind of in a daze. Moisés looked like a pile of bloody rags at the base of the wall, and people were exclaiming about me still standing there. Cassie was staring at me, as surprised and stupid as me. But Lieutenant Cano was laughing so hard he was nearly strangling, and slapping himself on the leg with his quirt.

Finally Cano said, "Great God and all the saints, Adams! I wish you could see the expression on your face!" And he quit laughing, but he was still grinning. He said, "Well, that's a good rehearsal, so you will appreciate it when they stand you against the wall in Chihuahua."

The train whistled in the distance, and they herded me onto the depot platform and turned me over to two soldiers to guard me on the trip to Chihuahua. A big ox cart drove onto the plaza and peones put Moisés on it. When they drove away, a lot of peones followed, and the women were crying.

The train had two coaches and a boxcar and a flat car with a machine gun behind a sandbag parapet. My guards shoved me into the back seat of a coach, and sat on the seat facing me. The passengers were army officers and a few civilians, and across the aisle, a civilian said, "He stinks! Can't you take him out on the platform?"

An officer told him, "They have their orders, man. He's a famous gringo gunrunner, and they're going to question him in Chihuahua before they shoot him."

It took three days to travel the two hundred miles to Chihuahua, because we kept stopping where the track was torn up by rebels. And every time, night or day, they shot at the train, and the machine gun cut loose at them. But it didn't make any difference to me, then, who shot who.

The train pulled into Chihuahua after dark, and they put me in an automobile and took me to the prison. Of course the Rurales had taken everything I had, but a guard searched me again, and an officer told them where to put me, and they marched me down a long hallway and through a door in a stone wall into a little room where five or six soldiers were sitting around. One of them took a key out of a desk drawer

and opened a door in the back and shoved me along a corridor that had one electric bulb in the ceiling. The stink got
worse the farther we went, and I began to hear voices, men
talking and coughing and somebody singing in a cracked
voice. We went past a lot of cells that didn't have any wall on
the corridor, just bars, and finally came to one where the
grating door was open. The soldier shoved me in and locked
the door.

I could barely see in there, but I found a plank bunk without any blankets and a tin can with a little water in it, and a
toilet bucket that hadn't been emptied for a long time.

I was in there fourteen days. The guards told me I could
have good food if I paid for it, but I didn't have a cent. They
would talk with me and the others up and down the line, and
I found out there was a big tank full of captured rebel soldiers, and sometimes we'd hear them yelling. The cells were
for special prisoners, reporters and Union organizers, and
spies, and it was from these cells they kept hauling men out
to be shot. That's what the guards said, and I never saw them
bring one back.

I lived in a kind of a daze. It was pretty chilly nights, but
not anything you couldn't stand, but the food was just thin
coffee, beans like pebbles that hadn't been boiled long
enough, and old, leathery tortillas. My belly bloated and my
ribs began to show, and my whiskers itched my neck. I got
one of the guards to lend me a tin basin and some rags, and I
cleaned up my face and nostrils the best I could. My nose
had a hump in it and was tender as a boil, but I could
breathe through one nostril, anyway. The bullet crease above
my ear was infected and oozing pus. I got a look at my face
reflected in the basin of water, and my cheekbone was still
swollen, and my nose was flatter and had a hump on the
bridge, and the whole left side of my face purple and yellow.
I had fleas and lice, too, and that was the worst torture.

Then one morning two soldiers came to my cell. The
guard unlocked the door and said, "Outside, gringo!"

I thought I was ready for it, that I could take it like a man
—but I began to shake, and they marched me down that long
corridor and up some stairs. They then stopped in front of a
door that had a soldier on guard, and said, "The prisoner the
Colonel sent for."

That guard said, "All right, get in there, you. Sweet Jesus
in heaven, couldn't you clean him up a little?"

Even to myself I stunk, and when he pushed me across a room with a desk in it and slid back a pair of double doors, I was ashamed, because there was a man with a big camera on a tripod fiddling around with a trough of flash powder, and another sitting by a big desk with a pad of paper in his hands, and behind the desk a Mexican colonel, and they were all washed and shaved and pressed. The colonel was very dark, I guess full-blooded Indian.

The guard saluted and said, "Sir, the prisoner," and went out and slid the door shut. The three of them looked me over and the photographer looked at the reporter and said, "Phew!" and held his nose.

Well, I was going to get shot, so what did I care? I made a motion with my hand, with my middle finger stuck out, and he sputtered and said to the colonel, "Did you see what he did?"

The colonel said, "He doesn't seem to like you, Señor Macías."

Then he said to me, real stern, "Stand at attention!", but I didn't give a damn about him either, so I just stood there slouched and stared at him.

He sighed, and said to those two, "I'll give you ten minutes with him, gentlemen."

They said their newspaper was going to tell the loyal public all about gunrunning and the treachery of the United States government stabbing Mexico in the back, and it would raise a smell all over the world.

I said I didn't know anything about gunrunning, and that's all I said. They got madder and madder, and the photographer took one picture of me. There was such a flash and a cloud of stinking smoke, the colonel wouldn't let him take another, and he chased them out in spite of all the squawking they did.

The colonel said, "How is your Spanish? It was hard to tell, because all you said to them was 'no'."

I said, "What does that matter to a man that's going to be shot?"

"Well," he said, "it is probably better than the Spanish in this letter. Here. Read it." and he handed me a grimy, wrinkled letter. "It came from Nuevo Casas Grandes a week ago," he said.

I looked at the signature, and there is was—"Castor Greenfield!"

It was such bad Spanish and awful spelling I could hardly read it, but it went something like this—

DEAR COLONEL DE LA TORRE,

You remember the American they caught in Agua Prieta that killed the Major by accident, and they said if he would join up with Guardia Rural they wouldn't shoot him? So I said I would and they sent me to Chihuahua because they said it was up to you. So you told me what I had to do and I joined the Guardia Rural. I have been a good loyal Rural and anyone will back me up. And it was me that shot the smuggler Kelly Adams and they sent him to Chihuahua. And I remember you said the Guardia Rural needed men that could ride and shoot and that was why they wanted me in the Guardia Rural instead of shooting me. So about Kelly Adams, he is a very good horseman and very good with a pistol. He killed a city marshal in Douglas, Arizona, and then in Nuevo Casas Grandes he killed that Spanish bullfighter. And he was smuggling guns to the rebels. So that shows he is mean and tough and don't mind killing anybody. So he would be a good man for the Rurales if he hasn't been shot yet. I hope you will send him to Nuevo Casas Grandes because my troop lost five men when we got him and them others and we need men, and him and me work good together.

CASTOR GREENFIELD

I handed it back to the colonel.

He said, "Well, is it true?"

I started to tell him I never killed Long Tom Mundt and I never meant to kill the bullfighter—then I figured maybe he'd want me for the Rurales if he thought I was a real killer. So I said, "Yes, it's true. I grew up with him and he knows me. And I killed the bullfighter."

Somehow he didn't seem to hate me like everybody else in Mexico. He told me, "General Orozco was Chief of Rurales in Chihuahua as well as army commander, and when he turned traitor most of the Guardia Rural went with him. So we are very short-handed, and have to take all sorts of riff-raff." He sat a while with his elbow on his desk and his chin in his hand.

Then he said, "Well, I hardly consider a Spanish bull-fighter much of a loss to Mexico. Now if I give you the chance to join the Guardia Rural, you know what is involved? You obey any order, or you die at once, because

your life is already forfeit. If it is to hand your sister over to
your Lieutenant, and cut your mother's throat, you will obey.
You haven't got a sister or mother here, of course, but that
will give you the idea."

"I understand," I said. "I know about the Rurales."

"Now what about this . . ." and he looked at Cassie's letter, "this Castor Greenfield. Can you work well with him?
Because it strikes me that the Guardia Rural might find some
special assignments for two authentic gringos."

All I said was, "We were raised together like brothers."

"Why were you helping the rebels?" he asked me. "I don't
understand why a gringo fugitive from justice would have any
special loyalty to one side or the other, in Mexico."

"I don't have," I told him. "When I got across the border,
I needed friends and a hole to crawl into, and those smugglers
offered what I needed . . . food, and a good horse, and men
to ride with, and I could get lost among them."

"Who offered you this refuge?" he wanted to know. "That
caporal of vaqueros on that hacienda . . . what is it called?"

"Yes," I told him, "the caporal at Los Cerritos."

"What about the girl, the daughter of the hacendado?" he
asked. "It seems . . . didn't someone say she was implicated?"

"I don't know," I said. "I worked in the mountains with
Lobo Barrera."

"Well," he said, "Lieutenant Cano has been yelling for
more men, so I am assigning you to him. But first you will
spend a few days in the infirmary for that squashed nose and
the wound on your head. And for the love of God, tell Doc-
tor Osmena to delouse you and give you a bath! And that I
said to give you a razor."

Cassie was pretty smart, finding a way to get me back
where he could get at me. It was the most important thing in
the world for him to finish me off, himself, never mind that
Colonel de la Torre would have had it done if Cassie
would've just kept his nose out of it. But no, he had to do it
personal, for Polly and for Letty and for the time I had them
holed up in that privy with my Bisley cutting holes around
them, and all the rest of it. Maybe I ought to tell him Polly
got loose—except it wouldn't make any difference, the way
he hated me. And maybe I should've told the colonel that
Cassie's letter wasn't for the glory of the dear old Guardia

Rural, but only for Cassie to get another whack at me, then maybe the Colonel would assign me somewhere else.

But if I went back to Nuevo Casas Grandes, it would cut two ways, and I'd get a whack at him—and I wouldn't dodge him, now, if they paid me a million dollars.

But mostly, I'd be near Lidia again—if she ever needed me.

CHAPTER 18

When they put me and three other recruits on the train a week later, I was in pretty good shape—at least they had straightened out my nose so I could breathe through it, and the bullet gouge above my ear was healing. They gave me a worn-out Rural uniform with a vest I couldn't button. The pants were too short, and the wide felt sombrero sat on top of my head so I had to hold it on with the chin string. The only thing that fit was the boots, and the leather sling for the short Remington carbine. Only they didn't give us the carbines, me or the other three murderers that had escaped the firing squad by joining the Guardia Rural. I guess they were afraid we'd kill our guard and escape. And again it took three days to get to Nuevo Casas Grandes, because the track was torn up in a dozen places, and one time the rebels or guerrillas or whatever they were, shot at the train with a machine gun. A couple of soldiers got killed before they got the track back in place so we could get out of there.

I got off the train a full-fledged member of the Guardia Rural, the *Acordada,* the most hated outfit that was ever in Mexico. And whatever was waiting for me, could only be bad.

Rurales met the train and marched us to the barracks like prisoners. They didn't trust any Rural that had been recruited the way we were till he committed enough crimes under orders so he didn't dare desert.

Lieutenant Cano went up like a skyrocket when he saw me. He said, "What are they thinking of, sending this man to me! Why didn't they shoot him? Are they all crazy in Chihuahua?"

He whacked that quirt he always carried against the hitchrack and the splinters flew. Men poked their heads out of the doorways, and some of them came to look at the new recruits, and one of them was Cassie. He grinned at me and made a motion like cutting his throat.

Cano stopped in front of me. "And you," he said. "You thought you saved your miserable life by enlisting, eh? We know you for a dirty smuggling cutthroat that killed two of my men in that Tarahumara village. How did you have the nerve to come back here? Because I guarantee you won't survive your first patrol!"

He walked up and down and whacked the hitchrack again with his quirt, then he hollered, "Lock him in the guard room!"

One of them shoved me with his carbine, and Cano said, "Just a minute! How did you work it to get back here, Adams? What are you planning? What lie did you tell, after they spared your life?"

I said, "Lieutenant Cano, ask that slimy little son of a bitch about the letter he wrote to Colonel de la Torre, telling him you needed me. Ask Greenfield why he wants me here!"

Cano walked over and stood in front of Cassie with his fists on his hips. The guard shoved me into the same room where they'd kept me and Moisés, and padlocked the door. I could hear Cano screeching, and I looked out the two-foot-square window that didn't have any glass, just mesquite bars set in the adobe. Two Rurales jerked Cassie's gun belt off then shoved him along with their gun butts, and unlocked the door and shoved him in with me.

Cassie leaned against the wall and said, "He'll cool down. I was going to kill you first chance, peg you out in the sun and cut your eyelids off, or hang you up like a hog and skin you, slow. But now, we'll wait till Polly gets here, so he can join the fun."

That startled me. Uncle Frank had wrote that Polly got away, but I hadn't thought about him coming to find Cassie.

Cassie said, "Kind of jolted you, huh? Yeah. I wrote to

Letty, a long time ago. Got an answer, too. She said Polly
didn't get killed by that deputy, just got shot up a little. And
they let her off on the charge of helping me kill the bastard,
and she was going to slip Polly a gun, and when he shot his
way out, they'd both come to Mexico."

"Yeah," I said. "So what happened?"

"Oh, they'll show up one of these days. You know us, Kel.
We work together."

"You're working alone," I told him. "I wrote to Uncle
Frank. You know what happened? She slipped Polly the gun
all right, and they're both dead. Letty just got in the way
when Long Tom Mundt let Polly have it."

I sure wasn't going to give him the satisfaction of knowing
Polly got loose. And I got set, too, because I knew he'd blow
up.

He did, too. His face went white, and he drew a deep
breath and held it, and then said, "You're a dirty stinking son
of a bitch *liar*, Kel! They ain't dead! You shouldn't never of
said that, Kel!"

He forgot that every time I'd fought him alone, I had beat
the hell out of him. He took a dive at me, and I hit him coming in, so hard it turned him clear over.

The guard began yelling outside, and the padlock was rattling, and Cassie got to his hands and knees, and braced his
hands against the wall and managed to get to his feet.

I let him get clear up and turn and stumble toward me,
and the door crashed open, and I said, "You broke my nose
with that rifle butt, Cass!" and I pivoted and smashed my
right fist into the middle of his face. He pitched onto his face,
just when three Rurales piled onto me and took me down.

I was hitting out and we were wallowing around on the
floor, and Lieutenant Cano came charging in with a pistol in
his hand and yelled orders, and they got off me.

I stood up, and Cassie still laid there on his face. When
Cano motioned for them to take him out, he was limp as a
rag, and his smashed nose looked like I'd rammed my carbine butt into his face.

Rurales were crowding into the room, and Cano snarled at
them to get out. He calmed down, then, and said, "Well, you
have punished him for me. I think it is adequate. He was
born to be a Rural. I wish I had twenty like him. You have
also given me whatever excuse I need for disciplinary action
against you. I will think it over." Then he went out, too.

I sat and stretched my legs out and leaned my back against the wall and waited.

If I ever stood a chance after Colonel de la Torre spared my life in Chihuahua, it was gone now. Cassie would kill me as soon as he could move around. But most likely, Cano would have me shot, tonight, out in the brush somewhere, because he wouldn't want people to know he had to shoot one of his own men. So once more I was waiting to be shot, but I felt a little better about it this time—I smashed Cassie's nose as bad as mine, and I was pretty sure I broke his jaw.

When Cano came back, in a couple of hours, he wasn't carrying a gun. A guard brought a chair for him and set a kerosene lamp down in the corner of the room. Cano told him to padlock the door and go away far enough so he couldn't hear us talk.

The guard left, and Cano sat in the chair. His shadow was huge on the wall and ceiling. He said, "It isn't because I trust you that I took my gun off. Just the opposite. I've seen a lot of men just before they were shot, and they will gamble. So I don't offer you that temptation."

I was still sitting on the dirt floor, and he looked down at me. "But," he said, "you don't have to die, Adams. You have something to bargain with. I received orders from Chihuahua to bring in Ángel and . . ." he paused and grinned at me, "your lady love, the enchanting Lidia. I will shoot Ángel, but she being the daughter of her father, will be tried for treason, and of course, shot later. But you are now in the Guardia Rural, and your sins were forgiven by Colonel de la Torre, playing Jesus. However, I can shoot you for your latest sin, the vicious attack on your fellow Rural. You can save your life only by cooperating."

He slapped the quirt against his leg and waited for me to answer.

"How?" I said, and I didn't believe for a second I could save my life—maybe for a couple of days, that's all.

He said, "You are well known to Ángel and the young lady. I might say on most intimate terms with her, eh? I've often wondered how she'd be. How was she, Adams? A hot one, eh?"

I wanted to knock him down and grind my heel on his mouth.

He went on, "So you will lead the two of them to where I can get my hands on them. Maybe on the pretense of a secret conference or to show them something of interest. I will leave that to you. Their capture will avoid a pitched battle, because Ángel's stupid vaqueros would fight. So you will be saving the lives of some of your friends, and of your fellow Rurales. Because otherwise, I will take the big house by assault. I have been waiting only for the replacements from Chihuahua. And in spite of getting only you and those three other miserable mongrels, I will surround the big house at Los Cerritos, with all my men, and take the girl if she is not in my hands by then. Ángel will be shot resisting arrest."

He kept fooling around with the quirt, flipping it around on the dirt floor and making little designs in the dust while he waited for me to make up my mind.

I sat up and said, "What's in it for me, Lieutenant?"

"Just your life, you stupid fool!" he said, and I got up and leaned against the wall.

The loop of his quirt was around his right wrist.

I said, "When are you planning to attack the place? So I'll know how much time I've got to work?"

"Daylight, next Friday, if you haven't got it fixed by then," he said.

I got a ten centavo piece out of my pocket, part of the change from five pesos they gave me in Chihuahua, to buy food on the trip. I kind of juggled it, like people do when they're thinking hard.

"I don't know what day today is," I said. "I'm hardly sure of the month."

"This is Tuesday, the tenth. September tenth," he said. "We will go to Los Cerritos on Friday. You have only Wednesday, because you must report to me by Thursday afternoon at the latest."

"Friday is the thirteenth, then," I said. "Some people think it's very unlucky."

He laughed, and I got clumsy and dropped the coin in front of him, and when I stooped down like I was going to pick it up, I grabbed the quirt with both hands and hauled him out of the chair, off balance. I hit him under the chin with my left fist and half straightened him up, then got my weight into it and slugged him on the side of his jaw with my right. He dropped on his face, like Cassie.

I heard the guard trotting to the door, and I snatched up the quirt and got the loop off Cano's wrist.

The guard said, "Lieutenant? Sir? Lieutenant Cano?"

I backed up to the wall so the door would open toward me, and said, "Get in here!"

He fumbled around with the padlock, then swung the door open and poked his head in. He stared down at Cano, and I looped the quirt around his neck and twisted it, and he dropped the carbine and began clawing at the quirt. I didn't want to kill him, and when he sagged, I let him drop. I grabbed up his carbine and put my hat on and pulled the door shut after me when I went out. I took time to snap the padlock on the hasp.

It was hard to make myself walk slow past the barracks, and around behind, because men were squatted cooking over charcoal fires and going in and out of their rooms. But I had my hat pulled low and kept my face down, and made it to the corral.

When I slipped inside, I took a halter rope off the fence and snapped it onto the halter of the first horse that let me get close enough, and led him out of the corral. I put the gate bars back, and then I had to lean the carbine against a post while I looped the halter rope over his neck and tied it to the ring to make reins.

I jumped and laid myself across his back, then swung my leg over and sat up, and then the horse guard saw me and asked me what the hell I was doing.

"Lieutenant Cano's orders," I said, and neck-reined the horse around. I reached down, but I couldn't reach the carbine, and the guard started trotting toward me, and I couldn't hang around. I squeezed with my knees and the horse went into a trot, and it wasn't till I turned away from the barracks across an open field that the guard began to yell.

By the time they got mounted, I was around the town and riding beside the river and past that big cornfield I had crawled through the night I killed El Niño. Two things I wanted to see—Narciso's Bisley Colt that I hid under a tile in the eaves of Ángel's quarters, and old Ángel himself.

In an hour, I guess it was about eight o'clock, I was walking slow and careful, leading the horse around the stone corral at Los Cerritos. I'd come across the *milpas* and the plowed fields, and a couple of dogs barked, but nobody bothered me. It wasn't a dark night, and I could see pretty good, and fifty yards from Ángel's place, I found some adobe bricks and put two of them on the halter rope to hold my horse.

I walked real quiet up to Ángel's window, which just had

wooden bars and open shutters. I was trying to hear whether maybe somebody else was in there with him, and he stuck his pistol in my ribs from behind. I must've jumped three feet straight up. He said, "Put your hands on the window sill and lean your weight on them, and after that, don't move. Not an eyelash!"

I did, and he felt for a gun, and I said, "It's me. Kel."

He didn't answer, but he whistled like a screech owl, then we waited, and in about five minutes, one of the vaqueros came. I didn't hear him, either, till he spoke to Ángel.

Ángel said, "Lucas? Go in and light the lamp."

In Ángel's room, he searched me again, while Lucas held his carbine on me. Ángel shoved his pistol back in the holster.

I said, "Ángel, Friday morning, Lieutenant Cano is coming for you and Lidia. He has orders from Chihuahua."

He spit in my face.

I was so surprised I just stared at him. And by the time I got mad and was going to hit him, Lucas had the muzzle of his carbine jammed into my kidneys. I almost hit him, anyway.

Ángel said, "Are you such a fool you think I would believe anything a Rural tells me? What kind of a murder scheme are you working, sneaking in here to lie to me after you have joined up with the Guardia Rural? What are you plotting with Cano?"

This shocked me worse than when he spit in my face. I said, "Listen, you brainless ape! I'm no Rural! They caught me! Up there with Lobo Barrera and Moisés and . . ."

He broke in, "That's the truth! And who survived? Only you! And Moisés for a little while. Him they shot, and you they sent to Chihuahua. This revolution has made many a filthy traitor. But you! You are the worst I ever heard of! Making love to Doña Lidia! Getting us to trust you! Well, you now wear your true colors, the uniform of the Guardia Rural, like the skin of a snake!"

Then Lucas made the mistake of getting enthusiastic and spitting in my face, too, and that put him in front of me.

Mexicans never expect to get hit with a fist. Their weapons are the knife and the pistol. My right hand was swollen, from clipping Cassie and then Cano, so I hit Lucas with my left. I really laid it on him, and he dropped the carbine and staggered back and brought up against the wall, and while Ángel was clawing at his pistol, I kicked him under the brisket, hard, and he gasped and sat down with a thump and gasped for wind. I got his pistol. Lucas look kind of crosseyed. He was on his hands and knees crawling toward his carbine.

I told him, "If you touch it, I put one through your hand," and he stopped. I opened the shutters and dropped his carbine outside the window.

For a one-time hired gun, I was sure using my fists a lot, lately. I had to use something, and I didn't have any gun. Anyway, they worked quiet, and didn't rouse up any nosy outsiders.

Old Ángel was retching, sitting in the corner, and Lucas got to his feet, but he was pretty rocky. I put my hand in his face and shoved, and he slammed back against the wall again and slid down so he was sitting with his back to it.

Well, I called Ángel every kind of a son of a bitch I could think of in Spanish, and there are more ways than in English. Then I told him, "I hope Cano gets you, Friday morning! But if you want to save Lidia's life, you better listen! I hope you burn in hell forever if your stupidity costs her life!"

I waited till the color came back in his face, and he quit gagging. I said, "I killed two Rurales when they hit Barrera's camp. You led them there, because you are too fat-headed to check your back trail! And they sent me to Chihuahua, and the prison commander gave me a choice, be shot or join the Guardia Rural. Which would you choose? Now, listen! I am supposed to trick you and Lidia into meeting me alone, and Cano will be there to take you. When I don't report back to him, he will bring his whole troop, Friday before daylight, to surround the big house and take Lidia. She will be tried for treason, and shot later. So you be ready! Whether you believe me or not! Tell me, you with a lump of tallow for a brain, what do I gain by lying about this? What do you lose by being ready?"

I waited, and he didn't answer, and I kicked him in the ribs, hard, and said, "Answer me! Why would I risk my neck, coming here alone?"

He said, "How do I know you are alone? I will never take the word of any Rural! If you told me my name is Ángel, then I will know it is something else."

There was no way to convince him. And as soon as I left, he'd have his vaqueros after me.

I made him tie and gag Lucas, and I made sure he did it right. Then I marched him outside and got Narciso's Bisley from under the eave tiles where I'd hid it. I took Ángel's pistol belt, because the .45 cartridges would fit the Bisley. I made him fill a goatskin waterbag from his wash pitcher, and give me a handful of jerky and a dozen tortillas from a tin box where he always kept a little something. Then I tied and gagged him.

I told him, "I think you will come to your senses when it is too late. But at least I will be back before daylight Friday, to fight for her." It was a bragging thing to say, but I meant it.

It was a chilly night, and I didn't expect to have a bed to sleep in, so I took Angel's *jorongo*—that's a short, wool jacket without sleeves—and put it on over my Rural coat.

I rode down to the river and splashed along in it for a ways to hide my trail. Then I threw the halter in the water and turned the horse loose. I walked back to the cuadrilla and sneaked into the granary. Up in the loft, I found an old tarp and some hay, and fixed myself a hiding place, and settled down to wait. I didn't think Ángel's vaqueros would find me right under their nose.

There was nothing stupid about Lieutenant Salvador Cano. He came Thursday morning!

CHAPTER 19

I was bundled up in all those clothes and still chilly, because the granary was cold as a tomb, so when I heard the shots and the yelling, way over by the big house, I just pulled on my boots and buckled on my gun.

I climbed down from the loft and ran out of the granary, and there was more yelling up by the house, and another shot. It was very early, not a bit of light, yet. I heard men calling back and forth, at the poblado on the hill. The black bull began bellowing in his corral.

I hurried as best I could, and heard men stirring around, and I cut in behind the wood shed behind the house, where Ángel and me stood off Cano and Narciso that night Paco died. Two men sort of appeared beside me. I felt them there rather than saw them in the dark, and I cocked the Bisley.

Then Ángel said, "Is that you, Kel?"

"Yes," I said. "And you're a fool!"

"You were right." he said. "But you told me Friday!"

"Cano told me Friday," I said. "But when I didn't report back to him . . ."

"Anyway, he tricked us." he said. "They're here. I had sentinels posted, but by the time we got here, they were already in position. There's a few under both arcades, and the rest in the house."

"What was the shooting?" I asked him.

"A couple of them by the kitchen door saw me and Lucas run behind the shed and had a try at us. Well, I blundered, even after you told me. I should never have let them get to the house. We have their horses, whatever good that is."

I stared toward the kitchen door, trying to see the two

Rurales he said were on guard there, but it was too dark to see anything.

Ángel said, "I thought when I yelled at Cano that we had the house surrounded . . . well, all he did was tell me to order my men away, because he had Don Hector and Doña Lidia and the priest for hostages, and he would kill them one by one if I didn't give myself up, too."

"What do we do, now?" I said. "They're in there with the stone walls and the tile roof and the food and water, where you said we'd be, if it came to worse trouble."

He said, "If Doña Lidia wasn't in there, we'd just kill them all (to the last man, and as far as I'm concerned), and that includes Don Hector and the priest."

"You couldn't get at them," I said. "The place is a fort."

He said, "Let it be a fort. There are wooden doors to burn down and windows to shoot through. I armed the peones. Thirty of them, with rifles. I told them to come tomorrow morning. Anyway, they're on the way now."

We could hear the peones talking and moving around, and the vaqueros giving them orders to go here or there.

"You wouldn't have any idea where Lidia is, in the house?" I asked him, because I was wondering if there was any way to get her out.

"She could be anywhere in there," he said. "Maybe we could rush the door, and . . ."

Somebody let go a shot, outside the house, and right away there were answering shots from the house, from the front arcade and an upstairs window.

Ángel yelled, "Stop shooting, you fools!" and the peones quit.

He said, "I don't know which they hate worse, Don Hector or the Rurales. Maybe it was a mistake to . . ."

He got interrupted again.

Somebody lit a lamp, in the kitchen. Salvador Cano had the guts, all right. He shoved Padre Arrellaga into the open window, plain in the light. He was holding a pistol to the priest's head, and he yelled, "Ángel! You there? The next shot from out there, I shoot the priest. Next will be Don Hector, and then Lidia. So let me hear you order your men to put down their arms, and let me hear them leave. Then you, yourself, will surrender to me, and we will all have a nice little ride to town."

The peones began to yell, and there were half a dozen

shots, the flashes bright in the blackness. I don't know whether they killed the priest, or if Cano did—because his pistol flashed, and the priest fell and hung over the window sill.

Lidia screamed, in the kitchen, and the Rurales were firing from windows and under both arcades, front and back, and everybody opened up, the peones and the vaqueros, too, and the racket was awful, and the smoke, gray in the dark, lit by muzzle flashes and rolling out the windows and from the lane, and behind the patio walls.

I began to trot across the rear patio to the kitchen door, but Ángel caught me by the sleeve and pulled me down onto the cobbles. I was about to tell him I was going to get her out of there, but he yelled in my ear, so I could hear over the racket, "There's two of them at the door! Have you got your Rural uniform on, under that jorongo?"

I saw what he meant, and I pulled the jorongo off and got up and sprinted, crouched over. Bullets were singing off the cobblestones, and Ángel was right behind me.

I yelled, *"Rurales!* Don't shoot!", and one of them at the door yelled, "My God, man, what were you doing out there?" and the other said, "We'd better get inside!"

I could make them out, because it was beginning to get light. One of them turned to grab the door latch, and Ángel dropped him with a shot from his pistol. He sprawled against the other one, and I slammed into the door with my shoulder. It crashed in, and I sprawled on the floor inside. Ángel was so close behind me he fell over me.

It was awful in there, the room full of powder smoke, and two Rurales at the window, swearing and shooting into the dark, and bullets whacking into the walls and splintering the tiles of the *brasero.* I was on my hands and knees, boosting Ángel off me, and Lieutenant Cano was swinging his gun to bear on Ángel. I shot him twice, from under Ángel's arm. He dropped sideways. Lidia was struggling with one of Don Hector's bodyguards across the room, and I didn't dare take a shot at him. Ángel rolled off me, and the Rural was trying to aim at me and hang onto Lidia. He fired, and missed because she jerked his arm. Ángel stood up behind him and slugged him with his pistol.

He got his arm around her waist and I grabbed her hand, and a bullet smashed the lamp on the table, and flaming kerosene spilled off the table and ran across the floor. Just before we rushed her outside, I saw Don Hector down on his knees, coughing blood.

We got her across the patio and behind the shed, and she hung onto me, her arms around my neck, and kept saying, "Kel! Oh, Kel!"

Ángel ran away, bellowing for everybody to stop shooting, but there was no stopping those peones. All the hatred and desperation of four centuries of slavery had broke loose, and they had guns, now, and their hated patrón was in that house, and a troop of Rurales trapped like rats.

The house was blazing, now, the fire like banners out the windows and spreading upstairs. It seems like a stone and adobe building with a tile roof and floors wouldn't have much to burn, but there are partitions and ceiling and rafters and furniture and curtains and wooden doors—and there was no stopping this fire, even if the peones would have let anyone try.

Salvador Cano was dead, the priest was dead, Don Hector was dead, and Cassie Greenfield had to be dead, too, even though I didn't see him in there—because nobody came out of there after Lidia, Ángel and me.

I led Lidia away to Ángel's place. She knew her father was dead, she'd seen him get hit.

It was light now. She stretched out on the bed, and I was afraid to touch her, because she hated me. So I sat in a chair beside the bed and looked at her and thought how beautiful she was, even with her face black with soot, and her clothes all rumpled and dirty. All the while, the carbines kept on firing, up at the house.

And I was thinking, I wonder if this ends it—if my worries are over. Because all my enemies were dead in that burning house, not one of them got out alive. So I could go home now, back to Uncle Frank and Lupe for a while, till I got straightened around and let some time pass.

I was thinking how beautiful it was, the way her long lashes laid against the curve of her brown cheek, and she opened her eyes and looked at me.

She said, "Can you still love me, after the awful things I said to you?"

I couldn't answer. She reached out and took my hand and held it against her cheek.

The big house was just a burned-out shell of stone walls

with two big chimneys sticking up, and a big heap of charcoal and broken tiles and melted glass.

The peones were gone, and only two vaqueros, Bartoloméo and Marcos, stayed with Ángel and Lidia and me. Four of the others got killed in the fight, and the rest of them, like the peones, ran away to the mountains because they were afraid the Rurales and the army would take some terrible revenge.

We buried the four vaqueros, but just left all the other dead in the ashes. They were just charred skeletons, and no way to tell which was which.

We turned the oxen loose, and the chickens and turkeys and goats and all the horses except one apiece, because we couldn't take care of them. But I had my little Gato again.

We were sure they'd send a new Rural troop from Chihuahua, so we moved five miles, to two charcoal burners' shacks, by a spring in a big stand of oaks. The shacks were just three sides and a roof, open toward a fire pit. We got blankets from the store and clay pots and jugs from the peones' village, and plenty of corn and beans and dried meat. The only chore we had was feeding the retired bull, Conquistador. He was too dangerous to turn loose, and too much for us to move to the bull pasture, and nobody had the heart to shoot him. Ángel and Barto and Marcos took turns standing watch, waiting for the Rurales to come.

And in spite of all the bad things that happened and all the men dead on both sides, and not knowing when we would be attacked, or whether the revolution was lost—this was the happiest time I ever had. Because Lidia moved in with me and lived with me. She said she was no better than a million other Mexican women that never got married, and God didn't seem to mind. Ángel and the vaqueros took it as the natural thing and left us alone as much as they could.

So I made love to her at night, and sometimes in the daytime, and sometimes she started it. And she was fierce and sweet and tender all at the same time. In all the talk about Heaven, in Uncle Frank's Bible, there was never anything like this.

We took long rides to exercise the horses, and sat around the fire in the evenings and watched the sparks twisting up to get lost against the stars. Lidia didn't say much about her father, but she was sorry, even if they hadn't got along. She said she had been a bad daughter to him, and cried for him.

She talked about the hacienda, and what she was going to

do after the war was over. It would all belong to her, and we would run it like a big cooperative farm, and it would be a good life for a thousand peones, and we would live well enough, but it would really be all for the Mexicans. She said that her father's safe was in the ashes of the big house, and we would dig it up when the time came, and there would be the money to get things started. She would have the hacienda officially made an ejido, and that was really what the revolution was all about.

We camped there for three weeks, until October, and the nights were cold and the days hot, and the oaks were turning, and way off in the foothills, the aspens were turning yellow. And all the time, I knew two things, but I wouldn't think about them—this wasn't going to last, because the Rurales wouldn't just let it pass, the wiping out of a whole garrison— and the reason Lidia was so loving and eager, and wouldn't listen to that iron conscience the priests had given her when she was a little girl, was because she knew it, too. Because we didn't know if we'd still be alive the next day.

Ángel took a trip to the mountains to see Aquiles Cerrudo, the *contrabandista* that was bringing guns in from the States, now, to tell him we couldn't handle them any more at Los Cerritos. When he got back, he said the army had pulled out of Nuevo Casas Grandes, and there wouldn't be any Rurales there for a long time, because the revolution was really warming up, and the troops and Rurales in Chihuahua had been pulled out to defend Monterrey over east in Nuevo León, where a big rebel army was about to attack. Zapata had defeated a Federal army in Morelos, and General Mondragón and General Gregorio Rúiz were raising hell on the Gulf coast, and Madero still wouldn't believe he was in trouble.

So the pressure was off us, and we moved again, Ángel and Barto and Marcos into Ángel's old quarters, and me and Lidia into the little house where I had lived a while beside Narciso. We set up a charcoal brasero, but she was a terrible cook, so I did the cooking.

Ángel said that with the Guardia Rural gone, bandits were coming out of their holes like toads after a rain, robbing and murdering in the outlying villages and towns in the sierra. That's what Aquiles Cerrudo told him.

Barto found fresh horse tracks around, twice—six or eight horses, and one day Ángel saw a bunch of riders watching him—just their head and shoulders showing over a rise. They rode away, and we didn't think much about it, because the country was full of homeless people and peones that ran away from the big haciendas.

Then things began to go wrong between me and Lidia. When I'd pat her on the rump, or grab her and pull her onto my lap and kiss her, she began to snap at me and tell me not to be silly. Half the time she wouldn't let me touch her in bed, and when she did, I could tell she hated it. Then, when I told her she was all I ever wanted, and I would try to be whatever she wanted, tears came in her eyes and her face kind of crumpled up and she said, "Kel, go away! Please go away!"

Well, that made me mad, of course, and I yelled, "I'll be glad to!" and buckled on my gun and my spurs and put on my coat and hat and went out. She stood leaning against the door frame, hunched over like an old lady, with her eyes closed. I wanted to take her in my arms but I was too stubborn. I started to walk away, then looked back, and her mouth was twisted like she was crying, but she wasn't making any noise.

Finally though, she said, "Kel? Kel?" and I started back to her. But she said, "Take Gato, Kel. To remember me by."

I saddled him in the dusk and rode past the black chimneys where the big house had stood. I wasn't thinking about what I was going to do, because tears were stinging my eyes, and I didn't see the black shape of the mountains to the west, nor the stars, nor the moon rising like a big, yellow, fire balloon.

Then I heard a horse galloping after me, and I stopped, and my heart skipped a beat, because I thought she had changed her mind.

CHAPTER 20

It wasn't her, it was Ángel. He spurred alongside me and said, "Kel, you better not go. It's that conscience of hers. When they're little kids, they get stamped into a mold by those priests, like an adobe brick, and there's no changing them. But all you have to do is marry her."

"We were going to," I told him. "But Padre Arrellaga acted like I was a mongrel. You're forgetting I'm a gringo and a heretic, and she's a Catholic and half Spanish."

"Kel," he said, "all she needs is to go through the motions, just the form of it. She loves you. And if a priest said the words . . ."

"No priest would do it," I said, "even if she would."

"Padre Guzmán will do it," Ángel said, "and I guarantee she will!"

And I remembered what I asked old Padre Guzmán and what he told me, in the mountains the day before Salvador Cano and Cassie Greenfield caught us cold. I was about to say something, and Ángel pulled his horse to a stop and got down and picked something off the road.

He stood up, and said, "Horse manure, Kel. It's fresh. And here's tracks crossing the road, six or eight horses."

I was about to ask him what was so interesting about fresh horse manure, and then I knew what he was thinking. I said, "Where are Barto and Marcos?"

"They rode into town," he said. "You think I ought to get them?"

"No," I said. "Come on!" and I reined Gato around and squeezed with my knees, and he grunted and sailed over the

163

rock wall beside the road and was going full gallop when he came down. Ángel was right behind me, quirting his roan.

She wasn't there.

The lamp was lit and there was a chair knocked over, and marks of a struggle outside the patio, and in the light from the doorway, we could make out the tracks of the horses. We followed them a short ways and lost them in the dry grass.

Ángel said, "It's no use till daylight. I'll go to Nuevo Casas Grandes and find Barto and Marcos."

When he was gone, I rode widening circles for an hour, but of course I couldn't find tracks in the dark. I rode back to the house and sat staring at the wall a long time, and finally lit the charcoal in the brasero and put the coffee pot on to boil.

I loaded a Winchester .44-40 carbine, and got Gato watered and fed, and had coffee, and as soon as it began to get light, I started riding circles again. Then Ángel hollered at me and came riding up past the bull's corral.

He said, "Marcos and Barto were in the cantina, half drunk, but I poured black coffee into them and we came back. As soon as it was barely light, Barto rode a circle to the east, and Marcos the other way, and Marcos found the tracks. They're following them."

I said, "Which way?" and started Gato moving, and Ángel said, "No! We'll wait! Not go charging into trouble! One of them will come back and tell us where they're taking her."

"No!" I said. "I'm not waiting!"

And just then Barto came riding over the hill, and we galloped to meet him.

"You know the adobe shacks by the bull pasture?" he said. "They're there, in the big one. Marcos is watching them."

"Why would they stop there?" Ángel said. "They had all night to get away!"

I began to get an idea, then. I'd been thinking Cassie Greenfield was just one more charred skeleton in the ruins of the big house—but maybe he hadn't *been* there! Maybe he couldn't go with Lieutenant Cano and the troop because he was laid up with a smashed nose and a busted jaw!

I said, "That gringo Rural wants me to come looking for her. She's bait! For me! My God! What are they *doing* to her? We can't wait around and . . ."

"They've had time to do it a dozen times," Ángel said. "It's saving her life that's important, not her virginity that doesn't exist any more. If it's you they want, Kel, we will offer you to them. Now listen! There is another little village of shacks, three on each side of the cart track, about three kilometers from where they are. The peones have gone from there, too. We'll put Marcos and Barto inside the first two shacks, each with two or three loaded carbines. You and I will go where they've got her, but I'll keep out of sight. Then you will ride into view and shoot at the adobe they're in, and if they are stupid enough, your gringo friend will lead them out to get you. You toll them down the cart track between the shacks where Marcos and Barto are waiting, and I will go and get Lidia."

I said, "You will lead them to Barto and Marcos, and I will get Lidia. You wear my hat and jacket, and ride Gato. He'll come!"

It took us to midafternoon to get ready, and I was scared half crazy for Lidia—but first Barto had to sneak in and get Marcos, then we had to get the extra rifles and ammunition for them from a cache in a cave by the river. Then we had to get the two of them all set in the little adobe shacks across the cart track from each other, and Ángel and I had to make our way without being seen to an arroyo about a hundred yards from the shack where they had her. Ángel had on my hat and jacket, and he was leading Gato.

I tied his roan that I'd rode, within fifty yards of the adobe, at the head of the arroyo, behind a *palo verde*.

There was a man leaning against the doorway. Ángel shot him, and he went to his knees, then fell on his face, and five men came boiling out of that shack and were yelling and fumbling around tightening cinches and untying their horses. Ángel shot into them and one of them went down. The other four got mounted and Ángel piled onto Gato and went spurring down the cart track. They went after him, pouring on the spurs and wasting cartridges. But Cassie wasn't with them.

I left my carbine and ran the fifty yards to the shack with the Bisley cocked in my hand, and dove in the door. I landed rolling and came to my feet squatted down, and I was looking right into the face of Polly Greenfield!

He was sitting on the dirt floor, leaned against the wall, and he had a black patch on his left eye, and his left arm hung kind of funny at the elbow, and his other arm was bloody from shoulder to elbow. He was white in the face and dirty, and dressed Mexican—but I knew him.

He was only wearing one holster, backward on his left side, and his pistol was on the floor in front of him. We stared at one another. Then I saw Lidia's blouse and skirt and her underdrawers, all wadded up on the floor, and I came within a hair of shooting him in the face.

"Where is she?" I said.

He licked his lips and didn't answer.

"Where's Cassie?" I said, and he didn't answer that, either.

I kicked him in the face. Not hard enough to knock him out, but so he'd get the idea. His head banged back against the wall, and his mouth started bleeding.

"He went away," he said. "Said he was going to look around and see if you were coming."

"Where's Lidia?" I said.

Well, he had guts—or maybe he figured it was too late to matter. He shut his mouth and wouldn't answer.

I slapped him hard, and he fell over in a faint. But maybe he was faking it.

Then I heard a long burst of firing, from way down the cart track—carbines going off in twos and threes, and then one alone, and then three or four, and it finally stopped. And I didn't know who had killed who. It stood to reason Marcos and Barto and Ángel got them, with two of them forted up and shooting out of windows, but I couldn't be sure. Maybe it was the other way around, and those four would be coming back. And Cassie was on the loose out there. I'd better take Polly somewhere where nobody would interrupt me, and pry some answers out of him.

I kicked him, and he didn't move. So I pinched his upper lip as hard as I could. It was swelling already from that kick I gave him, and he yelled and pulled away.

When I said, "Get up!" he did. He stumbled and staggered and made his way outside, and I helped him onto a horse.

I led his horse to Ángel's roan, and on the way, I said, "Did he kill her?"

He wouldn't answer, and I whacked his bloody arm with the barrel of my pistol. He yelled, then. He screeched, "No! No! She's all right!"

"Where is she?" I said.

"I don't know!" he screeched. "I got shot! I don't know! She ran out, after she . . . right after Cassie went out. And Policarpo was chasing her, but he came back and said he thought he saw dust way off on the cart track. And they got ready, but nothing happened. Not till you shot Eduardo, at the door."

"And good old Cass ran out on you, huh?" I said. "Old Cassie, the great gunslinger, he ran out on you! Maybe he saw something and decided not to wait around."

"He didn't!" Polly said. "You'll see, you filthy bastard! He'll come!"

I got on my horse and holstered the Bisley and took his horse's reins. I told him, "If you don't make that horse move, you'll be sorry."

I wondered who shot him, but there were more important answers to get out of him, and I spurred Ángel's horse at a gallop, up through the stand of oaks and then through cornfields and maguey fields using all the cover I could think of, and came back to the *cuadrilla*. I knew where I was going to question him, where no bandits and no Cassie would think to look—and after I got the answers, I wasn't quite sure what I was going to do with Polly—but I was going to find her. And after that, I was going to find Cassie Greenfield.

By the big corral, I told him to get down, and he almost fell off. I swatted his horse on the rump, and it trotted away. I stripped Ángel's roan and put it in the corral.

I shoved him along, stumbling and almost falling down, and when we got to Conquistador's corral, I pulled over the old crate that Ángel and I stood on once, and I climbed up and looked over the gate. Polly was too done in to make any break to get away. He just stood there swaying, with his eyes closed. It was hard to see Conquistador, he was so black, and it was getting dark, but he scraped the ground with his hoofs, and bellowed at me. I could see that plank door into his stone shed was shut.

I jumped down and shoved Polly along to the opening in the back of the shed, where they pushed the hay through. I heard the bull snuffling around the gate, so I grabbed the top of the window frame and swung myself in feet first, and made sure the door was barred. Conquistador got there fast and rattled his horns against the door.

I climbed out again and said, "You're going to answer

some questions. And if your *compadres* show up, we'll keep real quiet, and they won't find us, huh? Because if you don't keep quiet, you're dead, Polly. So get in there."

He whimpered, and told me Cassie would come and kill me, and he couldn't climb through the window. I boosted him and shoved him through, and he fell onto the straw inside. I was right there after him.

Polly was laying there crumpled up, and when the bull drew a long breath, sniffing at the crack under the door, he sat up and said, "What's that!"

It gave me the chills, too, and the hair on the back of my neck stood up. And when Conquistador gave a little moan in his throat and rattled his horns across the door, I was glad it was thick, and barred on the inside.

I said, "You ever see a fighting bull, Polly? Because that's why you're going to tell me where Lidia is, and where Cassie is. If you don't, I'll kick you out there."

"You . . . you wouldn't!" he said. He whispered it, and Conquistador snorted, against the door crack, and I said, "Wouldn't I, Poll? So now, tell me where she is."

He whined. He said, "I don't know! I told you. She ran out, right after . . ."

"Right after what?" I said.

"Right after she shot me in the arm!" he said.

"She shot you?" I said. "What for?"

He wouldn't answer. I could barely make out the shape of him, huddled there, and I hit his shot-up arm with the barrel of my gun.

He screamed and the bull bellowed, and thumped the door hard.

I said, "Tell me, Polly! Tell me what you did to her!" and I began to feel sick.

He didn't say anything. So I straightened up and moved the bar on the door. I said, "You going to walk out there, or do I kick you out?"

He drew a long, hissing breath and said, "No, Kel! God, no! I'll tell you!"

He began to talk, fast and stumbling over the words. "It was Cassie! He said we were going to kill you. That was after I came from Douglas and found him. From that letter he sent before . . . before I got out of jail and Ma got killed. And he couldn't go with the *Rurales* that morning when they went to get the girl because you cracked his jaw and broke his nose, and he couldn't hardly eat or breathe. That was the day before I got there, and I was going to join the *Rurales* with him, but then they all got wiped out in the fire."

Conquistador trotted away, and then came trotting back and snuffled along the bottom of the door.

"Go ahead!" I said.

"Well," he said, "we went to the mountains, and we got six men to join up with us. We raided a couple of villages and tried to wreck a train, but we couldn't. Then Cassie told us there was a lot of gold coin in the ruins of the house here in the safe . . . some house servant that ran away told him . . . and we'd come and get it because there was only you and the girl and a couple of men here. But him and me, we were going to kill you, for Ma and all the . . ."

I said, "Poll, if you don't quit stalling and tell me what you did to her . . ."

"No!" he said. "It was Cassie! He said you would come and try to get her back! And he said he might as well have a little fun, before you came, and he . . ."

He stopped. I was sick. I hit him with my fist, and he began to cry!

I said, "He tore her clothes off, and raped her! With you and those men holding her for him. Is that it? Is that it, Polly?"

He wouldn't answer. I said, "And then you, huh, Polly? After Cassie, you did it! And then everybody, huh, Polly?"

"No!" he screeched. "No! Not me! Not me, Kel! Because when I grabbed her, she got my gun! And she shot me! Right after Cassie got through with her, and went out to have a look around!"

He was whimpering and sniffling, and he said, "So I couldn't, Kel! And then she got away, she ran out! And then you shot Eduardo! It was Cassie, Kel!" And then he began to scream, because he knew what I was going to do.

And Cassie answered him. Quite a ways off. He yelled, "Polly! Is that you, Polly? I'm coming, Polly!"

I shoved the bar off the brackets and hauled him to his feet, and all the time he was screaming and scrabbling at the door frame with his good hand, and I put my foot in his back and shoved him out into the corral. I pulled the door shut and barred it and leaned my back against it, and I couldn't've stood up without it.

He kept on screaming. Conquistador's hoofs hammered on the hard ground, and I guess Polly dodged him once. His screaming got worse, and then it cut off, and there was a heavy thump and something slammed against the gate, and then all I could hear was the bull snorting and blowing.

Then real close, Cassie yelled, "Polly, What happened? Where are you, boy? I'm here!"

The bull bellowed, and Cassie said, not loud now, "Jesus! Polly! You in there?"

Then I didn't hear him for a while, and I opened the door and looked into the corral. But the bull snorted and charged me, and I slammed the door shut just in time.

Then there was a light flickering through the cracks around the door. I opened it just a crack, and Cassie had got a pitchfork full of hay on fire, and he was standing on the box outside the gate, holding it up.

Polly was just a dark lump on the ground. The bull was at the gate, shaking its horns at Cassie.

Cassie was saying, like in a dream, "Polly! Polly!"

He threw the burning hay, pitchfork and all, into the corral, and the bull backed off. Cassie jumped down into the corral and pulled a gun with each hand.

The bull charged him, and Cassie shot four times with one gun before he hit it at all, and then he broke its knee. It fell right in front of him, and was trying to hook him when he shot it in the head.

I swung the door in, and the hinges creaked, and he looked at me.

He dropped the empty gun and switched the other to his right hand, and began to shoot, too fast—and for some reason I wasn't scared. I took my time. He didn't hit me, not once. I shot him in the chest, and hit him again while he was stumbling backward, and killed him.

CHAPTER 21

The burning hay died down, and I walked around the dead bull and the dead twins and climbed over the gate, kind of numb in my head.

Somebody yelled, way off, and I walked down to our little house and lit the lamp and sat there. There wasn't anything of hers there, because everything she wasn't wearing that night got burned in the fire—only a comb Ángel had got for her from the peones' village, and a jorongo—but I could feel her there, and it was a weird feeling, and sad, because I thought I would never see her alive again.

Then Ángel and Barto and Marcos came pounding in at a gallop.

"We heard the shooting," he said. "What happened?"

I said, "I caught the gringo's brother, and the gringo came to find him, and they're dead. No sign of Lidia?"

"No," he said. "Those four bastards ran into our trap like sheep, and we killed them all. Then we went back for you, but there was nothing there. Only her clothes, and blood on the floor. We have been hunting ever since, for her and for you, and for that gringo Rural. What brother do you mean?"

"I'll tell you later," I said. "Let's get started."

"No," Ángel said. "We eat first. It is no use to hunt at night, but we will, anyway."

I said, "She got away from them, just before I got there. She's out in the chaparral somewhere. But she hasn't got any clothes on."

He stared at me for a minute, then said to Barto, "Get the brasero warmed up, will you? We'll make coffee. And I see you have beans and tortillas."

171

*   *   *   *   *   *

We took a couple of blankets, and rode back in the moonlight to the adobe shack. A couple of coyotes ran away from the body of the sentinel Ángel killed.

There was no use riding circles to cut for sign, because we could easy miss any tracks, even with the moon bright the way it was. All we could do was zigzag around and keep calling her. I didn't think she would've got very far, with no clothes on, and barefoot.

In about ten minutes, I rode right past where she was crouched in a clump of grass. But when Ángel crisscrossed my path calling her name, she answered him. He yelled at me, and I came back. He was off his horse and had her cradled in his arms, with her face buried in his neck.

I got down and said, "Lidia! Here, let me get the blanket on you."

She didn't answer, just hung onto Ángel all the harder.

I said, "Let me have her, Ángel."

He said, "Sure! Take her!" but she wouldn't let go.

He told her then, "Doña Lidia, we can't just stand here. You have to let me get on my horse, and you have to have the blanket around you."

So then she let him put her in my arms and get her bundled in the blanket. I put my face against her cheek, but she just hung in my arms like a sackful of grain. We yelled for Barto and Marcos, and they came to us. Ángel got mounted, and I handed her up to him and took his reins so I could lead his horse.

I asked Barto to go to the shack and get her clothes, and we took her home to our little house, and she never said a word all the way. Only when I turned up the lamp wick and Ángel laid her on the bed and patted her on the cheek and started to leave, then she reared up and begged him not to go.

I said, "I'm here, Lidia. I won't leave you."

"I don't want you here," she said. "Ángel, please stay!"

He said, "No," and went out. She turned her face to the wall and laid there like she was dead.

I got the fire going and put water on to heat, and pretty soon Barto came with her clothes. They were filthy, and the skirt was torn, and the blouse ripped almost in half. There was blood on it, and that scared me—but I found out later it was from Polly, when she shot him.

I filled a pot with warm water and got the cloth we used for a towel, and told her I was going to clean her up. She said, "No! No!" like I was going to rape her, too. I didn't want to get rough, God knows that's the last thing I wanted, but I had to make her behave. So I just went ahead. I held her the best I could with one hand and pulled the blanket off her, and began to sponge her off. For a few minutes, we had quite a wrestle, then she quit struggling and let me move her around like a doll.

She was scratched and cut, and her feet bruised and bloody and swollen, and I felt like crying. When I had her cleaned up, I held her for a little while, and at last she put her cheek against mine and sighed, and went to sleep. I laid her down on the bed easy, and pulled off my clothes.

But when I got in beside her, she pushed at me and yelled at me to get away from her, and she was crying. So I slept on the floor, wrapped in a couple of blankets.

All my bones were sore when I woke up in the morning. She was sitting on the bed huddled in the blanket, staring at me, and she wouldn't talk to me. It went that way for a week. I wouldn't sleep on the floor again, but she kept to her own side of the bed, and pushed my hand away if I touched her. I washed her clothes, and she had put her underwear on when I was out one day. She only got out of bed when she had to go outside. I made soup, and shot a couple of chickens and a turkey and a kid, and cooked them every way I could think of, but she hardly touched it.

Ángel, Barto and Marcos dragged the twins and the dead bandits away and caved in a cutbank on them. Then they hitched up a team and dragged Conquistador's body away, too.

I was sick in my guts about Cassie raping Lidia. I wished I could kill him all over again. And I felt kind of funny about her, too, for a couple of days, like I wasn't sure I really wanted to touch her—but I got over that. I was so sorry for her, and tried to understand what it did to her, and I wanted to hold her and comfort her and love her. But she wouldn't talk to me, and she didn't cry. She just lived like a wooden dummy.

And finally I got mad.

I stood by the bed and took off my clothes, clear down to the hide. Her eyes got wider and wider, and her mouth dropped open, and she said, "What are you doing?"

I said, "I've tried everything else. I've washed you and cooked for you, and slept with you and not touched you and this is a hell of a way to live! The only thing that makes any impression on you is rape. So I'm going to rape you. Then I'm going to leave and never come back."

I wasn't going to rape her, but I was going to get some kind of a response from her!

I jumped into bed and said, "Peel off your underwear! Because if you don't, I will!"

She gasped and scrabbled over against the wall and pulled the blankets up under her chin. Her eyes looked huge, and she was crying, with the tears flooding down her face and into her mouth.

She said, "No! Kel, no! You don't want me! I'm disgraced and shamed! I would have killed myself that day, only there wasn't any way to do it. And now I can't because it is a terrible sin! I'd go to hell!"

I reached for her, but she shoved my hand away.

"So you don't want me!" she said. "You can't love me any more! You despise me."

I grabbed her, then, and she wasn't strong enough to fight me off, and I held her close to my heart. I said, "Lidia, if you push me away, if you've quit loving me, what will I do? I will never love anyone else! I'm sick over what he did to you—not for my feelings, but for what it did to you. I killed him, Lidia. I've had to kill other men, but he's the only one I was glad to kill!"

The tension began to go out of her. I could feel her relax a little.

I said, "When you found out that the little whore in Agua Prieta raped me, you hated me. But I don't hate you because something happened to you that you hated but you couldn't help! No, I never stopped loving you!"

Well, she smiled a little. "I didn't know she raped you," she said. "I thought maybe you paid her."

She put her arms around my neck then, and hugged me. But she said, "When I thought we were going to be killed any day, after the battle and the fire, then I didn't care, and I went to bed with you and loved you because I thought it was the end for us. But, Kel I can't! Not again, because it isn't right. I love you, but I can't, because I can't marry you."

"Yes, you can!" I said. "I talked to your Padre Guzmán, in the mountains, and he said if it was an emergency, he would marry us! I will send Ángel to bring him here."

Well, she laughed then, and kissed me. She said, "If we haven't an emergency already, we can create one, can't we?"

So that is the story of how Letty Greenfield's horoscopes came true—even if they didn't foresee that I would find my beautiful girl in Mexico, and would be the husband of a very rich woman, and never go back to my own country—but work with her and old Ángel for her beloved peones. And because I haven't tried to tell the story of the revolution in Mexico, only what happened to me, I won't go on with how General Huerta murdered President Francisco Madero, and the vice-president, Pino Suárez, at midnight, February twenty-second, 1913, and how the American ambassador could have saved their lives, but wouldn't lift a hand to do it; and how those assassinations united all the old revolutionary generals that had fought for Madero and then turned against him, and how they fought Huerta and the wealthy landowners and finally won, after many bloody battles. The Revolution still goes on—not with fire and battles and executions, but in the courts and the legislature, and there is still a long way to go, but my foster country is now a great and united nation.

Kelly Adams.

FREE
Fawcett Books Listing

There is Romance, Mystery, Suspense, and Adventure waiting for you inside the Fawcett Books Order Form. And it's yours to browse through and use to get all the books you've been wanting . . . but possibly couldn't find in your bookstore.

This easy-to-use order form is divided into categories and contains over 1500 titles by your favorite authors.

So don't delay—take advantage of this special opportunity to increase your reading pleasure.

Just send us your name and address and 35¢ (to help defray postage and handling costs).

FAWCETT BOOKS GROUP
P.O. Box C730, 524 Myrtle Ave., Pratt Station, Brooklyn, N.Y. 11205

Name_____
(please print)

Address_____
City_____ State_____ Zip_____

Do you know someone who enjoys books? Just give us their names and addresses and we'll send them an order form too!

Name_____
Address_____
City_____ State_____ Zip_____

Name_____
Address_____
City_____ State_____ Zip_____